W9-CSH-754

WITHDRAWN

THE MAN WHO
HATED HICKOK

THE MAN WHO HATED HICKOK

C. M. WENDELBOE

FIVE STAR
A part of Gale, a Cengage Company

Farmington Hills, Mich • San Francisco • New York • Waterville, Maine
Meriden, Conn • Mason, Ohio • Chicago

LIBRARY OF CONGRESS CATALOGING-IN-PUBLICATION DATA

Names: Wendelboe, C. M., author.
Title: The man who hated Hickok / C.M. Wendelboe.
Description: First edition. | Farmington Hills, Mich. : Five Star, a part of Gale, a Cengage Company, [2019]
Identifiers: LCCN 2018059024 (print) | ISBN 9781432858179 (hardcover)
Subjects: GSAFD: Western stories.
Classification: LCC PS3623.E53 M36 2019 (print) | DDC 813/.6—dc23
LC record available at https://lccn.loc.gov/2018059024

First Edition. First Printing: August 2019
Find us on Facebook—https://www.facebook.com/FiveStarCengage
Visit our website—http://www.gale.cengage.com/fivestar/
Contact Five Star Publishing at FiveStar@cengage.com

Printed in Mexico
1 2 3 4 5 6 7 23 22 21 20 19

To Eric "Fireplug" Hyland and Scott "Mountain Man" Appley and Mike "Bomb Boy" Hieb and all the others who put up with me until I finally retired from law enforcement.

ACKNOWLEDGMENTS

Thanks to Daniek Long and the Cheyenne Frontier Days Old West Museum for staff knowledge and access to their vintage coaches and allowing them to be photographed for this novel; Peggy Sanders for providing much of the diligent and exhaustive research into the Cheyenne to Black Hills Stage; South Dakota Historical Society and the Wyoming State Library, whose help with research and local color enriched the writing of this work. To my editor, Alice Duncan, who curried the kinks out of my manuscript as surely as she curried the kinks out of a gnarly mustang. And to my wife, Heather, who stands by me every project.

CHAPTER 1

Ira Drang burst into the New Idea Saloon to laughter and the pained whimpering of a tormented boy. Drunks gathered in a circle, their hilarity focused on the naked form lying in the middle of the saloon floor littered with peanut hulls and cigarette butts. The lad tried covering himself with his hands as the crowd taunted him with nudges of boots, shouts of glee. Ira shoved a man aside and saw his brother curled up on the floor.

The laughter subsided, then stopped altogether when the rowdies realized it was Ira who squatted beside his bawling brother. Ira stripped off his vest and draped it around the slight, trembling body. "It's okay now, Jamie."

"He made me take off my clothes." Jamie wiped snot off his upper lip. "He took my pants. My long johns." He looked up at Ira. "What am I going to do?"

"I'll get you out of here in a minute," Ira assured his brother before he stood and confronted the crowd. "Who the hell made Jamie strip down?"

Drunks looked at one another. Down at the floor. At the back bar. Any place but at Ira.

He grabbed the closest rummy and shook him by the lapels. "How about you?" The canvas of the man's sourdough coat ripped, and Ira let the drunk go. "Who made Jamie strip—"

"Cool your heels," a scruffy man leaning against the bar said. He wiped beer foam off his salt-and-pepper colored beard, and a gray-back louse fell onto the floor. He looked at it curiously

9

before stepping on it. "Damn kid had it coming."

Ira sized the man up. He stood eye level with Ira, but his bulk under his dirty calico shirt showed great strength within the sixty-year-old body. The man's gaze darted around the saloon, sneaky-like, as if he were a ferret fixing to raid the hen house. "What the hell you mean, Jamie had it coming?"

The man chuckled, and Ira shoved another drunk out of the way. He stepped closer to the sneaky bastard and lashed out with a wicked slap across the man's face.

He staggered back.

The laughter stopped.

The crowd parted, leaving Ira and the man facing each other.

"Ed Mooney," Ira said, finally recognizing the man. He was one of many wanted men Ira had searched for when he was hunting bounty some years ago but had never found. Some other hunter had brought in Mooney, and he had twice been tried for murders in Colorado. And twice the witnesses failed to show to testify against him. Ira heard Mooney was working for some rancher around Cheyenne, but this was the first he'd had a run-in with him. "Back shooter, if the rumors are right," Ira said.

Mooney's face flushed red despite his dark complexion, and his hand dropped to his gun butt. His Colt hadn't cleared leather when Ira snapped his own gun from its cut-down holster. The sound of the gun cocking echoed loudly off the walls of the saloon, and men moved farther away from the two. Mooney carefully laid his pistol on the floor and raised his hands. He backed up three feet and ran into the bar. "Even here in Cheyenne, you can't get away with killing an unarmed man."

"I have half a notion to make you pick your gun up, and we'll finish this." As much as Ira wanted to do just that, he wanted even more to find out who had humiliated Jamie. "You do this?"

"Not me," Mooney said. "But I hope you find the man who

did. He'll ventilate you for certain."

"You got a name?"

Mooney smiled. "Hickok. And you won't be quick enough against Wild Bill," he said, laughing. "But every year on the anniversary of your gunfight with Bill, I'll go by your grave and piss on it."

Ira backed away and lowered his gun. "What the hell would Hickok have against my little brother? All Jamie does in here is empty spittoons and sweep floors. Tidy up the cribs when the upstairs girls come down to work the floor."

"The kid came up on Hickok's back side," another drunk at the end of the bar said.

"That's right." Mooney carefully withdrew a cigar from his vest pocket and grabbed a match from the bar. "The kid came up and stuck his finger in Hickok's back. Told him not to turn around." He grinned. "Kid might have just been joking, but Hickok took exception to it. Stripped the kid naked and told him to dance in the middle of the floor."

Ira holstered his gun and knelt beside Jamie. Ira kept an eye on Mooney while he wrapped his arm around the boy. He helped Jamie stand, but his legs buckled. "It's okay," Ira whispered. "I got you." Ira brushed peanut hulls and pieces of cigarette butts off Jamie's backside.

"Where'd Hickok go?" Ira asked as he started for the door.

"Out." Mooney waved his hand at the door. "Go on the hunt for him. But be careful—you might actually find him."

Ira took off his shirt and tied it around Jamie. He slipped his vest around the boy before he led him from the saloon. They passed a wolfer on the street, who gave them little more than a passing glance, as did two cowboys sporting new, flowered shirts as they headed for an afternoon of debauchery in one of the many saloons.

"I'm sorry," Jamie said, swiping his hand across his snotty nose. "I was just joshing Wild Bill—"

"Let's just get you to your room and clean you up."

They waited to cross the street until a carriage adorned with the flowers of a wedding party trotted down the street, pulled by matched Morgans. The driver—dressed in a flowing coat—looked down at Jamie and shook his head as his coattails flapped against the head of the new groom. They knocked off his top hat, and it rolled in the dirt, but the man ignored it as he snuggled closer to his wife. She had "catalog woman" written all over her face as she looked indifferently at the groom.

When the carriage had passed, Ira led Jamie across the street toward the alley, avoiding onlookers stopping to stare at the half-naked boy. They entered the alley in the back of the Bella Union Theater, where Jamie had a basement sleeping room in exchange for cleaning after performances. Ira helped his brother down the narrow stairs and into his dank, one-room sleeping quarters.

Ira lit a lamp and turned the flame high, illuminating the bunk with its wafer-thin mattress. A tattered quilt hung over the sides of the bunk, but it was neatly made. Beside the bed a bushel basket sat overturned and used as a table in front of a rustic chair Jamie had carved from a tree stump. When Ira brought Jamie to Cheyenne, Ira wanted the boy to bunk with him at his rooming house across town above Pease and Taylor Grocery—small, but three times the size of Jamie's room. And it actually had a working window one could open to draw out the stale air, unlike this room. When their parents died in a buggy accident in Ohio four years ago, Jamie had no place to go. "Jamie musta' been dropped on his head as a baby," their father often said, " 'cause the kid's a little lacking," and he'd tap the side of his head.

But that mattered none to Ira. After the tragic accident, he had insisted Jamie come out west where Ira could watch over him. He had quit the bounty-hunting business and taken odd jobs around Cheyenne to be close to his brother. At once the boy insisted he live on his own, to prove to Ira he wasn't a dummy like folks whispered. He'd insisted on sleeping in his own room, working his own job, proving his independence. Ira had sheltered hope that the boy would one day be able to make it on his own. Until this morning.

Jamie sat on the tree stump and looked up with tears streaming down his cheek. "Hickok hurt me," he said as he reached under the bed for a clean shirt. "Hurt me bad, Ira. I was just funnin'," he said as tears carved rivulets down his dirty cheeks.

Ira looked the boy over, with his bare legs sticking out of Ira's shirt that barely covered his butt, and his underdeveloped arms jutting from Ira's vest. He saw no injury and realized Jamie was talking about Hickok hurting his pride.

Ira took a pair of denims from Jamie's makeshift dresser and held them to the light. The knees had been worn through, and the seat of the pants was ripped. "Put these on." He handed the pants to Jamie. "And we'll go buy you a new pair."

"You mean a pair of store-boughts?" Jamie said, his shoulders shaking uncontrollably.

Ira draped his arm around Jamie. "The finest we can buy," Ira said before he realized he was a little shy of money at the moment. But he'd worry about that when the time came to pay for them. "That will make you feel better."

Jamie buried his head in his hands, and Ira bent and patted the boy on the shoulders. "Nothing will make me feel better," Jamie said.

"It will," Ira said, "soon's I get some money. You gonna' be all right here for a couple hours?" He fished a nickel out of his pocket and handed it to Jamie. "Go down and get a bowl of ice cream from Ellis's parlor and come back here. That'll help."

Jamie held the nickel tight and swiped his hand across his eyes. "Hickok hurt me bad, Ira."

A Union Pacific train whistle two blocks over blew loud in the bar as Ira leaned over the faro table. Shingle and Locke's had a reputation of being the one gambling house in town that ran an honest game. But Ira knew better. A faro dealer running an honest game would break even, have a *slight* edge, at best. But the dealer had won eleven of the last fourteen plays, far more than mere chance would dictate. And if Ira expected to buy Jamie a new set of clothes, his luck would have to change.

Five other players stood around the table and placed their bets on different cards. Ira grabbed his last dollar and placed a card on a ten of spades while he watched the dealer intently. He *knew* the dealer was cheating for the house. He just didn't know how.

The dealer—folks called him Nebraska Slim because he weighed as much as the state of Nebraska—swiped his hand over the next card in the dealer's box. The bar dog came around and set a fresh mug of foamy beer beside Ira, who flipped him two bits when . . . light reflected off the beer mug for a moment.

Just a fleeting moment, and it was gone.

Gone when the dealer brought his hand away from the Faro box containing the cards. Ira left his beer mug sitting on the green felt and waited until Nebraska Slim covered the box with his hand once again. And once again light reflected off Ira's mug.

And he knew how the fat man was cheating.

He leaned across the table and snatched the dealer's box from Slim. "What the hell you doing?" the dealer demanded.

"You're cheating," Ira said. "The damn box is gaffed."

Ira held the box to the light and spotted the small mirror affixed to its bottom—a mirror that told Slim what the next card on the deck was to be dealt. Slim—standing in the center cut out of the faro table—threw the gate up and waddled out. He lunged for the box just as Ira lobbed it against the wall, shattering it. "You cheatin' son-of-a-bitch—"

Instantly, a small, silver gun shot out from a holster under Slim's shirt. He growled like an angry bull and pressed the gun hard against Ira's chest.

Slim pulled the trigger just as Ira jammed his hand between the frame and the trigger. The hammer dug into Ira's gloved hand, tearing his flesh, but he kept his grip. Slim hit Ira hard on the side of the head. Ira shook off the blow, wrestling for control of the gun.

They fell to the floor, rolling over one another. Nebraska Slim pressed all his weight atop Ira, losing his grip on the gun, grunting when . . .

. . . the shot erupted loud in the saloon, surprising Ira. But he wasn't as surprised as Slim, who looked wide-eyed a final time at the man who had killed him. Then he slumped dead on top of Ira. The peanut hulls littering the floor crackled and snapped as Ira rolled Slim off him, showing a small hole in Slim's white shirt just above his breast.

"You're gonna' swing for this!" the bar dog yelled. He reached for a double shotgun under the bar, but the barrel got hung up on his half-vest.

By the time he had freed the shotgun, Ira had drawn his gun and aimed it at the bartender's head. "Best put that double down, or your wife will be cooking for one tonight."

The bartender laid his shotgun on the long bar, and Ira motioned for drunks to move aside. He picked up the shotgun and shucked the shells out before sliding the gun across the floor away from the bar.

"You're gonna' swing for this!" the bar dog yelled again and hollered to an old woman sweeping the floor. "Best go fetch the law."

"But you all saw Slim pull a gun on me—"

"You got other troubles." A man burst through the door, stopped beside Slim, and looked down at the body. " 'Bout time, cheatin' bastard." He turned his attention to Ira. "I did everything I could." He breathed heavily. "Kid was still kicking when I walked past his open door. I cut him down, but it was too late—"

"What the hell you blabbering about?" Ira said.

"Your brother," the man in bib overalls answered. "Better come see."

The bar dog yelled at Ira to wait for the law, but Ira paid him no mind as he brushed past the farmer and ran the three blocks to Jamie's basement room. Two soiled doves Ira had visited a time or two at the New Idea stood, shaking their heads, in the doorway. They cried into silk handkerchiefs as they stared into the room. "He was always nice to us," one said. Ira pushed them out of the way.

He stopped stone still just inside Jamie's room. The boy lay crumpled across his thin mattress, a partially-melted bowl of ice cream on the floor. The tree-stump chair lay tipped over beneath a piece of hemp dangling from one rafter where the farmer had cut him down, the other piece encircling Jamie's frail neck. Ira snatched Jamie and held him in his arms, shaking him, as if shaking the boy would cough him back to life.

But he'd seen enough men die by strangulation to know there was nothing he could do for Jamie. Ira fought back tears as he held the body close, slowly rocking back and forth, cradling the boy's lifeless head as Ira sat on the edge of the bed.

"Sorry, but you got to come with me, Ira." A man filled the doorway, his vest barely covering his thick chest, where a deputy sheriff badge was pinned.

"I'm not leaving him—"

Bobby Wells cocked his gun and held it loosely beside his leg, ready to bring it up if need be. "I'll make arrangements with Graves down at the funeral home to take care of your brother. What you got to do now is come on with me."

"Come with you where?" Ira held Jamie tightly. "For what?"

"Killing Nebraska Slim."

Ira made no move to leave as he continued rocking, holding Jamie, knowing this would be the last time he would hold his brother in his arms. "Slim pulled a gun on me when I caught him cheating. We wrestled for it, and it went off when I tried to get it away from him."

"Folks down at Shingle and Locke's tell different versions as to how that faro dealer was shot."

"You think I murdered Slim?" Ira shouted. "What about Jamie? Hickok killed him as surely as if he'd cinched that rope around my brother's neck. You gonna' go after Hickok, too?"

Deputy Wells shook his head. "Not on your life. Onliest other man I'd rather not meet in a square fight is seated right in front of me."

CHAPTER 2

Sheriff T. Jeff Carr had come to Ira's jail cell a month ago on the day Jamie was to be buried. He told Ira that the eight upstairs girls at the New Idea had passed the hat so Jamie could have a proper service. "You give me your word you'll come back, I'll let you out to go to your brother's funeral."

After the funeral, Ira had detoured while going back to the lockup, visiting businesses and bars asking about Wild Bill's whereabouts. He got no answers—folks were afraid to say anything. Afraid a showdown might happen on their precious street that had been civilized not five years ago.

Ira agreed—as soon as he found Hickok, there *would* be blood spilled, though the idea of fleeing Cheyenne after the boy was laid in the ground had crossed his mind more than a few times. But thoughts of escaping were fleeting, and he returned to jail that afternoon. Ira could have outrun Sheriff Carr. He was certain he could outshoot the man, too, if it came to that. But besides Sheriff Carr being a master tracker who would eventually bring him back in, Ira had given his word that he would return to his jail cell after the burial.

So Ira sat in the eight-by-eight foot cell in the sweltering heat, his fate in the hands of the only lawyer in Cheyenne who would take his case, John Branner, who now walked ahead of Deputy Wells through the long hallway. They stopped in front of the cell door while Wells fumbled with the keys. Ira's attorney—hired because he was the only lawyer in town who would take a

18

horse and tack in trade for services—stood aside while Wells opened the door.

Ira stood and held onto the bars. Yesterday, Deputy Wells had brought Ira his only clean shirt and trousers for the trial, and he had slicked his long hair back with brilliantine. "Trial time?" Ira said and grabbed his hat.

"Not going to be any trial," Branner said.

"But—"

"All the witnesses left town." Wells stepped aside to allow Ira to leave his cell. "Seems like they got gold fever. Every damned one I was going to call as a witness cut a choggie for the gold strike in the Black Hills. Damned fools. Indians will get them more 'n likely."

"So, Judge Slaughter *had* to drop charges," Branner said. "You're free to go."

"I got no place *to* go," Ira said. "All I want to do is find Hickok. Probably hanging around bragging in one of the saloons what he done to Jamie—"

"Hickok left town," Wells said over his shoulder as he led Ira and Branner down the hallway and into the outer office.

"Left when?"

"About a week after I tossed you in the hoosegow."

Wells opened a safe and came away with Ira's belt rolled around his holstered pistol. "Seems like Hickok and his friend Colorado Charlie Utter went north with a freight train packed with dry goods and picks and shovels, flour and sugar, too. Figured on tapping into the miners' money up Deadwood way."

Wells handed Ira his rig. He checked the pistol before he strapped it on and positioned his Bowie just behind the holster. "Then that's where I'm going." Ira turned to Branner. "I'll pick up my horse now."

"I don't think I can do that."

"What do you mean, you can't do that?"

"I sold your buckskin for my fee." Branner waved the air. "And that ratty saddle as well."

"But you didn't have to do anything to earn it if the case was dismissed."

Branner shrugged. "Sorry, Ira, but I had no use for another nag." Ira grabbed Branner by the lapels and shoved him against the wall. Branner struggled to break free as Ira lifted the fancy man off the ground. "I had bills to pay—"

"Let him down," Deputy Wells ordered.

Ira pondered if it was worth another week in jail for knocking the lawyer senseless, finally concluding that would be one more week during which he couldn't get Hickok in his sights. He let Branner down, and he smoothed the lapels of his coat. Branner looked a final time at Ira before scurrying out of the office.

Ira shook his head as he watched Branner scamper out the door. "Is that even legal?"

"Did you give him a bill of sale?"

"I did."

"Then you've just been screwed by a lawyer." Wells handed Ira a tin cup. "Why'n't you sit and have a cup of coffee while you cool off."

Ira dropped into a captain's chair missing an arm and held the cup out. "Bobby, what the hell am I gonna' do? I need to get up to Deadwood before that son-of-a-bitch Hickok leaves for some other mining town."

"The sooner you get to Deadwood," Wells said, "the sooner Hickok will kill you."

Ira blew on the hot coffee, steam rising, clouding his vision as he eyed Bobby. "I don't see it that way. I'm pretty handy with this Colt my ownself. 'Member?" And Ira was sure Bobby 'membered.

While hunting the UP train robber Jubal Wright and his clan, Ira and Bobby had crossed paths, agreeing to partner up in chasing Jubal's gang. They had cornered them in a sheepherder's cabin at the base of the Shining Mountains, and a gunfight ensued. As Ira recalled, he had killed three outlaws to Bobby's one, splitting the bounty and going their separate ways—Bobby here working for Sheriff Carr; Ira giving up bounty hunting to watch over Jamie.

"Folks hereabouts claim you're faster than Hickok was at his age."

"See—I'll be the one walking away."

Bobby smiled and propped a boot on an open desk drawer. "You might be fast and accurate—hell, I've seen you hit a dollar flipped into the air at ten paces—but that don't mean you're cagier than him. That Hickok is as wily as they come. Folks tell how Wild Bill maneuvered those soldiers down in Kansas a few years back so they had to look into the sun. And you know how he ventilated them." Bobby leaned across the desk. "Bill needed a witness for his marriage here last March, and Sheriff Carr was away. So I had to go. I tell you, there is just *something* about Hickok that makes one pause. And you should, too, before you wind up like those Kansas troopers."

"All the same, I got to get to Deadwood. But I got no money to buy a horse."

Wells reached onto the stove and grabbed the coffee pot. "I don't know why I'm telling you this," he said as he refilled their cups. "It'll only get you closer to a shootout with Hickok. But the stage is hard pressed to go north without a shotgun messenger."

"I thought George Hawn was riding shotgun—"

"George got hisself killed. The stage had just left the Harding Ranch station when a Sioux war party attacked them. George and one of the passengers on their way back to Cheyenne got plugged."

"Damn Indian attacks have been picking up lately."

"Ever since the Sioux beat hell out of Custer up on the Greasy Grass, they've been emboldened." Bobbie bit off a corner of his tobacco plug. He offered Ira a chaw. When Ira waved it away, Bobbie put it back into his vest pocket. "That's why the stage hasn't been running regular of late. The stage company can't find anyone fool enough to ride shotgun." Wells held up his cup in a toast. "But I got the feeling they just found someone dumb enough to do just that."

Ira walked past the new Inter-Ocean—the fancy hotel he'd never have the money to stay in. A couple sat outside sipping tea, the woman twirling her parasol. She giggled as she bent close to another lady bustled-up in her finest. They spotted Ira in his threadbare clothes and bent to whisper to a man across the table. They laughed at Ira as he walked past, but Ira paid them no mind as he continued west on Sixteenth Street to the stage office.

He beat dust off his dungarees and took off his hat before walking through the door. A clerk stood stooped over papers as he jotted down figures, while a corpulent man sat behind an enormous mahogany desk reading that day's edition of the *Cheyenne Daily Sun*. The fat man looked over his half-glasses at Ira and jerked his thumb at the door. "Stables are on 29th and O'Neal," he said and returned to studying his newspaper. "Manure's been piling up for days, waiting for you to come clean the stalls."

"Not here to clean stables," Ira said. "I'm here for that shotgun messenger opening I understand you have."

The clerk stopped writing then, and the man behind the desk dropped his newspaper. He stood and approached Ira, looking at his boots, with one toe worn through, and his trousers hosting more dust than a Badlands' wind storm. He snickered and smiled when he looked at Ira's faded shirt with one torn pocket.

"What makes you think you can protect my stage all the way to the Black Hills? You ever been on the box before?"

"Can't say I have."

The man took out the makin's from his pocket and began rolling a smoke. "Stuttering Brown was kilt in April, and Jack Harker bought it on the Hat Creek to Red Cloud leg. Along with many more drivers and messengers I can't name." His smile faded. "Between the damned Sioux and road agents, folks just don't want to travel like they did when gold was first yelled about." He waved the air. "So, get on your way. Unless you're up for cleaning manure out of the corrals."

"I can't say that Ira Drang's ever shoveled shit for some piss-ant hiding behind his desk."

The man paused, his match close to his cigarette, the flame shaking in time with his trembling hand. "*You're* Ira Drang?" he asked, once again looking over Ira's shabby attire. "No offense, but you don't exactly live up to—"

"What folks say about me? I've had a bit of bad luck as of late." Ira leaned across the counter and blew out the match. "I need a ride to Deadwood, and the only way I'm getting there is on your stage. 'Cept I ain't even got the ten dollars for a third-class ticket."

"You could take a freight wagon up there. I hear the Swede is gathering a thirty-oxen train—"

"Too slow. Now, you want someone to ride shotgun or not?"

The man lit another match on the edge of the counter. "Be here in the morning. I'll give you that ride *and* that ten dollars if the stage makes it to Deadwood. And Ira"—he motioned to his clothes—"take a bath."

CHAPTER 3

Ira looked a final time at his one-room sleeping quarters before he slung his saddlebags and his Winchester over his shoulder. All he owned he carried with him. If Hickok killed him, so be it. But he didn't expect to lose. Either way, he'd not come back here to Cheyenne. As soon as he took care of Wild Bill, he thought he'd try his hand at a sluice box on Deadwood Gulch.

He had started across the street when riders—galloping past him and nearly running him down—thundered past. A piece of dirt clod hit Ira on the cheek, and he brushed it away. He ran across the street ahead of a scurrying mongrel, and the riders nearly ran over a man and his missus crossing the street carrying a bolt of muslin cloth. For a brief moment Ira recognized Logan Hatch leading the pack before disappearing around the block. But Logan stayed to his ranch west of town, content—it was said—to count other men's stolen horses he kept in his corrals only long enough to sell them. What had brought him to town in such a rush?

Out of curiosity, Ira walked to the end of the block and peeked around the corner of the Planter's House Hotel. They reined their horses in front of the sheriff's office: six men with no good in their manner. He shielded his eyes with his hat against the harsh sun. Ira recognized Ed Mooney, Dutch McMasters, and Handy Johnson, as much from reputation as from stories each man carried with him. Whoever the other three were he didn't know, but he recognized their kind—hard men all. Any *one* man would be dangerous to go against; all of them together would be suicide, he was certain. Even for Ira Drang.

And it certainly would be for Bobby Wells. Ira decided to hang around. He figured the least he owed Bobby was to be there in case there was gunplay. Not that the odds would be much better if he joined in.

Bobby emerged from the jail with a shotgun resting across the crook of one arm, his other hand nervously stroking his mustache. Logan dismounted and approached Wells, while the other men sat their horses, looking about as if they expected trouble. Or wanted it. Ira strained to hear what Logan and Bobbie talked about, but a Union Pacific train whistle drowned out anything they had to say to each other.

Bobbie shook his head, and Logan spat a string of tobacco that hit Bobby on the boot top, yet the young deputy remained calm. Within moments, Logan said something to his men, and they each rode off in different directions through Cheyenne. Ira waited until they had disappeared around the corner of Sixteenth before walking across the street to where Wells stood on shaky legs. "Maybe *you* ought to have a seat," Ira said, "before you fall down."

"And that bunch of owlhoots wouldn't cause *you* to be just a little nervous?" Bobby asked. "Especially since Logan Hatch promised to kill the man who murdered his little girl."

"Maybe we better talk inside," Ira said. "If Logan sees you with me, he won't invite you to his next barn dance."

Inside the jail, Ira dropped his saddlebags and propped his rifle in a corner before he poured Bobbie a cup of coffee. He kept watch out the door and motioned to a chair. Bobby took the cup in shaky hands and sat behind his desk.

"Now what's this about Logan's daughter getting killed?" Ira asked.

"Logan went to church yesterday morning, like he always

25

does on Sunday—"

"Logan goes to church?"

"I suspect it's not to keep up his spotless image in these parts." Bobbie forced a laugh. "Anyways, he and his daughter, Cassie, always go to Sunday meetin's together—something about a promise he made to his wife before she died that he and Cassie would go to Sunday meetings regularly. I just never knew he actually did."

"They always go?"

"Apparently," Bobbie said. "Except yesterday. Logan left his girl at home. Seems like she was sick—food poisoning or something—he never really knew. She felt puny, so Logan went to the meetin' alone." Bobbie stood and walked to the window as if expecting Logan and his men to come busting back. When he faced Ira again, tears clouded his eyes. "When he came back to his ranch, some son-of-a-bitch had raped and strangled Cassie right in his ranch house."

"I've been to his ranch once," Ira said. "Had a notion of killing Logan my ownself 'bout three years ago when I learned he'd bought land in these parts."

"Why'n't you kill him then?"

"I wised up and got the hell outta here when I realized Jamie would be left by himself. If I recollect right, his ranch hands got 'em a bunkhouse next to the main ranch. If his girl started screaming or anything, they'd be alerted."

Bobby shook his head. "I took a ride out thataway this last spring looking for some cavalry mounts the garrison at Camp Carlin reported stolen. I didn't find the horses, but I did find out that Logan was so protective of his Cassie that he built a new bunkhouse a hundred yards from the house, give or take."

"What the hell for? When I was there, the bunkhouse looked just fine—"

"I tossed one of his ranch hands in the hoosegow for fighting a couple months ago. He got to flapping his gums, what with the amount of rot gut he'd drank. He said that Logan built a new bunkhouse when he realized his daughter was . . . coming into her age. When he realized the hands were taking notice of the way Cassie was filling out, he figured the best thing to do was keep daughter and horny cowboys apart.

"A few moments ago, Logan demanded that Sheriff Carr find his girl's killer. I said he was out of town, but that I'd start an investigation. He said he'd shoot the first lawman who stepped foot on his ranch."

"Guess he's afraid you'd find some stolen stock there. But he's not helping you to find the killer and bring him in?"

"He don't want me to bring the murderer in," Bobby said. "Logan wants me to find Cassie's killer and turn him over to him."

"But, of course, you can't do that."

"I cannot. So, Logan said he'll find the man and give the killer a dirt nap hisself." Bobby glanced out the window. "Sure wish Sheriff Carr was back in town. Army lost another eight head of horses, and the sheriff went out looking for them. Jeff figures Logan and his men would be good for the thefts."

"I'd put him at the top of the suspect pile." Ira knew the rumors about Logan's rustling business were based on fact. Logan was smart enough—and cunning enough—to rustle horses whenever he found them and evade the law. But that was none of Ira's business, especially now that he had a line on just where Hickok had gone.

Ira leaned against the wall next to the window. He pulled the curtains back and watched the street. Now Bobby had *him* jumpy. "Logan's saying someone just came riding into his ranch and waltzed up to the house, and no one noticed?"

"Logan gives his hired hands Sundays off," Bobby said, "so they can all recuperate from their hangover from the night before. With the bunkhouse being so far away from the house . . . well, it's sure that no one heard her."

"Did it ever occur to Logan that any of the men riding with him today would be capable of raping and murdering a young girl? Hell, I'd wager each one has done worse than that a time or two in the past."

"But not with Logan Hatch's kid." Bobby shuddered. "He'd skin them alive and feed them to the Sioux if he caught anyone even looking at his Cassie thataway."

A hulking figure walked out of a saloon, looked about, and entered the one next to it. Ira recognized the Canuck, an overlarge Canadian rumored to be wanted by the law north of the border for murdering a Shoshone family living peaceably there. "That Canuck—he's got a hangman's noose with his name on it, from what I hear."

"We heard that. But we got our own problems to worry about," Bobby said. "Sheriff Carr figures the Canadians can come down here and put the grab on him if they really want him." Bobby wiped coffee from his chin stubble. "The sheriff figures it ain't none of our business, long's he keeps to himself."

And it wasn't Ira's business either. "What are Logan's men doing—looking in every building?"

"They're turning the town upside down looking for her killer, what else?"

"So, he *knows* who murdered his girl?"

"He does not. Dutch McMasters worked out a blood trail inside the house."

"Then what makes him think Cassie's killer came to Cheyenne?" Ira asked.

"Maybe you don't know just how good a man-tracker Dutch is."

But Ira knew *just* how good the man was. During the war, Logan and Dutch had hired out to southern plantation owners to track down and bring runaway slaves back to their masters. Or, kill them, if they had to. Seemed like they resorted to the "had to" part more often than not. "Even as good a man-tracker as Dutch is, he wouldn't be able to track footprints all the way to Cheyenne."

"No, but he could track a buggy," Bobbie explained. "Cassie's killer rode onto his ranch in a buggy, which Dutch tracked back here. A horse and buggy Hap Barnes rented from the livery Saturday afternoon."

"Hap the drunk? Where'd he get money to rent a rig?"

Bobby shrugged. "Your guess is as good as mine. Never knowed him to have even the price of a drink in his pocket. But the buggy was abandoned in back at the livery."

"Now Logan is on the hunt for Hap?"

Wells nodded and finished his coffee. He stood and grabbed his shotgun as he headed for the door. "And the only thing stopping Logan from stringing the old man up when he finds him is me." He paused in the doorway. "You wouldn't want a part-time deputy job by any chance?"

"Thanks for the offer," Ira said. "But I got a stagecoach calling my name. And Hickok is whispering in my ear."

Chapter 4

As Ira walked the three blocks towards the Inter-Ocean, Handy Johnson emerged from the grocery. He looked at Ira and stopped, his one hand poised beside his holster, the other hand left somewhere on the battlefield at Gettysburg. He smiled at Ira and continued walking toward him. "Thought that was you."

Bobby had told Ira that Handy had spouted about how he intended killing Ira if Ira beat the murder rap on Nebraska Slim. "So, you watch your backside," Bobby had advised. "The man fancies himself a gunny."

Ira didn't worry about Handy too much, though. He'd heard the six men Handy had already killed had been sitting down or running away. "I thought I smelled a back shooter," Ira said.

Handy took the loop off his holster when he stopped in the middle of the street and glanced past Ira.

Ira chanced a look behind. Dutch McMasters walked toward him. The tall, lanky man with a smile on his amiable face ambled toward Ira with a thumb hooked into the pocket of his dungarees. Yet Ira knew better than to be lulled into thinking Dutch was just another friendly farm hand. More than twenty men had already made that mistake—letting their guard down in front of Dutch. It was said the killer carved scallops on the butt of his gun while still standing over the body of each victim.

When Ira looked back at Handy, the man had disappeared into one of the other stores that lined the street.

"Thought that was you in your damn tattered clothes. You

look like a bum," Dutch said, a match twitching between his teeth as he talked. "Heard you crawled out from under some rock. Been living here in Cheyenne for a time. I been meaning to come look you up. Just for old time's sake." He nodded toward where Handy had disappeared. "That damn fool thinks he's good enough to take you." Dutch laughed. "I should have let the idiot try. Never liked the sneaky bastard anyhow."

Ira shifted his saddlebags and rifle, his gun hand inching toward his holster. If Dutch decided to make his play, Ira wanted at least a fighting chance. Not that it would matter. For as fast as Ira was, Dutch was that much quicker. The only chance Ira would have was if Dutch lost his temper. Which he was known to do. "I heard you're still working for Logan Hatch."

Dutch shrugged. "Where else *would* I go? Me and Logan's been together for so long—"

"That's right," Ira interrupted. "Have you and Logan hunted down any unarmed runaway slaves lately?"

The match twitched faster. "You got a big mouth."

Ira forced a laugh, blading his stance, his hand now just over his gun butt. "You're just pissed 'cause I got away from you two fools."

Dutch's face flushed red, and his match jerked between his teeth. After the war, Logan and Dutch had been hired by a Nashville family to track down Ira and bring him to them. He and a prominent Nashville lawyer had sparked the same woman, and the lawyer had made the mistake of drawing down on Ira. For three years after the war, the family kept the reward money outstanding. It was only when the lawyer's mother died that the surviving family decided it wasn't worth money to bring Ira to justice, and they retracted the reward. "Only thing that's stopping me from drilling big, gaping holes in your chest is that we're on the hunt for Cassie's killer."

"I heard you peckerwoods were sleeping it off Saturday night and didn't even know the girl was being attacked," Ira said. "If it were my ranch, I'd fire the lot of you."

Dutch tossed his match aside. He squared up to Ira as Handy burst from an alley. "We found Hap!" he yelled at Dutch as he waved him over, one empty shirt sleeve flopping at his side. "Logan says for you to come. Quick."

Ira smiled. "Guess you'll have an easier mark there in the alley."

"Like I'd have a hard time with you?" Dutch said. He started toward where Handy waited at the end of the alley. "Another time," he said over his shoulder and disappeared around the corner.

Ira's legs buckled, and he found a bench along the street. He brushed off pigeon crap and sat down, setting his saddlebags beside him while he took deep, calming breaths. *If* he had provoked Dutch enough that it would throw his shot off, Ira *might* have had a chance. *Might.* He sat, thinking what the outcome of a gunfight with Dutch would have been. And thinking he might never have gotten his crack at Hickok.

"Lucky you didn't draw down on that one." A soldier with quartermaster chevrons on his sleeve sat beside Ira. He bit off a corner of tobacco and offered Ira a chaw, but he waved it away. "Don't you know who that tall drink of water is?"

"I know," Ira answered and motioned to the soldier's sleeve. "Camp Carlin?"

The sergeant nodded and looked to where Dutch had disappeared. "Seen that one a couple weeks ago at the Keystone dance hall there in Chicago. A private from Fort Russell drew down on him but never cleared leather before he was looking down the tall man's gun barrel."

Ira had once been to the area of west Cheyenne the soldiers had dubbed *Chicago,* where most anything was available, and the law rarely stopped by. Ira even had the price to take one of the upstairs girls to her crib for the night. Once.

"I know him. Dutch McMasters. He's as good with that target rifle of his as he is with his Colt. What did the commanding officer of the fort say when one of his men was killed?"

"That Dutch never killed the private," the sergeant said, working the chaw around in his cheek. "Never even shot him. The tall man there *could* have drilled him, but the . . . lady on his arm saved the private." An empty army supply wagon stopped beside the bench. "That's my ride," he said and hopped in the wagon's back with ten other soldiers.

Ira waited until the dust of a freight wagon packed with bags of flour and sugar passed before he walked the rest of the way towards the stage office. Even before he cleared the corner of the block, he heard violin music filter above the everyday noises of Cheyenne. Old Zip Coon sat on a chair in front of the office, an old man in oversized buckskins, one boot lost—somewhere, sometime, he wasn't sure—his eyes closed as tears ran down his dirty face. Ira waited until the old man finished "Shenandoah" before walking up the steps. " 'Fraid I don't have any money for your hat," Ira said. "If I did, I'd sure as hell give you some. That was purty playing."

Old Zip Coon smiled through perfect pearlies. "That's all right—I heard you been having troubles as of late. Heard about your brother hanging himself, and you getting railroaded for killing Nebraska Slim. That fat ass deserved it. Sorry about all that." He looked around him. "And now that Logan Hatch has been turning the town upside down looking for Hap Barnes—"

"Sounds like they found old Hap," Ira said as he watched the stagecoach kicking up dust rounding the corner of the block, nearing the station, six matched horses stepping strong in the street. Horses, Ira heard, bought in the St. Louis horse markets just to pull the stages. "What did they want with Hap?"

Old Zip Coon took out a chunk of resin and rubbed his fiddle strings. "Logan thinks Hap killed his daughter. That man-tracker—that Dutch McMasters—tracked the buggy he rented back here to Cheyenne," he said, plucking strings as he tuned his violin. "But Hap never drove that rig. All he did was rent the horse and buggy for some feller."

"What feller?"

The old man shrugged. "Just some man who gave Hap two dollars to rent the rig for him. Never bothered to say what his name was."

"Didn't that seem odd to Hap? Some stranger asking him to rent a horse and buggy?"

"Hap, he always is a mite too trusting." Old Zip Coon laughed. "Or a mite too drunk to pay any attention, as long as he got him some drinkin' money. All Hap does most days is wear calluses on his elbows inside the saloons—whenever he's got him the price of a shot of whisky."

"When was the last time you saw Hap?"

Old Zip Coon looked up at the clouds as if the answer were there. "Last I seen him, he was going into Delmonico's with his two dollars for a bottle yesterday." He pulled the violin tight to his neck. "Only now you say they found Hap. Hope they go easy on him. I'd damn sure help him. But what am I going to do to help him with this?" He held up his violin and pointed to Ira's gun with his fiddle bow. "Now *you* could make a difference. I heard about you—"

"Not today," Ira said. "I'm headed up to the Black Hills in that." He nodded to the stage rolling to a stop in front of the depot. A short, fat man cursed the team of horses in a thick London brogue as he hauled on the brake lever. He tied the reins off and stepped down from the bright red coach, the clean running gear reflecting yellow paint. Above the hunting scene painted on the door was the name of the stage: "Belle of Custer City." The driver patted dust off his overalls and looked at Ira through one good eye, the other as white as the driven snow. Dead. "You a passenger?" the driver asked. " 'Cause we ain't been getting many riders nowadays, with the Indian raids and all."

"And don't forget the road agents that's been picking you clean." Old Zip Coon laughed right before he began a sad song, a funeral dirge played in a minor key.

"I'm your shotgun messenger," Ira said.

The driver rested his hands on his hips and looked Ira over. "You figure you are up to the job? You're a bit . . . skinny. No offense."

"None taken," Ira said. "Most folks think I look perpetually hungry." He rubbed his belly. "Which I have been as of late." The wind shifted, and Ira got the first strong whiff of the driver. He was—as Ira's mother used to say—water shy. In need of a good scrubbing. "I hope to find at least a decent meal somewhere along the way."

"Then welcome," the man said. He smiled wide, and Ira could count the man's remaining teeth on the fingers of one hand. "I was worried we couldn't get anyone fool enough to ride shotgun, and we'd have to cancel another run." He pulled his glove tighter and held out his hand. "Folks just call me Sally . . . short for Salvatore. That's if I believe my late mum." He crossed himself. "Let me stow your saddlebags in the boot."

When he disappeared around the back of the coach, Old Zip Coon waved Ira over. "Be careful of that one," he whispered, covering his mouth with his violin. "Heard he skipped England right ahead of a lynching. Rumor is he got into some argument with a street whore, and it ended up bad for her."

"I'll keep that in mind."

Sally waddled back to the front of the coach and swiped his hand across a stubbly beard crusted with dried tobacco juice and that day's breakfast. He fished a pocket watch from his vest and cursed. "Damn near seven. Ain't nobody on time nowadays."

"I am." A man walked out of the stage station, coughing violently. He produced a bottle of Tubercolozine from his back pocket and took a short sip. He corked it and put it back in his pocket before offering his hand. "Dan Crane. But folks hereabouts just call me Preacher."

Ira hesitated before shaking Preacher's hand. He wasn't sure how contagious consumption was. "Ira Drang. Riding shotgun for this trip."

"So, we may actually get under way today," Dan said. "Good. There are souls up Deadwood way that need a little guidance."

"I suspect Preacher Dan there would dearly love to get away from Cheyenne," Old Zip Coon said, "where his reputation stays with him."

Preacher turned his back on the old man. "He is referring to my . . . alcoholism. But I have since slain that dragon."

Old Zip Coon plucked "Dixie" on his violin. "But not that other dragon of you'rn. I'm talking about that Quantrill dragon."

Preacher's complexion turned ruddy. "What I did in the war I'm not particularly proud of." He faced Ira. "But, to the old man's satisfaction, I am going up to Deadwood and minister to the lost souls. I'm to meet my good friend Preacher Smith"—he tipped his hat—"who drifted up that way just last month to minister to miners on the gulch. At least I'll find men who are actually salvageable. Unlike here. Now I think I'll sit in the coach. The stench is overwhelming." He nodded at Old Zip Coon before stepping inside.

"I got to see a man about a horse," Sally said as he headed for the outhouse. "Then we'll get under way."

"Why would anyone single out Hap to rent a rig?" Ira asked Old Zip Coon when Sally had disappeared around back. "He'd be the least likely feller I'd trust with a job like that."

The old man set his violin across his lap and grabbed a hip flask. It looked a lot like Preacher's medicine bottle. And it smelled a lot like it, too. He offered Ira a nip, but he waved it away. "Hap would do anything for a drink." The old man laughed. "And he'd forget what the hell he did a minute later. I always thought the booze pickled what few brains he had. If I didn't want to be remembered, Hap's just the man I'd ask to rent a buggy for me."

Sally emerged from the station office buttoning his trousers. "Dispatcher said a couple cowboys bought tickets, but they ain't showed—"

"We're here." A small man in his twenties ran around the corner of the building, with a man twice his size stumbling behind him. "Dauber Nelson," the small man gasped, out of breath, as he handed the stage driver two tickets. Sally exaggerated looking Dauber over. "What we got here is your garden variety Monkey Ward cowboy, don't 'cha figure?"

Ira had no argument with that. Dauber was dressed in a sequined, double-breasted shirt and denims pressed so sharp, a man would cut himself if he ran his hand over them. His bright red and yellow bandana seemed out of place with his Montana Peak that sat atop his head at a rakish angle. He did—as Sally said—look just like the models in the Montgomery Ward catalogue.

"But don't call my partner there a cowboy." Dauber nodded to the big man, who towered over him. "Gordy here's a farmer."

"Ain't gonna' be no farmer no more." Gordy smiled at Dauber. "Now I'm fixin' to go to Deadwood and be a miner."

Sally looked the pair over. "Where's your gear? Your saddle?"

Ira wondered if they'd lost their gear to a fast-talking lawyer like he had, until Dauber said in almost a whisper, "We lost them in a poker game last night."

"That's right," Gordy said. " 'Sides, we don't need no

saddle—we're fixin' to be miners. Won't need no horse when we get there, neither."

"All right then," Sally said. "Have a seat inside beside Preacher. We'll wait a bit more—some man and his wife bought tickets. If they don't show in a few moments, we'll roll to the Black Hills with a half-empty stage."

Sally broke off another chaw of tobacco and stuffed it inside his vest while he opened the stage door. He rolled down the oiled curtains that would block some of the dust. "Dispatcher in the office said Logan Hatch's men have been bulling their way around town."

"That's nothing new," Old Zip Coon said. "That's what they do every time they come into Cheyenne."

"But this sounds serious—roughing folks up. Tearing up the place looking for his girl's killer," Sally said.

"You'd think Logan would want to keep his gunnies on a short rope," Ira said.

Sally laughed. "Letting off a little steam is healthy. I'm just grateful I'm on the trail whenever they come into town." He cinched his gloves tighter and looked around a final time before climbing onto the seat. "Guess that couple's not going to make it."

Ira propped his Winchester against the seat and climbed up beside Sally. He grabbed for the brake lever when a couple ran around the corner of the stage office, as much as a woman could run in those fancy lace-up boots, and him with steel-toed shoes. The man stood taller than Ira, but he looked even taller and heavier in his double-breasted suit and pressed trousers. Younger than Ira—in his thirties, perhaps—his bowler sat at a wicked angle over hair pasted down with wax to match his blade-thin mustache. He looked fit, but the man's pale complexion was as white as that of the woman he followed, and

Ira was certain he'd never toiled under the hot sun a day in his life.

But it was the woman who held Ira's attention. She appeared to be a few years younger than her partner. Slightly built, she held her dress—riding over shapely hips—out of the dirt as her bosom strained against the fabric. Blond curls bounced on her chest as she shuffled toward the stage. With formal clothes so unsuited for travelling, Ira thought it just a matter of time before she shucked the gloves riding past her elbows and traded in her bustled skirt for something more practical.

The couple stopped, out of breath, in front of the coach and looked about. The man fished inside his coat pocket and withdrew two tickets he handed to Sally. He squinted and grabbed a pair of spectacles from his shirt pocket. After he compared the list from the way pocket to the tickets, Sally tore them and handed the man their half. "Frank Warner."

"And my wife, Beth." Frank Warner smoothed his hair pasted back with tonic and brilliantine.

"You better wash that crap outta' your hair," Sally said.

"Why would I do that?" Frank asked.

Sally shook his head. "Trail gets mighty dusty."

"So?"

"Suit yourself." Sally nodded to the coach. "Better get in. We're late as it is."

Sally issued the pair dusters—supplied by the stage company to keep the infernal road dust off them—and watched as they climbed into the stage. "Anyone else want a duster?" Sally asked. Preacher accepted one, but the cowboy and farm kid declined.

He stowed the unused dusters in the front boot and whispered to Ira, "I'd wager a quid that if fellers around Cheyenne saw that little lady riding the stage, we'd be packed."

"No doubt," Ira said. "Especially since she's dressed like

she's going to some kind of formal ball. What's the story on them?"

Sally uncoiled twenty feet of bull whip. He shook it out while he grabbed on to the reins. "I mind my own business." He shrugged. "But I'm sure we'll find out before this little trip is over."

CHAPTER 5

Dutch followed Handy through the alley and around back of the livery. Wind whipped stalks of hay into the air, swirling around Logan as he leaned on the top rail of the corral. Horses snorted and clustered at the far end of the enclosure, watching Logan smoke a cigarette. He stared down at a dead man who had been shoved under a juniper bush in back of the stables. "Hap Barnes?" Dutch asked, though he already suspected it was.

Logan nodded. "What's left of him."

"He tell you anything before you . . . ?"

"I didn't kill him." Logan snubbed his butt out in a pile of fresh manure and waved swarming flies away. He motioned to Handy. "Go fetch the others and tell them we found Hap. And Handy—after you've found everyone—bring that old man with the fiddle back here."

They watched Handy until he disappeared around the corner of the alley. "Hap was dead when I found him. Strangled." Logan kicked a rock, and it flew into the fence. "Like Cassie was. Not ten yards from that buggy he rented. Son-of-a-bitch! Don't make any sense."

Dutch turned around and sat on the fence rail. "You can bet it wasn't Hap who killed Cassie. That old bastard lived for his next drink. Doubt if he was ever sober enough to even *drive* a rig. And I never even seen him with a woman."

"Cassie wasn't a woman!" Logan snapped. "She was just a

little girl." Then he waved the air. "Sorry."

"Understood," Dutch said. "But my point still stands: Hap was all about drowning in his next drink. Besides, Cassie lived all her life on a ranch. If some old man like Hap tried to get frisky . . . well, she was stout enough to fend him off."

Dutch took off his hat and ran his fingers through his wispy hair, recalling the thick, naturally wavy hair Cassie had, and he drove the thought from his mind. Later—after they had caught and killed her murderer—he would allow himself to think about his friend's only daughter.

"I know you're right," Logan said. "Cassie would have fought him off. There'd be evidence she did so. Still, the buggy . . . this close to his body. Reins all bloody. My gut tells me whoever Hap rented the rig for killed him and stuffed him under that bush."

The buggy still stood beside the corral fence where it had been dropped beside other buggies awaiting rental. Dutch didn't know which horse had been hitched to it—it mattered little. All he wanted was to be able to work out the sign. He waved away blowflies that had been attracted to the body and squatted. He studied the ground around the corpse, but there had been too much commotion from the horses milling about. Any sign that might have told him something about Hap's killer was obliterated. He lifted up Hap's boot, but it didn't match the bloody boot tracks shuffling through the house.

Handy followed the Canuck into the alley as he dragged the screaming Old Zip Coon by an arm to where Logan and Dutch waited. The Canuck tossed the old man down in the pile of horse manure. "I checked with the livery man. He said all he knew was that Hap paid with two half-eagles."

Logan pulled his gloves on tighter over his knuckles and knelt beside Old Zip Coon. "Where'd Hap get the five-dollar pieces?"

Zip Coon's eyes darted from the Canuck to Dutch to Logan.

"From that feller who wanted to rent the buggy."

"Give me a name."

"I don't know who it was. Hap didn't know the man, and he never described him."

"Ed Mooney says him and Hap were bestest pards," the Canuck said, kicking the old man in the side. Old Zip fell backward, screaming in pain, and flies flew into his mouth. He spat them out and stared wide-eyed at the Canuck, who was donning his own gloves. He shook his fist under the old man's face. "He knows. I'll get the information out of him, even if it kills him."

The Canuck jerked Old Zip erect, but Logan shoved him aside. "I do my own asking."

Dutch leaned on the top rail, his back to Logan and the old man. He didn't envy Old Zip Coon—Logan was killing-mad. Dutch had been with him enough years to recognize that look, the same look he saw yesterday morning after he came back from church. Dutch had seen Logan's horse tied to the rail in front of his house, and he headed from the bunkhouse to talk to Logan. They had a buyer for the eight head of army horses they'd "found" running loose just outside Camp Collier. When Dutch entered the house, he expected his boss to be pleased they had a buyer willing to buy stock with changed brands.

But Dutch found anything but a happy man inside. What he found was Logan crouched in Cassie's bedroom, where she had fallen, holding her tight, her nightshirt pulled up over her naked torso. Logan held the dead girl as tears streamed down his leathered cheeks. In all the years they had been together, Dutch had never seen Logan cry. Even when cholera took his wife nine years earlier.

Blood. There had been enough on Cassie's face and staining her chest for Dutch to tell Cassie had put up a fight. The hard hand print on her face where her killer had tried to silence her, pressing his hand over her mouth hard enough to bruise, showed clearly. The scene was surreal—Logan holding his dead daughter while dust motes filtered through the bedroom light and settled on the two. But the blood wasn't Cassie's—it was her attacker's, and skin and blood on the girl's teeth indicated she had bitten him sometime during the attack.

That day had floated by as if in a dream for Dutch. Logan wouldn't let anyone else touch Cassie, insisting himself on changing his daughter's clothes into something appropriate for her final rest. That had not been unusual—Logan had kept such a tight rein on Cassie since she started developing, he would kill anyone who even saw her naked. He'd flown into a rage this spring when that cowhand from the Circle G south of Cheyenne delivered the bull Logan had bought. The cowhand rode up to Cassie as she saddled her horse and suggested they go for a ride.

Before they could traipse off together, though, Logan stormed out of the house. He ran across the yard to the horse barn where the cowhand was sparking Cassie, but the boy had wisely galloped off to safer pastures. Logan would have ridden after him and likely killed him if Cassie hadn't stopped her father.

While Logan was preparing Cassie to be buried, Dutch had studied the blood trail leading from the house to where twin wheel marks showed where a buggy rode quickly away from the ranch. And, after Logan and Dutch and the ranch hands had shoveled the last of the dirt over Cassie's body, that frightening look of a father possessed returned—the same look Logan now displayed as he grabbed Old Zip Coon and squeezed his face in his powerful hand. He turned the old man's head to where Hap's body lay. "That's your friend stuffed under that bush," Logan said. "Who'd he rent that buggy for?"

"I told you, Hap never seen the feller before," Old Zip Coon said. "He never told me what he looked like. And I didn't ask."

Logan backhanded him, and he fell over backwards. "Once more: who paid him to rent that rig?"

"Like I says, Mr. Hatch, Hap didn't say. Alls he said was that it was the same man paid him to rent the rig who paid him to buy fare on that there Cheyenne to Black Hills stage what left this mornin'.'"

"That buggy came back here with blood on the seat. And Hap there's got blood aplenty over his shirt front from whoever killed him. Surely Hap must have mentioned that."

"I never *seen* old Hap after he bought the ticket for that feller," Old Zip Coon said, and a sad look crossed his face. "I guess I was about the last person to see Hap alive."

Logan cocked his fist, but Dutch caught it. "The old man don't know anything more." It mattered not at all if Logan beat Old Zip Coon to death. What did matter were the horses they needed to sell, and more stolen ones coming down the trail from the Dakotas soon. Beating the old duffer would only bring the law down on them. And that was bad for business. "We know they left on the morning's stage," Dutch said. "All we got to do is catch up with it. We'll find Cassie's killer."

Logan turned Old Zip Coon loose, and he fell to the ground. "Find the others," he told Handy. "Tell them to meet us at the livery office. I'm going to find out what they know."

Logan leaned over the counter and slapped it. "I need information."

"What the hell . . . ?" The heavyset line supervisor looked up from his newspaper. He stood abruptly and approached the counter warily. "Sorry, Mr. Hatch. I didn't know it was you."

"What do you know about that buggy out back? The one with the dried blood on the reins and smeared on the seat?"

"Not much *to* tell. I come out this morning, and there it was. I unhitched the mare and turned her in the corral."

"And you never saw the man who rented it?"

"It was Hap."

"And it didn't seem odd the old drunk *had* money for the horse and buggy?" Dutch asked.

The supervisor shrugged. "He paid in gold. What can I say?"

"And a dead man stuffed under that bush never tipped you off that something wasn't right?"

"D-dead man?" the supervisor stammered. "I never seen no dead man. Oh, God." He started pacing the floor. "I gots to go fetch the law."

Dutch tapped Logan on the shoulder. "Maybe the stage office will know something."

By the time they walked to the stage office, Logan was fit to be wrestled to the ground. His face was crimson, and his teeth gnashed as his frustration grew. "Tell me what the hell you know about the stage that left for Deadwood this morning," he said to the office man.

The heavy-set man looked up over his newspaper. He saw Dutch and Logan and stood abruptly. "What's to tell?"

"Who boarded it?"

The fat man donned glasses and looked at a sheet of paper hanging on the wall. "A couple cowboys. A man and his wife. That evangelist who used to spread the gospel with Preacher Smith before Smith went to Deadwood."

"That's all?"

"Except for the driver and the shotgun messenger."

Dutch pulled Logan aside. "He don't know any more than Old Zip Coon did. This fool never saw whoever paid Hap to buy the stage ticket, either."

Logan nodded. "You're probably right." He had started for the door when he turned back to the counter. "Who's your jehu for this run?"

"Sally. But don't ask what his last name is, 'cause he never gave one. He's a limey, is all I know. But he's our best driver."

"Who's riding shotgun?"

"Ira Drang," the company man answered.

Logan waited until he and Dutch stepped outside before he spoke about Ira. "I heard that son-of-a-bitch was awaiting trial for murdering a faro dealer last month. Did he bust jail?"

"Case got tossed out," Dutch answered. "Judge dismissed it when all the witnesses lit out for the gold fields up north."

"Just our luck—Ira riding shotgun on this run."

"Don't worry none about him," Dutch said. "I can take him most any time I want."

Logan looked up at his friend. "Maybe you forget how many times he gave us the slip back in Tennessee. That's one foxy bastard. Don't underestimate him. Too many men who have are now resting on the other side of the grass."

Ed Mooney, Handy Johnson, and the Canuck rode toward them, leading Dutch's and Logan's horses. "If we ride hard, we ought to be able to catch up with them by the time they get to Horse Creek Station." Logan turned to Ed. "Ride hard to the ranch, and tell Matt and Miguel. Tell 'em we'll stop the stage outside Horse Creek at the narrow spot we found that time going to Spotted Tail Agency."

"Then what?" Dutch asked.

"Then we line them all up," Logan said, "and see who the hell Cassie bit."

CHAPTER 6

Sally hauled back on the reins and rode the brake as the stagecoach started down the steep slope leaving the Pole Creek Ranch. They headed north, going past Fred Schwartz's barn with its huge, round frame. They had stopped at the ranch eighteen miles out of Cheyenne. While the horses rested and took in grain, the passengers stretched their legs, none talking to one another as if each held their own secret they wished to keep to themselves.

"They'll friendly-up to one another before the trip's finished." Sally nudged Ira. "That's how it always is—folks open up once they got nothing else to do but stare at the inside of the coach." He held up one hand. "But I'm not one to pry."

For a man who minded his own business, Sally was more than a little nosey. And talkative, something Ira found annoying, for all he could think of was finding Bill Hickok and killing him for what he'd done to Jamie.

"Now you take those two kids that boarded together—that ranch kid and that big farm boy—it's mighty odd that they didn't even have a saddle and bridle to their names. A man don't travel this country without riding gear."

"Preacher and that fancy couple don't have any either."

"That's different. They're not . . . western folks. You can tell that by lookin' at 'em."

"*I* didn't have horse gear," Ira said, feeling the Concord rolling and rocking gently on thick, leather cushions as the stage rode over the hard mud ruts. "Does that make me odd, too?"

"But you got a good reason for not travelling with any gear. That shyster, John Branner, took it for your defense." Sally spat a string of juice, but the wind brought it right back. It splatted against his cheek, and he wiped it off with his glove. "Just don't seem right, him taking your horse and tack to defend you, and the case being dismissed before it even got to trial. And before Branner had to even lift a finger to help you."

"Bad luck seems to follow me."

"But dammit," Sally said, and cracked his whip over the heads of the leaders. "A man ought to have at least a saddle with him in this country."

Ira laughed. "Right now I couldn't afford to put a horse under one anyhow."

Sally tickled the reins expertly, his bull whip cracking just over the ears of the horses, never coming close to hitting them, and for a moment he kept quiet. That was all right with Ira—he needed to think, to plan what he would do once he got to Deadwood; once he faced Hickok in the street. Or the saloon. Wherever. It mattered none to Ira. He just wanted this rage within him to run its course as he looked down at Hickok's body.

Just after leaving Horse Creek Station, where the fifty-cent meal left passengers and Sally and Ira a little sleepy, Ira's eyes drooped, and his head nodded as the rolling of the stage lulled him to sleep.

Until movement off to his periphery caught his eye.

He half turned in the seat and pulled his hat low over his eyes to shield them from the sun. "Riders approaching." He picked up his Winchester propped against the seat and looked through the shimmering heat and dust at the men fast approaching. "And there's not a friendly smile among 'em."

Sally followed Ira's gaze. Seven riders rode down a gently sloping hill, five riding close together with two outriders. Flankers. Like they had military training or experience. Ira said, "Folks don't come riding hell-bent for a stage if they have good intentions."

"No use trying to outrun them," Ira said. Sally slowed the coach as he snatched his shotgun from the seat. He leaned over and yelled to the passengers below, "You men down there, fill your hands. Riders coming hell-bent-for-election, and I don't think they want a friendly chat."

Frank Warner moved the curtain aside and poked his head out the stage door window. "I didn't pay fare to be your protector."

Ira spread his attention between Frank and the riders. "If you don't throw in with us, you might be walking to Deadwood. Or worse, depending on what those fellers want."

"What the hell *do* they want?" Frank said. "You're not carrying a strongbox." Many stages were stopped and robbed returning from the gold fields. On the trip up *to* Deadwood, all they carried were passengers.

"All the more reason to arm yourself," Sally said. He spat a string of tobacco that trailed off and slapped a horse on the rump. " 'Cause the only thing I can think of is that they intend to rob each and every one of us."

Sally stopped the coach on a flat, level part of the road and turned in his seat to face the riders. "Be ready," he said and clutched his shotgun tight.

"Me and Gordy are ready," Dauber said. He opened the door and stepped out, followed by the Nebraska farm kid, who was nearly too big to squeeze through the door. He held a pistol that looked like a derringer in his big paw in front of him like a divining rod.

Ira swore under his breath. "You'd better be ready," he said as he reached for more rifle rounds in his pocket. "Because that's Logan Hatch leading that bunch of hired guns." Ira recognized some of the riders—the Canuck riding a roan fifteen hands high that seemed to struggle under the weight of the big man, and Handy Johnson, who rode his bay as expertly as any man with two hands. Ed Mooney sat his gray, and Ira noticed his saddle scabbard was empty. "Who's the kid riding the brown?"

"Matt Ales," Sally said. "He's some contract buster who showed up at Logan's wanting a job breaking horses. Folks say he'll ride anything with hair on it. And I'd bet that horse he's riding was stolen."

Probably from some army post down south, Ira thought as he looked at the Spanish rowels adorning the man's spurs, far too large for any cowboy this far north. And the short rope tied to the saddle horn as if he were still looking to throw a loop over some Texas longhorn hiding among the brush.

A man with a sombrero pulled tight by the chin strap rode a pinto thirteen hands tall. "Who's that on the tobiano?"

"Watch that one close," Sally said "That's Miguel DeJesus. Loves his blades. And loves showing off his collection of Indian scalps."

Ira's attention quickly turned to the man riding a dapple gray, a smile pasted across his face, the same grin he'd flashed Ira in Cheyenne. Ira had seen that smile more times than he wanted. Folks claimed Dutch always smiled before he was about to kill someone.

Dutch, riding flank, wandered off as they neared, but Ira knew better. He knew the man intended working his way around to the back of the stage. "Dutch McMasters is coming up on our backside," Ira said, losing sight of the tall man when he rode over a hill.

"Shit! That's all we need is him agin' us," Preacher said. He stepped from the stage and walked around the far side, putting the stage between him and the riders. He threw aside his duster before he checked a short-barreled pistol concealed inside a hogged-out bible. He closed the book and drew his sidearm.

"Watch for Dutch. If he gets the chance, that bastard'll back-shoot any of us."

"That any way for a preacher to talk?" Bethany Warner stuck her head out of the window of the coach. "For what it matters, I've got a hide-out gun in case they get too . . . friendly with me."

"That's the least of your worries," Ira said. He set three more rifle cartridges on the seat beside him. He stood, looking the way Dutch had disappeared, but could not spot him. "Logan Hatch is all about killing men. Not molesting women folk."

Logan and his men slowed their approach, and Ira wondered if they were giving Dutch time to work around behind them. "That tall man on the dapple gray," Ira called down to Gordy and Dauber. "Watch for him. If you see him, don't try him on by yourselves, or Sally here'll be two passengers short."

Logan turned in his saddle. He said something to Ed Mooney, who peeled off and rode in the opposite direction Dutch had. "You set, Preacher?" Ira asked.

"Got two Navy Colts," Preacher answered, taking up a position by the rear boot for cover. "And I believe I still know how to use them."

"That's about far enough," Ira ordered Logan when he had come to within twenty yards of the coach. Ira shouldered his rifle and pointed it loosely in Logan's direction. Logan's chestnut seemed to falter under the weight, as he reined in to one side of the stage. Logan's own rifle lay loosely across his saddle, but Ira knew he could bring it to bear in a heartbeat. "I'd hate for this thing to go off on account of you robbing us."

Logan reached inside his vest pocket, and Ira snapped his

rifle up. "Kinda' touchy, ain't ya'?" Logan said. He came away with his bible and showed it to Ira. "Hate to get drilled for building a smoke." Logan peeled off a paper and began rolling a cigarette, trickling the tobacco from the pouch. Taking his time. *Stalling,* Ira thought. *For Dutch and Ed to get into position?*

"I heard you was riding shotgun," Logan said. He lit a match on his saddle horn and touched it to his cigarette. "Dutch said you were out of jail. How you skirted that murder charge of Nebraska Slim is beyond me. But whatever—I should have taken care of you back in Tennessee."

"If you could have caught me," Ira said. He kept the area where Dutch had disappeared in his periphery, while staring down Logan Hatch. It had been more than ten years since he'd last seen Logan. But except for the graying hair around his temples, and the slight paunch holding up his long barreled pistol, Logan looked the same. *Dangerous.* "Now whyn't you and your gunnies turn around and ride away. No one on this stage has enough money to make robbery worthwhile."

Logan shook his head. "I can buy and sell anyone on this stage. This ain't about a robbery."

"Then why the hell you ride up here with bad intentions written all over your faces?"

"Cassie," Logan answered, and his eyes flicked to the far side of the coach.

He's expecting Dutch and Ed to make a move any moment, Ira thought. "I heard someone murdered your daughter. Sorry to hear it."

"You'll be even sorrier if you don't turn over her killer." Logan turned his head and swiped a hand across his eyes. Ira felt for the man. Losing a child would be the worst kind of living hell. Still, Ira didn't feel sorry enough for him to let his guard down.

"Ira," Dauber whispered. "I think our friends are putting the sneak on us now."

Ira caught the almost imperceptible movement of a blue bandana among swaying prairie grasses to one side of the stage. He shouldered his rifle and centered the sight on Logan's chest. "You want to die right here? Right now?"

"A man's got to die sometime," Logan answered. "But I suspect I'll be the one riding away in one piece."

"Not if your two gunhands sneaking up on us don't show themselves."

"You drill me, and it's you who won't make it to the end of the day."

"A man's got to die sometime," Ira mocked Logan. "If you get me, Sally here's sure to pull both triggers."

Sally cocked the hammers of his shotgun. "And, being one-eyed, I'm not much with a shooting iron, but even *I* can't miss at this range."

"Don't let him buffalo you, eh," the Canuck said. "They can't get all of us."

"Nothing I'd like better than to have Ira Drang's scalp hanging from my saddle," Miguel said. He took off his sombrero and let it dangle on his back by the chin strap. "The Canuck is right, *Caporal*—he cannot get all of us."

"No?" Ira said. "Look a little closer."

Logan met Ira's eyes for long moments before he broke the stare and looked the stage over. Frank had both of his gambler's guns pointed at Logan. Preacher and Gordy stood behind cover of the coach, aiming their pistols at Logan's men, while Dauber stood with his back to the stage, watching the way Dutch had disappeared.

"All you gotta' do to start the dance is let your boys get closer." Ira thumbed the hammer back on his rifle, and his trigger finger tightened. "I'd call them out, but my finger might accidentally let this Winchester go. I get almighty nervous with a couple back-shooters hiding in the grass behind me."

Logan's jaw tightened, and his face flushed red. After several tense moments, he gave a short whistle, then a longer one and—out of the corner of his eye—Ira saw Dutch and Ed stand up in the tall grass. They walked to the crest of a rolling hill where their horses were staked.

"Come out around here, so's Ira I put an eyeball on you," Logan said. "By the looks of him, Ira's plumb scared. And scared men make mistakes."

"About as big a mistake as you stopping us," Ira said.

"Yeah," Sally said. "Just why the hell *did* you stop us?"

"I told you—someone murdered my girl yesterday while I was away to the Sunday meetin'. And her killer is on your stage. Now if you just hand him over, the rest of you can go on your way."

Dutch walked beside his horse and stopped next to Logan. He stuck a stalk of grama grass in his mouth and gnawed on it. "I should have taken care of you back in Cheyenne," he said, his southern drawl as thick as Sally's British brogue. "And we'd have Cassie's killer by now."

Ira ignored him and spoke to Logan. "Your daughter's murderer is not one of us. We just left Cheyenne five hours ago."

"He's here," Logan insisted.

"You ain't told us anything convincing," Sally said.

"All right, then." Logan's neck and face flushed crimson, and his jaw muscles worked overtime. "When I came home from church, there was my Cassie—raped and strangled. There was blood on the bed, and the floor—"

"Cassie's?"

"Her killer's," Logan said. "Put his hand over Cassie's mouth—surely didn't want the ranch hands to hear her screams—and Cassie bit his hand. Bad enough he bled all the way out of her bedroom and throughout the house. Found blood on the buggy he drove from the ranch."

Dutch reached inside his vest, and Ira swung his rifle to center on his chest. Dutch smiled and came away with a pouch of tobacco. He stuffed his cheek before putting the pouch back. "Kind of jumpy, like you don't trust ol' Dutch."

"About as far as I can shoot you," Ira said.

Dutch tried squaring up to Ira, but Logan stopped him. "Don't try any gunplay. I'm still looking down the barrel of that old man's shotgun and Ira's rifle."

Logan's gaze darted past Ira to the back of the stage. He paused, seeming to measure his options. "I should have killed you when I had the chance ten years ago," Dutch said.

"Then why didn't you?"

"I figured I'd kill that horse of yours first," Dutch said. "Let you taste a little fear before we caught you."

"Bullshit," Ira said. "You missed me that day and shot my dun by accident."

Dutch winked. "I never miss."

Ira felt his anger rise from deep inside up his neck to his face, flushed hot with the memory. The only time Logan and Dutch got close enough to cash in the reward money in Tennessee. They had caught Ira as he topped a hill and shot his horse out from under him. A man didn't shoot horses, especially a fine Tennessee mare. Ira had gone underground then, living in the back woods, doing everything he could to shake Logan and Dutch. He evaded them long enough to reach a hobo camp, where drifters riding the rails hid Ira out until the next train rumbled west. "Except you peckerwoods lost my trail."

Dutch turned his horse so he faced Ira. "You son-of-a-bitch—"

"I said leave it be," Logan said. "All I want now is Cassie's killer."

"You still haven't said why you figure your girl's killer is on my stage," Sally said.

"You deaf?" Logan said, and Ira caught an almost imperceptible nod to Matt Ales and Handy Johnson. They eased their horses toward the back of the stage. Ira had been in war long enough to recognize a flanking maneuver, and he whispered over his shoulder to Dauber and Gordy, "Watch those two. I suspect they got a plan in mind that we can't live with."

"Blood," Logan repeated. "Whoever attacked Cassie had a sizeable chunk of his flesh bit away. The handprint covering her mouth probably came when she tried to scream, and he clamped his hand over her. Dutch followed a blood trail to where the buggy tracks left my ranch."

Ira knew that if Dutch tracked the killer through the house to a waiting buggy, it was just what happened. No one confounded a track when Dutch worked it out, and it was said he could run a track over water.

"Hap Barnes rented that rig, but he didn't kill my girl. He rented it for her killer. Who bought a ride on *this* stage."

"Then it ought to have been easy to just ask Hap who paid him."

Logan took off his hat and ran his fingers through his sweaty hair. "Hap was dead when we found him. Someone snapped his neck like a twig, right there in that alley back of the livery."

Sally laughed. "So, some dead man just up and whispered to you that Cassie's killer boarded my stage."

Logan leaned over, his rifle still lying across his saddle. "No. Old Zip Coon—when he found out his pardner Hap was dead— said the same person who paid Hap to rent the horse and buggy also paid the old drunk to buy fare on this stage."

Ira motioned to Beth and Frank Warner, to Preacher and Dauber and the farm kid, Gordy. "Nothing you have told us can show who the killer of your little girl is. Sounds like even

Old Zip Coon has no knowledge—"

"But as soon as your passengers line up and show their hands," Logan said, "I'll know. As soon as the killer with the chunk out of his hand—"

"And those boys of yours who meandered off somewhere," Ira said. "Tell them to meander over here where I can keep an eyeball on them."

A shot behind Ira made him jump, and he turned in the seat. Matt Ales lay on the ground beside his horse, clutching his shoulder, blood seeping through his shirt. Dauber stood pointing his pistol at Matt. "Damn fool tried to put the sneak on you," he stammered.

"Watch for the one-armed guy," Ira said. When he turned back to confront Logan, the outlaw had leveled his Henry at Ira's chest. "I don't figure to miss at this range."

"And neither will I." Preacher stepped from behind the coach, a Navy Colt cocked and pointed at Logan's head.

"Drunken Dan Crane. I heard you got out of prison after that last little episode with Quantrill. Still hitting the sauce, are you?"

Preacher extended his arm and sighted down the barrel. "See how steady my aim is? You might say I confronted my demon and am a reformed man. Found Jesus. And Jesus is right here alongside me, guiding me, telling me just where to put this .36 caliber ball into you. I think you know I am quite capable of doing just what I say I'm going to do."

"I'll kill Ira before I die."

Preacher shrugged. "Then he'll get his just rewards a mite earlier than he planned on." He winked. "But I'll still be here to say some words over his grave. And yours, too."

Logan's rifle muzzle drooped slightly, and he looked to his right and left, weighing the odds.

"He can't get all of us," Dutch said. "Say the word, and we'll clear leather."

Logan paused, and his muzzle dipped even lower.

"And *I'll* get off one shot before I'm dead," Ira said.

"Boss—"

"Shut up!" Logan said to Dutch. "Some of you might survive this little dance, but I damn sure won't."

"Then stand down, and leave us to go on our way," Ira said.

Logan looked to the back of the coach and called out: "You all right, Matt?"

"He'll live," Dauber said. "And this one-armed man you sent with him." Gordy had joined Dauber and stood covering Handy with a beat-to-hell cap and ball Ira was certain didn't even shoot.

"There you have it—a Mexican standoff." Sally laughed. "Even though the only Mexican within killing distance is Miguel there."

"Come on out here," Logan said at last.

Out of the corner of his eye, Ira saw Dauber and Gordy lead Handy and Matt away from the back of the stage. When they got close to Logan, they shoved them. Matt fell to the ground, clutching his shoulder, blood soaking through his shirt and vest.

"What'll it be?" Ira said.

"We can best them," Dutch prodded.

Logan's jaw muscles bulged, and the gnashing of his teeth could be heard across the few feet that separated him and the stagecoach bristling with gun barrels pointed his direction. He lowered his rifle and slipped it into the saddle scabbard. "Why the hell you protecting a child rapist and murderer?" Logan asked. "I got little respect for you, but I never knowed you to side with the likes of that."

"I got no problem seeing a child killer swing," Ira answered, his trigger finger relaxing. "I'd kick the horse out from under him my ownself. But not the way you want him to swing—

without a trial."

"Who needs a trial?" Logan said.

"Cassie's killer is damn sure wearing gloves to hide his hand that was bit all to hell."

"We're all wearing gloves," Sally said.

"That's my point," Logan said. "The killer's damn sure hiding his wound."

"That's nonsense," Preacher said. "Everyone wears gloves in this country." He motioned with his pistol. "Hell, every one of your men are wearing gloves right this minute. Are they suspects, too?"

"You got some proof your man is aboard this coach, you report it to the territorial marshal," Ira said. "Hell, take your whole crew to talk to the law." Ira grinned. "Might thin your ranks by a few men, though, when they start looking through wanted posters."

Dauber handed Handy and Matt their empty guns. He kept a close eye on Handy as he helped Matt into the saddle.

"This ain't over," Logan said. "On my word—you'll never make it to Deadwood."

"Logan's damn sure right," Handy said. "It ain't over."

Logan glared at Ira a final time before he turned his horse and rode off, with the others following.

Except Dutch. He calmly reached inside his waistcoat and withdrew his makings, turning his back against the wind while he built a cigarette. "Logan is right. Your coach will never make it to Deadwood unless you turn over Cassie's killer." He shrugged as he blew smoke rings overhead. "Don't much matter to me. I'm rather partial to getting the killing out of the way. Ain't I, Dauber?"

Dauber's hand began to tremble, and Dutch winked at him. "Dauber there can tell you just what Logan is capable of." He tossed his butt on the ground. "Thought I wouldn't recognize you with your hair cut and them fancy duds, didn't you? Logan might not, but I *never* forget a face."

"Ride out," Ira ordered.

"Sure," Dutch said. "Sure. But mark my word—the next time you and me stand this close across a patch of grama grass, one of us will be fertilizing it for the next season."

Dutch spurred his horse toward where the others had ridden over a hill five hundred yards to the west.

"Thank God that's over," Beth said as she slipped her tiny gun into a garter holster.

Preacher decocked his Colt and concealed it back inside the hogged-out Bible. "It ain't over. If I know Logan Hatch, it ain't over."

CHAPTER 7

"Preacher's right." Ira kept an eye on Dutch's backside. "Logan's not finished with us yet. When he set out to track down runaway slaves during the war, folks said he never stopped pursuing them. Him and Dutch even chased a group of runaways into British North America. Not surprising, few runaways ever made it back south alive after they were caught." Ira continued watching Dutch. Only when he disappeared over the hill with the others did Ira lower the hammer on his Winchester. He propped the rifle on the seat before he climbed down.

"Sounds like Logan ain't much better than Preacher," Frank said. "I heard about those Bushwhackers during the war—Lawrence, Kansas. Raiding into Missouri—"

Preacher broke out into a coughing fit, eased with a sip of Tuberculozine. "No secret now that I rode with Quantrill." He capped the medicine bottle and stowed it back inside his coat. "Even got myself shot and captured at Wakefield Farm, same's Quantrill. Some folks even said I was on the same side as Logan Hatch and Dutch—we both hated slaves, and those that wanted them freed. But even Logan and Dutch were unwelcome riding with Quantrill. They were just too . . . merciless."

"Merciful like that massacre at Lawrence?" Frank said.

Preacher shook his head. "Can't say as I was proud of that now. But the Union sent me to Camp Douglas when I was caught. Damn Jayhawkers turned me in. Point is, Logan Hatch is one mean son-of-a . . . man."

"Then we'd best keep our eyes peeled," Sally said. "Hand me that tub of Frazier's from under the seat."

Ira handed Sally the can of axle grease, and he began slapping it on the axles. Last thing they needed now was a hot box from too much friction. "Maybe you can say a little prayer that Logan leaves us be and goes to the law with his suspicions," Ira said.

"Like you're going to the law over your dispute with Hickok?" Frank asked. "The way you've been flapping your gums how you're going to kill Hickok, the last thing you want is the law getting in your way. Just like Logan doesn't want the law interfering in his revenge." Frank slipped a hip flask out and took a nip while his wife glared at him.

"We don't need you drunk on top of it," Beth said. She grabbed for the flask, but Frank held it high out of her reach.

"No," Frank said, taking another short pull before slipping the flask in his back pocket. "But we do need a man riding shotgun with something on his mind besides killing Bill Hickok."

Ira bit off a corner of a plug. He stuck the rest of the tobacco into his shirt pocket and stepped closer to Frank. Ira had to look up slightly, and Frank had him by twenty pounds. But it was a gambler's pounds, not earned by back-breaking work. Ira had known dozens of Frank Warners in his lifetime, each taking the easy fork in the road, and he feared Frank not at all. Still, Ira hadn't lived this long by underestimating folks. "You have nothing to worry about, fancy-man," Ira said. "Comes time for gunplay, you'll get your money's worth."

"I'd add that Frank—and each one of us—best keep our guns handy," Preacher said, reaching once again for his medicine. " 'Cause with that bunch riding with Logan and Dutch, we may need every gun we've got."

Beth moved to stand next to Gordy, her elbow touching his.

If Frank noticed, he said nothing. "Do you think Mr. Hatch will try anything," Beth said, "this close to Ft. Laramie?"

Sally wiped excess grease on the leg of his dungarees and stowed the can back under the seat of the coach. "Not likely." He nodded toward the north. "We'll stop for a bit at Bear Springs, ten miles on. And the swing station's not more 'n twenty miles past that. That puts us near thirty miles from Ft. Laramie." He looked to the north and thoughtfully scratched his groin. "We haven't had any trouble with Indians or road agents on this leg of the route, not with the army being close. With patrols crisscrossing this area, I doubt Logan will pull another stunt like he just did."

"What about *after* Ft. Laramie?" Beth sat on a fallen log and fanned herself with a floral-patterned hand fan. Her skirt rode over her boots, revealing shapely legs, and Ira looked quickly away. "What happens then?"

Sally ignored her and walked to the front of the team, where he acted as if he were adjusting the leaders' martingales. That might have been the closest the driver had gotten to a woman lately, Ira thought.

Beth asked Ira, "If Mr. Sally does not have the decency to tell us about what dangers we face, maybe you do. What happens *after* we leave Ft. Laramie?"

Ira kicked a dirt clod with his boot. Beth was right—she and the other passengers had a right to know. "Most of the Indian attacks this past year happened north of Ft. Laramie, where the cavalry patrols rarely go unless they have to."

"Don't forget the road agents," Preacher said. He swiped his hand across his nose, and blood streaked his glove. He tipped the last of his medicine and tossed the bottle aside. "That's where *all* of the robberies have occurred, if saloon gossip is accurate."

"So, we're being hung out to dry?" Frank said.

"Like Preacher said, we may need all the guns we have," Ira said. "If Logan is going to stop us again, it'll be after Ft. Laramie."

Thirty-eight miles north of Cheyenne the coach rolled over plains and rolling hills to the well-sheltered, well-timbered Chugwater Valley. Ira scanned the high bluffs on either side of the stage route, noting the aspens clustered together along the road rutted by stages and freight wagons, clusters dense enough to hide riders. Ira half expected Logan and his men to set an ambush there, even though Ira had reassured the other passengers that, if Logan made another play for the stage, he and his gunnies would do so after Ft. Laramie. Yet, in his gut, Ira knew Logan would think Sally and Ira would be lulled by the safety of nearby army patrols and let their guards down. Ira stood in the seat and scanned the valley.

"I don't figure Logan will make his play with the army on the move hereabouts," Sally said, his cracking whip snapping over the heads of the horses, the sound echoing off the high bluffs.

Sally was wrong, Ira knew. Logan might be wary of the army patrols. But, in the end, he would not give up until he had stopped the stage and killed all aboard, if need be. And even though Ira despised the man for stopping the stage, for threatening the life of everyone on it, he knew he would do the same thing if he were in Logan's boots.

But he'd never been there. Never married. Never had a loving family to stand by him, to protect. Ira's life had been one of going from one dangerous event to another. From Union soldier to buffalo hunter to bounty hunter. As he thought about Frank and Beth and what children were in the future, he admired them. Like he admired Logan.

They passed the ranch of Portugee Phillips, past the groves of willow and box elder and cottonwood among chokecherry bushes, places Logan could be lurking.

"Can we stop, Mr. Sally?" Beth called out from the coach. "I have to visit one of those trees."

Sally slowed the coach, but Ira urged him farther along. "Stop by those cottonwoods next to that cliff face."

"You're almighty sure Logan will make his play even though the army is operating hereabouts?" Sally asked. " 'Cause I wouldn't want to scare the passengers."

"Let's just say he is as unpredictable as he is ruthless."

Sally stopped the coach beside several large, gnarly-limbed cottonwoods sitting next to a tall butte. Buffalo grass grew tall beside the cliff, and Sally hobbled the leaders there to graze. "Anyone else need to take a pi—uh, visit the trees, best do it while you can."

"I do," Gordy said. He grabbed a corn cob from the basket hanging on the side of the coach. He walked past Beth. She dug in her travelling bag and handed her husband something. "What'cha got there, Miss Beth?"

She showed Gordy a flat pack of paper. "It's for . . . when one is done."

"Done with what?" Gordy asked.

"What the hell you think it's for?" Frank said.

Ira held out his hand, and Beth handed him a pack of paper. "Geyetty's Medicated Paper," he read. "For the water closet."

"What's a water closet?" Gordy asked.

Frank snatched the papers and started for the trees without looking back.

"A water closet's an indoor toilet," Preacher explained. "A room where folks go when they got the urge."

"Get outta' here," Gordy said. "You mean folks . . . do their constitutional inside?"

"Back East they do," Preacher answered.

"Whoowhee!" Gordy said. "That must be a powerful odor in

that room if folks do that."

Ira looked after Gordy heading for the trees and shook his head. Had he ever been as ignorant of the world as that big farm kid? He thought not, though he knew better. He was once just as naive as that boy.

Ira put his hands on the small of his back and stretched. Riding atop the coach, on the rock-hard seat, took as much out of a man as a hard day's branding, while at the same time lulling one to sleep. He had forced himself to remain alert, and it took a toll on his energy. At least Sally would be able to leave the stage and relax soon. Once they reached Kelly's Ranch, another driver would take the stage the next sixty miles. "Guess it's a good thing that kid left the farm. Might learn the ways of modern folks," Ira said.

"Guess we all got to leave the farm eventually," Preacher said and headed off with pages torn from a Sears Roebuck catalog.

Dauber looked around and waited until the others were gone before he approached Ira. "Can we jaw a little?"

"Sure," Ira answered.

Dauber motioned Ira away from the coach, even though there was no one to hear him. He lowered his voice while he rested his hand on his gun butt. "I ain't never even fired this thing since I bought it from that mercantile in Scottsbluff."

"But you done good."

"That man back there—that Matt Ales . . . I ain't never shot a man before."

"And you're wondering if you did the right thing?"

Dauber nodded.

Ira draped his hand over Dauber's shoulder. "That coyote was putting the sneak on me and Sally. If you hadn't stopped him, he might have killed us. Besides, you *didn't* kill him."

Dauber's trembling subsided. "But he could bleed to death."

"Not if Logan gets him to a doctor, he won't. Now go join

your friend soon as he gets back from his break. And keep your eyes open. Logan and his bunch are still with us. Somewhere."

Dauber walked back to where Gordy emerged from the trees buttoning his overalls. Ira recognized Dauber's doubts about shooting another man. Ira had those same doubts as he'd lain in the grass on a hill above Shiloh with others of the 6th Ohio waiting for the fighting to erupt in a bloody battle.

"Time to wonder if'n you're doing the right thing," a grizzled sergeant next to him said, "ain't now. The time to think things out is *before* you really need to make a decision on killin'. Take a moment right now and think about what those gray legs mean to do to you if'n they get the chance."

It had been good advice then, and it was good advice now: If Logan or Dutch or any one of Logan's other gunnies got the chance, they'd as soon kill the whole lot—Ira and Sally and every one of the passengers. That realization took all doubts away from Ira. And he'd sleep just fine, no matter which of Logan's bunch he had to kill.

Ira untied the back boot and grabbed a piece of pemmican from his saddlebags. He had learned how to make the trail food of dried meat and berries from the Crow that winter he was laid up after the buffalo trampled him. He watched the others reappear from the trees as he nibbled on it.

"I overheard what that ranch kid said." Preacher took a long pull from a fresh medicine bottle before slipping it back into his pocket. "I'm not particularly worried. If Logan and his bunch rode up hell-bent-for-election I'd ventilate whoever I could before they dropped me. With the things I've been through, I'm long overdue to meet my Maker. But the rest of those folks over there"—he chin-pointed to Beth and Frank huddled together and whispering, at Dauber and Gordy playing mumblety-peg with a pocket knife like they were youngsters. "They have no idea what we're facing with Logan."

"All the more reason to keep your eyes looking up into the hills when we start again. All we have to do is reach Hi Kelly's, where we can wrangle a cavalry escort the rest of the way north."

CHAPTER 8

"Just wrap up his damned arm!" Ed Mooney said.

"It is not that easy." Miguel sat on a rock next to where Matt Ales bled from the gaping shoulder wound. "The bullet . . . it did not pass through. It is still in Matt's arm," Miguel said.

"Can you get it out?"

Miguel shook his head. "He should have a doctor. All I can do for him now is stop the bleeding."

Matt looked up at Miguel. "Dig it out, and get me the hell patched up—I'll make sure that son-of-a-bitch Dauber takes one from my Colt."

Handy Johnson squatted by the fire and turned the heated blade of his Bowie over in the hot coals. "You can have Dauber. All I want is a crack at Ira Drang."

"You'll have to wait until I'm done with him," Ed Mooney said. "The way that bastard slapped me in front of everyone in the New Idea, I owe him some lead."

Dutch smiled. For all his men's bravado, he was the only one who could go against Ira in a stand-up gun fight. He was certain he was faster, more accurate than Ira. But even he had his doubts, and he brushed aside the rumors of Ira's quickness with his gun, rumors passed around campfires at night by frightened men. Like telling tales about Indians sneaking up and slicing throats in the middle of the night. Talk that kept men looking over their shoulders. Alert.

Just exaggerations. "I don't know why you didn't just take

him right then and there when we stopped the stage," Dutch taunted Handy. He knew if he could keep his gunnies worked up, there'd be more incentive for them to take the stage. And get back to thieving horses. "Been me, I'd have forced his hand. And ventilated him right where folks could walk over his dead body."

"Come again?" Ed said. "If what folks say of Ira is right, you *may* be the only one who can beat him. But if the man ain't afeared of Hickok, he ain't afeared of you neither." Ed smiled. "And, as I recall, you had your chance at the man back there in Cheyenne, too, and . . . was wise enough not to try it."

"That's enough!" Logan said, and he nodded to Miguel. "Can you take out the bullet in Matt's shoulder?"

The color drained from the Mexican's face. "I . . . I have never done this. He needs a doctor."

"How about it, Matt: do you want one of us to take you to a sawbones?"

Matt spat tobacco juice that hit the embers with a *hiss*. "Just take the bullet out, and patch me up. We need to find those bastards."

"Miguel—"

"Understood *caporal*," Miguel said and took the hot blade Handy passed to him.

Logan walked away from the others to a clump of bushes. When he finished and buttoned his trousers, he walked fifty yards off and sat on a log.

Dutch looked after his friend. Logan had begun taking time away from the others and now sat on the fallen tree, his shoulders visibly shaking even at this distance. As Dutch neared, he cleared his throat, and Logan swiped a hand across his eyes before he stood.

"Matt getting patched up?"

"As best as Miguel can. The man's no doctor."

71

"I told Matt he was free to ride back to Cheyenne or on to Ft. Laramie to find a sawbones, but he refused."

"Kid's tough," Dutch said. "If we had figured the passengers would join the party, we might have come up on the stage differently."

"So, you think I did things wrong?" Logan asked.

"All's I'm saying is that . . . rage has a way of invading a man's clear thinking." He bit off a piece of tobacco. "I'm not blaming you for anything."

"But you think I should have thought things out better?" Logan said and held up his hand. "You don't have to answer, 'cause you're right. I wanted to find Cassie's killer so badly, I bulled my way onto the stage. Shit!" He kicked the rotted log, and a piece flew into the tall grass. "That's why I keep you around—you've always been the clear head between us. And I was a heartbeat away from getting myself killed on top of it. If I'd have blinked, Ira's trigger finger would have tightened just a smidgen more and . . ." He ran his finger across his throat.

"And I should have killed him back in Cheyenne. But there'll be another time," Dutch said as he put his gloves back on. "Another place. The road to Deadwood is long. And, next time, we'll plan things out better."

Logan jumped when Matt screamed. He had started for the campfire when Dutch stopped him. "Let it be."

"But Matt—"

"You won't be able to help him any. Let Miguel do what he can."

"But the kid—"

"I understand. But let Miguel do his work." Dutch patted Logan on the back, recalling how he had taken in the wandering bronc buster when he'd first ridden into the ranch looking for work. "I can ride anything with hair on," Matt had bragged.

"I'll ride the kinks out of any damn mustang you put under me."

Logan had smiled at Matt and called his bluff. He led him to a small corral where a two-year old mustang pawed the ground at their approach. "Rope him, and we'll see just what you can do."

"And the job?" Matt asked. "Can you offer me something permanent? I'm tired of going from ranch to ranch begging for work."

"What do you think?" Logan had asked.

Dutch rolled a smoke as he readied himself for the entertainment. "If he can ride *that* ornery horse, I'd say give him a job."

And Matt had. The mustang sunfished sharply and threw Matt the first time he swung a leg over him, but that was the last time the two year old did that. By the end of the day, Matt rode the horse around the cattle pens like it was born to work cows.

Through the last year, Logan had taken Matt under his arm more and more, sometimes referring to the kid as "son." And when Cassie began showing an interest in Matt, Logan didn't discourage her.

"Where are *you* going?" Logan asked as Dutch started to where the others hunkered around the fire.

"That planning we just talked about," Dutch answered. "I'm going to find out how far along that stage is. We need to jump them and get on with our business."

Dutch and the Canuck rode back into camp. They dismounted and tied their horses off on a fallen tree away from the fire. Ed Mooney lay sleeping under the shade of a cottonwood, while Miguel sat with Matt Ales, who was moaning and holding his shoulder. Logan stood from the campfire and met Dutch at the horses. "Well?"

"Let me get coffee first," Dutch said. He squatted on his heels b y the fire and poured a cup. "They're making good time. That station master was right—that old one-eyed driver *is* good." He picked up a broken branch and drew a map in the dirt. "We crossed some Sioux tracks here just north of Hi Kelly's ranch—"

"Dammit! I don't want Indians finding that stage before we do," Logan said.

Dutch waved the suggestion away. "Tracks were eight, ten hours old. And shod tracks atop those. Some army patrol out there might not catch the Sioux, but at least they'll keep them on the move."

"Any chance the army'll escort the stage into Ft. Laramie?" Logan asked.

Dutch recalled the cavalry tracks he and the Canuck had spotted crossing the stage route. "Doubt it. They're busy enough just trying to find them Lakota to worry about a stage full of civilians."

"Think they'll stay to the road?"

"If it were me—and the Hatch gang was after me—I'd find another route. It would be slower, but it might just throw us off enough so's we'd lose the stage. Concord coaches are pretty rugged. That old Cyclops driver *might* try it."

"We need to keep an eye on that stage . . . Ed!" Logan yelled.

Ed Mooney took the hat from his face. He stood and rubbed the sleepers out of his eyes. "Yeah, boss?"

"How's Matt?"

Ed looked over at the young horse thief lying under a horse blanket. Even at this distance, Logan saw how the young man trembled. "Miguel dug the bullet out. Cauterized the hole. What's to tell?"

"Can he ride?" Logan asked Miguel.

"That one, he is tough," Miguel said. "But he got a fever. He will be able to ride in a few hours, but now . . ." Miguel shook his head. "He better rest up until the fever breaks."

"All right, then." Logan motioned to Ed. "Take Handy and Miguel. Find the stage and shadow it. Dutch will draw you a map where him and the Canuck saw the Indians' tracks, and where the army patrol might be."

Ed smiled. "We'll make *certain* they stay in one spot." He patted his gun.

"I do not want you to get into a gun fight with them. Understood?"

Ed nodded. "Okay, we'll just keep them spotted. But if there's a chance to slow them down?"

"Slowing them down would help," Dutch said. "Give Matt a little time to feel up to sitting a saddle."

"Okay," Logan said. "But remember what I said—"

"I know," Ed said. "Don't get into a shootout with them."

CHAPTER 9

Ira jumped at every snort of the team, every loose rock rolling down onto the road. He knew from past experience that Logan would stop at nothing to exact his revenge. He aimed to stop the stage and ferret out his daughter's killer, and pity the poor bastard who had some recent injury to his hand. He'd dismissed Logan's claim that the killer was one of the passengers, yet he thought about each one.

Men wore gloves these days, from the lumbering farm boy, Gordy, to the stage driver, Sally, to the gambler, Frank; everyone wore gloves. Wearing gloves was one of the few things a person could do to protect himself while he worked. Even Beth wore gloves, albeit ones that made her look like she was about to visit a theater for some nightly performance. But which one could be Cassie's killer . . . he stopped short of thinking *anyone* could be the killer. Logan had made his accusation based on something Old Zip Coon said about Hap—an old man who was known for what he'd do for a drink.

The horses seemed to know their time on the route was over for this trip, and they stepped quicker against Sally's hauling back of the reins. As if they knew a well-needed rest awaited just past the herd of shorthorns in a pasture off to one side of the rutted road.

The well-built brick station with its store and hotel was situated among elm trees. Hi Kelly's house peeked between the shelter—built a half mile above the station where a company of cavalry were garrisoned—and the tree line. It reminded Ira of a fortress, though Kelly didn't really need one. He was far south enough that Sioux war parties rarely passed this way and, if they did, Kelly's Lakota wife would talk her magic, and the Indians would move on. Still, these were not normal times. Not more than a month ago, the Sioux, Cheyenne, and Arapaho had beaten Crook to a draw on the Rosebud, and a week after that wiped out Custer's 7th. The Lakota were emboldened, and Ira knew he could not drop his guard for even a moment.

By the time Sally set the brake in front of the stage station, the horses were lathered from the run. They breathed heavily as tails swatted flies circling around them. Sally looped the reins around the brake and slapped Ira on the back. "We made it. Now we can get an army escort the rest of the way."

"You look beat." The man said little, but whenever Kelly's brother-in-law spoke, it was usually something profound. Like Sally being tired and beat from wrestling the team. Maxwell handed the long lines to the hostler, a young feller half his age. "And that team looks worse."

Sally coiled his whip and set it on the seat before he climbed down. The passengers stepped from the coach and headed into the station for a meal. "More'n beat," Sally said. "More like looking forward to a hot bath and a good night's sleep."

"Well, you're not going to get a rest anytime soon," Maxwell said, drawing his explanation out like a trained actor. "Shawn O'Brien's been killed." Maxwell jerked his thumb over his shoulder at the small cemetery Kelly maintained in back of the stage station for such purposes. "I buried his body this morning, him and a drover from Yankton. Without their scalps, of course."

Sally's shoulders slumped, and he hung his head. Ira knew the driver was looking forward to some rest while the relief took the stage to the next home station fifty miles farther. "What happened?"

"Same thing that always happens—Sioux war party happened onto them. Damn fools went out hunting prairie chickens." Maxwell pointed up the hill to the long brick enclosure that housed a company of cavalry. "Soon's Captain Davis's soldiers found the bodies, he took his troop out looking for the Lakota. They've been out since this morning."

"So, we can't expect any help from them?" Sally asked. He explained to Maxwell about Logan Hatch and his bunch stopping the stage, and how he expected Logan to make another try down the road.

"The cavalry rationed-out for a week," Maxwell said. "You're more'n welcome to stay here until they get back if you want an escort."

"You know I can't do that. If it was just me and Ira, I would. But I got passengers."

"Understood," Maxwell said, scratching his crotch.

When Ira fought during the war, he'd always seemed to know—or thought he knew—when a surprise ambush would take place, or when an attack was imminent. He wasn't always right. But more than half of the time he was beating mathematical odds. And on those occasions when he felt the hair on his neck stand at attention, the attack *would* come. Those hairs stood on his neck now, and he told Sally to pull up.

"What are we stopping for?" Frank yelled out the window.

"Ira's got one of his feelings again."

"And is he going to be wrong like he was the last four times?"

"Just get your fool head back inside before some Indian shoots it off," Sally said.

Frank began arguing with Sally, but Ira drove their conversation from his mind.

To concentrate.

To figure out why those neck hairs kept standing up. Perhaps he was wrong again, like the other times on the route when he got the feeling they were being watched. The feeling that hostile people followed. Was it that fleeting glint of something metal he had sworn he saw through the trees right after Kelly's ranch? Or the snort of a horse he was certain came from high on the hill overlooking the stage route? Or the rock that rolled onto the road from high overhead? In those cases, he *wasn't* sure he'd just imagined things. A fella's mind plays cruel tricks when he's on edge, and Ira had been on edge since leaving Hi Kelly's. And, as in the war, Ira more often than not just wanted the fight to come to him, so he could get the bad feelings out of his system. So he could take a moment to relax, however short, afterward.

"Let's get past the Point of Rocks quick," Ira said. He turned in his seat, his rifle ready as he looked up at the high, round formation rising from a tall, perpendicular cliff. It would be the perfect spot for Logan to launch an attack: high ground that would be hard for the stage to defend against. Logan would have taken stock of the armament pointed in his direction when he confronted the stage, and he would know only Ira carried a rifle. All Logan had to do was stay out of pistol range while he picked off passengers and driver at long range.

And Dutch. As fast with a Colt as he was, his skill with a rifle at long range was something men whispered about at night over campfires and in saloons. For all the deaths that had earned Dutch another notch on his gun butt, the men he had killed with his buffalo gun totaled even more.

But they passed Chimney Rock and the cliffs and made it to the Bordeaux station without incident. Ira breathed a sigh of relief as they stopped in front of the stage station. Opened as a relay station this past June, the low-roofed building was just large enough for the passengers to enter for a quick meal.

After the passengers climbed out of the stage to stretch, the hostler took the lines from Sally. He led the coach to the corral, where fresh horses waited.

"Meal is on the company," Sally said and followed Ira inside the station house. Sheets hung suspended from the ceiling to catch dust, and the floor was lined with bear skins, the hair positioned toward the door so that a broom would easily *swish* the dust outside.

A tall, raw-boned woman, who introduced herself as Lucille, entered the room. She balanced biscuits and a bowl of beans and beef in one arm, spoons and plates in the other, and set them down in front of the passengers. Gordy was first to reach across the table. He grabbed the biscuit plate but stopped as he realized the others watched him. "What?"

"Preacher wants to say a blessing," Ira said.

Beth folded her hands and closed her eyes. "Thank God there's some civility here on the frontier."

Gordy looked sheepishly around the rough-hewn table and bowed his head.

Ira bowed his, too, but watched the others out of the corner of his eye. Surely, he thought, gloves have to come off to eat. Gloves made eating awkward, yet no one took theirs off, and when Preacher gave an "Amen," Ira realized he'd left his on, too. He cursed himself under his breath for thinking Logan might be right, and cursed Sally's constant questions as to who the killer was. *Cassie's killer is not among us,* Ira thought.

As they passed the bowl of food around, Lucille emerged from the kitchen with a pitcher of milk. She nodded to a pie safe in one corner of the dining room, legs set in kerosene-filled cans to prevent pests from getting to the gooey food. "Crab-apple pie when you're finished." She began pouring milk in glasses in front of each passenger when Beth stopped her. "I appreciate it, Lucille, but I break out in a rash if I drink milk.

Always get a reaction to it."

"That's quite all right, honey," Lucille said, filling up the other glasses. "You're not the first one today who was allergic to milk."

Ira dunked his biscuit in the beans and bit off a corner. "Milk disagrees with you or Elias, too?" he asked.

Lucille used her apron to wipe up a spill on the corner of the table. "Not us. That Holstein cow out back can't hardly keep up with milk for us. No, a couple drifters came through here a few hours ago. I thought they were looking for a handout, but they paid. Even gave me two bits extra." She shook her hand. "At least that Mexican appreciated good cooking. More than I can say for that one-armed feller."

"One-armed, you say?" Ira asked, those neck hairs standing up once again.

Lucille nodded and looked at the ceiling for a moment. "His Mexican partner was a friendly feller. And polite." She lowered her voice, as if the two drifters were within earshot. "Now his partner . . . he was one to watch, looking around all beady eyed. He was the one that couldn't drink milk. He wanted whisky. Got a little antsy when I told him we had none."

Ira paused and put his spoon back in his bowl. "Tell us more about that one-armed man."

"He was a nosy one. Slopped his beans and wiped his mouth with that piece of sleeve dangling from his stump. Asked me a lot of fool questions about other folks who might have stopped today. Wondered about the stage," Lucille said.

"What did you tell him?" Sally asked.

Lucille shrugged. "Nothing *to* say, except you folks was overdue. Even if I knew more, I wouldn't have told that one a thing. He was sneaky—like you'd think of a mangy coyote being sneaky." She shook her head. "Had his gun tied low so he could reach it faster. As if he needed it here."

"Handy Johnson and Miguel DeJesus," Sally breathed.

Lucille snapped her fingers. "That's what the one-armed feller called his partner—Miguel. They rode out not an hour before you folks arrived."

CHAPTER 10

"It's your call," Ira told Sally after they had stepped outside. "You're the permanent employee of the stage line."

Sally looked at the sun setting and picked dried food out of his scraggly beard. "If I'm to be on schedule, we need to get going."

"Except traveling at night—with Logan's bunch being close—just might prove fatal."

Sally kicked a dried horse apple with the toe of his boot. "We're pretty well armed. We held off Logan last time. Even managed to wound one of his gunnies."

Ira thought that over. They had prevailed last time because they caught Logan by surprise. But now Logan knew what kind of weapons they had and how many were fighting men. If it were just him, Ira would chance it. The longer he delayed getting back on the road, the longer it'd take to get to Deadwood. And to Hickok. But with passengers to think about . . . "The only one we can really count on in a gunfight—someone who's seen the elephant—is Preacher."

"Dauber shot Matt Ales last stop."

"But he's having second thoughts," Ira said. "The kid's just too . . . decent. Now if he was a cutthroat like Preacher, I'd have more faith in him."

"Maybe Handy Johnson and Miguel are the only ones Logan ordered to dog us," Sally said. "We'll be able to handle those two—"

"At night? They will pick their time, pick their place. And, even if the rest of Logan's men weren't along, those two just might catch us by surprise."

Sally stuffed tobacco in his cheek and put the pouch back into his waistcoat. "I think we need to take the chance. We're behind schedule as it is."

Ira noted the sun was nearly down. They would have an hour of daylight at best. "Then we'd better get loaded up. The sooner we leave, the sooner we'll be safe at Ft. Laramie."

Sally stuck his head inside the station house. "We need to get back on the road, folks."

Beth and Frank left the house first. She whispered something to him, and Frank walked to the water trough. He stuck his head in the water and worked his fingers through his hair. Beth hung back, and she motioned to Ira to step away from the others.

"Looks like Frank's finally taking Sally's advice to wash that brilliantine out of his hair," Ira said.

"He looks like a fool," Beth said. "All the dust in the territory must have been stuck to Frank's head." She looked over her shoulder and shook her head. "Lucille just described two of Logan Hatch's men, didn't she?"

"She did."

"We *will* be safe travelling, won't we?" She laid her hand on Ira's arm. " 'Cause I'm more than a little frightened." She stepped closer and looked up at Ira. Her cologne drifted past his nose, and he felt excitement rise within him. *If* he were alone, and *if* his business with Hickok were done and over, and *if* she weren't married to Frank, he could easily get lost in those green eyes. Ira stepped back before he did something stupid. "We'll be all right," he said. "Now you'd better join the others."

"If that's what you *really* want."

After a long moment, Ira nodded. "It is."

Beth smiled. "All right. But perhaps we'll have a chance to talk later." She jerked her thumb at Frank. "Without my husband around."

Ira didn't answer as he watched Beth turn and head for the coach. Right before she climbed inside, she looked back at him and smiled again.

"Intoxicating, isn't she?" Preacher took a short nip of his medicine before putting the bottle back in his pocket. "She came on to me, too. When Frank wasn't looking."

"Now why would she do that?" Ira asked. With a large scar running down one cheek and one missing ear lobe, Preacher wasn't exactly a man a woman would fantasize about. "No offense, but you're not exactly every woman's dream."

Preacher held his hand over his heart. "I'm hurt." He smiled. "But you're no work of art yourself." He looked at Beth disappearing inside the coach. "But in answer to your question about why she would flirt with us when she has a handsome bastard like Frank—I guess it's like if you had prime beef steak for every meal, even venison would taste good for a change." He took another pull of his medicine and wiped blood dripping from his nose. He coughed into his bandana and followed Ira's stare. "Don't mind me. Just getting a mite worse is all," he said and took another longer sip of his medicine.

"Better take it easy with that," Ira said.

Preacher capped the bottle. "Or else it'll kill me?" He laughed. "Before Logan's men do? We all heard Lucille describe two of Logan's gunnies." He nodded to the coach. "Only a fool would start off at night with them nearby." Preacher shrugged. "Don't much matter to me. I'm already dead." He grabbed his bandana from around his neck and coughed into his hand. He wiped blood off his lips and pocketed the neckerchief. "But I can't figure out why those other folks want to get to Deadwood so bad they'd throw caution to the breeze."

"Gold fever . . . what else?" Ira said. "In any event, I need you to keep your wits about you. Once Logan realizes we didn't lay over for the night, he's likely to set up an ambush."

The coach pulled into Eagle's Nest Station and stopped only long enough to change horses and let the passengers stretch their legs. While the hostler led the stage over to the corral, Sally stomped around the yard and bitched because he had to take this second leg of the route without a relief driver. "The stage better give me a bonus, is all I got to say," Sally said. "Ain't good for a man to drive this damn thing this far without—"

"Let's go inside and grab some coffee while we can," Ira said and led Sally into the station master's house. The others walked around the room, stretching, while the station master's missus sat beside a large oil lamp, knitting. "Help yourself to the pot," she called out, not missing a single knit nor purl.

Ira grabbed the coffee from the top of the Franklin and poured Sally and himself a cup. Ira nearly spat the coffee out—if what he poured could be called coffee. The woman hadn't made coffee with Arbuckle's or anything akin to coffee but instead made that frontier concoction of parched peas and barley.

"Molasses on the counter," the woman said, her knitting needles *click-clicking.* "Some folks like their coffee sweet."

I'd just like coffee of any kind, Ira thought as he spooned some molasses into the cup and stirred, then added another spoonful just in case. He sipped the coffee, grateful for *any* bitter and piss-warm liquid, appreciating anything that might get him to relax. He had been on high alert since leaving the Bordeaux station, expecting Logan Hatch and his men to surround the coach and demand his daughter's killer.

Ira heard the hostler lead the stage toward the station house, and he stepped outside.

"I figure we're out of the woods," Dauber said, following close on Ira's heels, "being this close to Ft. Laramie." He watched Ira's face and set the coffee pot back on the stove without pouring any before following him outside. "Even Logan Hatch wouldn't attack a stage this close to the fort."

"Don't bet on it." Preacher stood in the doorway looking up at the Eagle's Nest situated high atop a sandstone cliff overlooking the road. The top was barely visible in the partial moon, and Ira thought that to be the perfect spot for an ambush. "If we're lucky, lightning will hit them while they're watching us." Preacher pointed up. Lightning to the west illuminated the cliff face sporadically, bringing heavy thunder clouds with it.

"When're we gettin' on the road again?" Gordy said, scratching his groin like he had grain chaff down there. "Logan ain't coming, and me and Dauber gots to get to Deadwood—"

"We *all* need to get to Deadwood." Frank turned to Ira. "But I agree with the big dumb . . . farm boy—Logan done gave up and rode back to his ranch."

"And you think two of his gunnies being at the Bordeaux station was a coincidence?"

"Maybe they split with Mr. Hatch and lit out for the gold fields like so many others," Beth said. "Surely pays more than stealing horses."

Sally took the reins from the stock boy and uncoiled his whip. "They'll know that once we get to Ft. Laramie, we can get army protection." He motioned to the others standing beside the coach as the first sprinkle of rain came. "I'm figuring, if Miguel and Handy are still around, they're going to shadow us is all. Let Logan know where we are. That might give us time enough to make it to the fort in one piece."

Ira waited until the last passenger—Preacher—had boarded the coach before wiping water off the seat and climbing up beside Sally. Sally wrapped the whip's leather thong around his hand and took the brake off before he snapped his whip over the heads of the team.

"As much as I'd like to get to Ft. Laramie quick," Ira said, grabbing the side of the seat as the coach lurched forward, "I'm still convinced Logan's men will try something."

"I don't know," Sally said. "I'm beginning to think Frank's on to something—Logan gave up." Sally turned the coach on the road north. "Miguel and Handy Johnson are probably just on their way through to the gold fields. Like we ought to be doing, rather than making money doing this."

Ira sat on the edge of the seat, watching the road ahead, watching the moon peek through the clouds illuminated by frequent lightning. He squinted against the rain drops as he stared ahead, wishing he could see farther down the road. If he were alone on horseback, he would welcome the darkness. But with Sally driving the coach at night, he'd need all the light he could get. And the lightning and moon only seldom peeking from the clouds helped him little.

"That woman down there ever come on to you?" Sally said between cracks with his whip.

"She did," Ira said. The wind came up, and Ira pulled his hat down lower on his head. "She flirt with you, too?"

Sally laughed. "I'm just a bit plug ugly. Now that big farm boy down there's another matter. She started sidling up to him, and I could tell Gordy was embarrassed. He stood looking anyplace but at her, his big hands stuck in his back pockets."

"Wouldn't you be if you were not quite twenty and some beautiful woman flirted with you?"

Sally shook his head. "Can't say. I was just as homely when I was twenty. I *always* had a hard time getting a woman interested." Ira thought back to what Old Zip Coon had said about Sally fleeing just ahead of a necktie party in England. Fleeing for killing a woman.

Or not. Ira never put much store in rumors.

Ira knew men didn't talk about themselves in these parts of the country, and that other men didn't ask. Sally's thick British brogue and homely appearance might just cause men to speculate about most anything. Like his background. Or, why he left England.

"You see it?" Sally asked, urging the horses to pick up speed. He pointed to the top of the high sandstone cliff that Indians called Eagle's Nest. "Or, am I imagining things?"

"I saw it, too," Ira answered. He shifted in the seat and shouldered his rifle. A glint of metal, or the reflection of glass in the moonlight. Someone watched from atop the cliff—Ira was certain; someone who figured his presence wouldn't be detected in the darkness. And, when lightning flashed, Ira spotted it once more. But he also knew whoever was watching them from above would play hell making it down the side of the cliffs before the stage rode past. Especially if the trail were getting muddy with the rain. "If these horses are up for it, I'd get through Eagle's Nest canyon as quick as we can," Ira said, digging his slicker from under the seat and putting it on. "I'd feel a whole lot better to be away from these cliffs."

They urged the horses past 9 Mile ranch, bypassing George Hawk's place and fresh horses, wanting to get to Ft. Laramie as fast as possible. Sally was babbling on about something, but Ira paid little attention to him as they crossed 6 Mile Creek.

A flash of lightning. A flash briefly illuminating their path.

And they saw too late a fallen tree lying across the road.

Sally hauled on the brake and set himself against the reins. The horses stumbled in the traces, kicking mud up over Ira's head. Clods struck his cheek and chest, and he braced himself. The coach bowled over the tree and came down with a jolt. The horses fought the reins. Ira and Sally clung to the seat. Passengers yelled, their screams heard over the thunder. The coach listed to one side as Sally got the team under control. An axle dug into the ground, slowing the stage, and it jarred to a stop in the mud.

Frank was the first out of the stage. He took Beth's hand and helped her down. "What the hell happened?" he asked as he pulled his hat low and turned his back to the rain, now pelting with a ferocity that stung Ira's back even through his slicker.

Sally climbed down from the seat and walked to the back of the coach. He shielded his eyes from the rain with his hand as he examined the damage. "Son of a bitch." He turned to Beth. "Pardon the French, ma'am."

"What is it?" Preacher asked.

"Looks like we broke an axle," Sally said. "Damned if the wind didn't knock that cottonwood over." He kicked the side of the coach. "Of all the times—"

"Can we fix it?" Ira asked.

"I carry a spare axle lashed under the stage," Sally answered. "But it'll take everyone helping."

Preacher started stripping off his coat. "Guess we all better get ready to lift this pig off the wheel." He nodded to Frank. "Those duds will just get in the way. I'd take the coat off and help."

"Help, how?" Frank asked.

"Help with the axle, fancy man," Dauber said, returning Beth's smile.

"I didn't pay good money to—"

"Frank," Beth said, wrapping her arms around herself, "just do whatever Mr. Sally wants. I for one don't want to be stranded out here with a bunch of savage Indians around somewhere. And in the middle of a thunderstorm."

Sally grabbed tools from the front boot and crawled under the coach. "Gordy," he said from below, "I'll need the strongest man close to the stage. Then Frank and Preacher." He crawled out from under the coach, dragging another axle. He dropped it on the ground beside Dauber. "When they pick the coach up far enough, you and me'll have to swap axles afore they poop out and drop the stage. Can you do that, boy?"

Dauber nodded and bent to the axle as Gordy and Frank and Preacher positioned themselves on one side of stage.

"Where you going?" Frank asked Ira as he walked away from the coach. "Sally said we'll need everyone—"

"My job is to protect you folks," Ira said. "Not get tied up with my hands on the stage."

Frank started speaking, but Beth interrupted. "Just never you mind. If Mr. Drang says he needs to be free in case there's trouble, then I trust him."

Ira walked the twenty yards back toward the downed cottonwood, a medium sized, stunted tree that seemed out of place, falling across the road, and he squatted beside it.

The moon peeked through the clouds, and he shielded his eyes from the rain as he ran his hand over the break in the trunk. But it had *not* snapped with the wind.

It had been chopped down.

He knelt and examined the deep drag marks barely visible in the mud, marks that came from the tree line forty yards away.

"Shit!" he yelled. "Logan's here—" But gunfire cut his warning short. Muzzle flashes erupted from the tree line. A rifle bullet whizzed past his ear, and he ran back to the coach, diving for cover as bullets tore chunks of wood off the side.

Frank threw himself under the stage, pulling Beth after him. He drew his pistols and fired blindly at the flashes.

Gordy ran for the safety of the stage when he was hit and went down. Dauber ran to his friend. He snapped shots towards the trees as he dragged the wounded man toward the stage.

Preacher squatted beside the coach, pistol drawn, while Sally struggled to control the team. He threw a blanket over the heads of the leaders, and they settled down.

"Two of them out there, if I'm figuring their shots right," Preacher said. "Both rifles. We'll never be able to hit them from here with our handguns."

Ira handed Preacher his Winchester. "When I'm ready, give me about twenty seconds and start levering rounds towards those trees fast as you can."

"Where you going?"

Ira motioned to the fallen cottonwood back down the road. "My guess is they're not paying any attention to that tree they cut down. If I can get back to it without getting my ass shot, it'll give me some cover to make it to that tree line."

Ira low-crawled to where Frank lay beside Beth. "You hit?"

"Not yet," Frank said, plucking rounds from his gambler's gun and shoving fresh cartridges in.

"Keep winging rounds in that direction."

Ira bent to Gordy and pulled his hand away from his bloodied leg. "Bad?"

Gordy shook his head, but Dauber grabbed Gordy's bandana from his neck and handed it to the injured man. "Here. Hold this on it." He snapped another shot and quickly opened the loading gate of his Colt. "He ain't going to bleed to death, but Gordy's hurting bad," he said, digging fresh cartridges out of his vest pocket.

"If all goes right, we'll be able to roll into Ft. Laramie and get the post doctor to patch him up," Ira said. "Soon's I work my way around back of them."

"When?"

"Now," Ira said. He waited between flashes of lightning to belly-crawl toward the fallen cottonwood, while Frank and Dauber kept up a steady fire.

When Ira reached the tree, he lay behind it, catching his breath. He parted branches and saw where the shooters' flashes came from. The sky was dark, the flashes momentarily diminishing his night vision, but when the clouds drifted past and moonlight shone, he clearly saw Ed Mooney and Handy Johnson firing their rifles from the safety of the trees. Chunks of coach blew off as they kept up a steady barrage, keeping the passengers' heads down.

Ira waited until he heard Preacher firing his Winchester before he scrambled along the mud, reaching the trees just as Preacher's firing stopped. Empty. He was thankful that thunder masked his movements.

Ira peeked around a willow, waiting until the moon went behind the clouds before he ran hunched over. He slipped in the mud and caught himself. When he reached trees, he was thirty yards away from Ed and Handy. Pistol range.

Ira stood with his back against a tree, breathing deeply, calming himself, looking through the grove of trees. Preacher was right: there were only two shooters—Ed Mooney and Handy Johnson. But Miguel was nowhere to be seen. Did he ride to meet up with Logan? Would the others be riding down on them before the fire fight ran its course?

Ira took a last deep breath and started picking his way closer. He needed to get both men close together. He might have only the one chance to kill them both.

A thick Russian thistle stood twenty yards between Ira and the shooters, and he squatted behind it as he drew his Colt. Handy knelt beside a boulder, levering his Henry, shooting faster than many men with two arms could shoot. He reloaded every few shots, the lull being taken up by Ed shooting his pistol two handed, taking his time.

Ira picked his way carefully, inching closer, timing his steps to coincide with claps of thunder. When he stepped on a dry branch between claps, Handy's head snapped around. He turned, and Ira snapped two shots at Handy. Bullets careened

93

off the rock and drove pieces of boulder into Handy's cheek and face, and he dropped to the ground. He scrambled to get behind the rock as Ed spun around, firing until he was empty and dived behind a tree.

A bullet whizzed past Ira's ear, and he crouched. Handy had thrown his empty rifle aside and thumbed the hammer back on his Remington, firing again and again. Missing again and again.

Ira didn't. He cocked the hammer of the big Colt and took up trigger slack. The slug tore into Handy's chest.

Handy slumped to the ground clutching his chest, and the shooting stopped. Ira crouched, looking for Ed, when Ira heard him riding fast away.

Ira reloaded his spent rounds before he advanced on Handy. The man's gurgled breathing spewed foamy blood onto his shirt front, and his lips moved as if in silent prayer. Ira knelt beside him. "Was it just the two of you?" Ira asked, but he didn't expect an answer. Even if Handy wasn't close to death, he wouldn't have said.

"Just you two?" Ira repeated as he shook Handy's shoulders. "Where's Miguel?"

Handy smiled weakly a moment before his head lolled to one side. Dead.

Ira stood on wobbly legs, as he often did when he had faced death and won. The firing from the stage stopped, and he holstered his Colt. He bent over to catch his breath.

As soon as the others realized the threat was over, they'd start changing the axle. But for now, Ira paused, his heart thready, the veins on his temples throbbing. If he had been but a heartbeat slower, Handy might have killed him. Or Ed, if he hadn't run off scared.

Ira straightened and was stumbling toward the stage when a gun cocking behind him sounded as loud as a thunder clap. "If I was you, my friend, I would stay real still."

"That you, Miguel?"

Miguel DeJesus emerged from the cover of the trees ten feet away from Ira, his pistol pointed at Ira's head. "Looks like you got me cold," Ira said.

"So it would seem, my friend."

"Now you're just going to kill me?"

"Dutch would not be very happy if I did this," Miguel said. "He wants that pleasure for himself."

"He and the others close?"

"No," Miguel said. "He sent us ahead to find out where the stage was. Matt Ales, he caught a fever after he was shot. So hot. He cannot ride just yet. *Senor* Hatch, he will be very unpleasant, too, if I killed you outright. Now if you drew on me I would have no choice, no. Turn around."

Ira turned towards Miguel's voice. His pistol was held at arm's length, centered on Ira's head. "You need better people to hang around with." Ira nodded to Handy. "He was a crappy shot."

"I cannot argue with that. He *thought* he was game." Miguel shrugged. "Obviously, he was not."

"So, you are going to murder me?"

"My friend, murder is such a . . . unfriendly word, no? I am going to give you a chance." Miguel held up his thumb and finger. "But such a small chance."

"So you and me . . . you think you are faster?" Ira said.

Miguel laughed again. "I know that I am not as fast with this"—he nodded to his pistol—"as Ira Drang is. But, nonetheless, you will soon be resting in some *campo santo.*"

"Maybe it is you who will wind up in a graveyard," Ira said, looking around for anything that might give him a distraction just long enough to draw. He was too far away to expect anyone from the stage to come busting through the trees, and he'd never make it if he rushed the Mexican. Ira's only hope was that Miguel's bullet was off by just enough that it hit nothing vital—that it would give Ira time to draw before Miguel's second shot.

"That gun, my friend—be very careful and take it out of the holster. Toss it into the trees."

"I thought you intended facing me like a man."

"I do." Miguel smiled. "Toss it away."

Ira hesitated. With his gun out of his reach, there was little chance of reaching it if Miguel fired.

Ira grabbed the butt of his Colt by two fingers and tossed it into the grass next to some willows. "I never figured Miguel DeJesus for a cold killer. Never figured him for a coward . . . killing an unarmed man—"

"But even now you *are* armed. That Bowie on your belt . . . it is a weapon, no?"

Ira shrugged. "I mostly use it for slicing kindling for the fire. Opening cans of peaches. Sometimes scaling a catfish. But if you're asking me if I can defend myself with it—"

Miguel grinned wide and holstered his pistol. He slowly took off his gun belt and drew his own knife, a long, thin blade that glistened wickedly each time lightning flashed. "We shall see, my friend, how well you and your knife survive this night. I think that you will not." He chin-pointed the direction Ed had ridden as he stepped closer to Ira. "I will kill you just so I can meet up with that coward, Ed Mooney, once again."

Miguel held his knife low as he circled, and Ira recognized the maneuver. He had recuperated in the camp of a Crow head man four winters ago when a herd of buffalo turned on him and trampled him. The warriors thought it good sport to tease the white man in their game of who-can-flick-the-flesh off their guest. Ira had gotten pretty good at the game, flicking flesh off the Indians now and again, though he never quite won. He was hoping Miguel wasn't as adept with his knife as the Indians.

"Ever see a man's guts hanging out of his stomach?" Miguel said, and when Ira began to answer, the Mexican darted in and sliced his knife across Ira's stomach. He barely jerked back in time, and the knife ripped through his vest. He could feel sticky blood trickle down inside his shirt, and he cursed himself. *Don't talk when you ought to be thinking. Get that little bastard to talking.*

"Hurts, my friend, does it not?" Miguel said as he tossed his blade from one hand to the next, Ira fighting to figure out which hand would attack with the knife when . . .

. . . Miguel rushed in and backhanded his knife to Ira's throat. Ira blocked the blow, and his foot slipped in the mud. The tip of the knife opened up a nasty wound on the side of his neck. "Hurts, does it not?" Miguel said again and nodded to the ground. "A big man like you does not keep his balance so good."

Rain pelted Ira's face, stinging as he stood. He circled, matching Miguel's movement, fighting to remember what the Crow did to gain the advantage. They talked incessantly and—when Ira answered them—they'd rush in for the flesh. "Ed Mooney's going to ride back to Logan and claim he beat me in a fair fight. He'll get the credit for killing Ira Drang."

"He would not do that—" Miguel said as Ira feinted one way, then darted in as Miguel was talking and drove his knife at the Mexican. Miguel jerked back. Ira's wide Bowie missed his chest but cut a shallow furrow across the Mexican's shoulder. He howled in pain as he leapt back out of range of Ira's knife.

Ira grinned. "Hurts, does it not, my friend?"

"You do have some moves," Miguel said, flicking his blade at Ira's arm that clutched the knife. It cut across Ira's forearm, and he dropped the Bowie. Miguel rushed in, sensing Ira's predicament.

He thrust his knife low, knowing Ira could not block it.

But Ira *could* land a crushing blow to Miguel's nose that shattered cartilage. Blood spurted onto his face and chest, and when Miguel wiped blood from his eyes, Ira dove for his Bowie. He snatched it and rolled across the ground.

Miguel lunged for him.

Slipped. He fell face down in water and muddy gumbo. And, as Miguel gathered his legs under him to rush Ira, Ira lunged at Miguel, driving his knife into Miguel's stomach and ripping up violently. Hot bile and blood spilled onto Ira's hand, and he looked up into the Mexican's dying eyes. Miguel dropped his knife and fell onto his knees at the feet of his killer. He felt his broken nose, rain washing mud off his face, and he stared in disbelief at Ira. Miguel tried talking, but already the shock of such a painful wound shut off anything he could say. He fell onto his back.

Ira had seen men die of such open gut wounds during the war, and it wasn't pretty. Sometimes, it took many long, agonizing moments for the victim to die, all the while being in such excruciating pain, they could not even whisper. Ira looked at Miguel and crawled to sit at the Mexican's head. Taking Miguel's head in his hands, Ira twisted it hard, and Miguel's neck snapped.

He liked to think Miguel would have done the same for him.

CHAPTER 11

Ed Mooney fell sprawling onto the mud and rolled in the fire. His hat flew off, revealing the full head of black hair with the gray stripe down the middle. Like an old civet cat. He rolled out of the fire and batted the embers from his shirt as Logan cocked his leg to deliver a gut kick.

"Whoa, boss," Dutch said. He stepped closer to Ed but did not come between him and Logan. Dutch had seen Ed Mooney fight more times than he could recall, and he was good. Though not as brutal as the Canuck, Ed could hold his own with anyone. Even Logan on most days.

But this was not most days.

This time was different. Logan was as furious as he had been the day when they had missed the shot on Ira Drang ten years ago. Dutch could usually calm his friend down. On most days. "Let's hear Ed out."

Logan's face glowed as red as the coals, and he took deep, calming breaths. He wiped rain water out of his eyes and backed away to give Ed room to stand. "This had better be good, or I'll be down another man."

Ed stood, his hand flexing, rubbing his cheek that had already begun to swell from Logan's blow. "It was Handy," Ed sputtered. "I tried to get that one-armed bastard to back away, but all he thought about was how pleased you'd be if we stopped the stage right then and there."

"I ordered you to shadow them and report back. Nothing

more. Surely not kill them before I got a chance to learn who killed my Cassie."

"But what could *I* do? Handy thought he was *some* gunny. He was like a crazy man when he saw Ira."

"Handy had no chance again' you if you had forced him to stand down—"

"But Miguel fell in with him. I couldn't hardly stop *both* of them set on springing an ambush." Ed shrugged. "And, Lord knows, I tried."

"He's got a point," Dutch said.

"Point, hell! I got two men dead . . . you did see Miguel die, too, did you not?"

Ed's mouth turned downward. "Poor Miguel. He had no chance. Ira disarmed him, then shot him in the back of the head."

"And just how the hell did you survive such a deadly killer?"

Ed's hand dropped to his gun, and Logan stepped closer. "Careful now just how you grab that hogleg."

Ed took hold of his pistol with two fingers and handed the gun to Logan. "Check my gun. It has only empty shells. I winged rounds Ira's way until I was empty. I'd given my last ammunition to Handy when he ran dry." He looked down at the ground and kicked mud. "Poor Miguel. While Ira was busy murdering him, I made my escape." He looked at Logan. "Miguel's life meant that I lived." Ed's fists clenched and unclenched. "And Ira will rue the day he killed that fine, young Mexican *compadre*. I will never forget him." Ed crossed himself.

Logan looked at Dutch, who nodded. "Sounds like he had no choice. Man runs out of ammo . . ."

"Sure you didn't kill any of the passengers, or Ira?"

"Handy wounded one. I tried to stop him, but he shot that big farm kid."

"Bad?"

Ed nodded.

"Shit! Hope he don't die." Logan turned away. "There's ammunition in my saddlebags. Load your damn gun."

Ed walked to Logan's horse and took a box of .44-40 rounds from the saddlebags. He opened the loading gate and thumbed fresh cartridges into the empty cylinder.

"You feel like travelling?" Logan asked Matt.

"I can ride," he answered. "Just help me on my horse."

"Good." Logan looked around camp. "Where the hell's the Canuck?"

"Went to the trees for a minute."

"Well, get his ass mounted, too. Ed, get over here."

Ed holstered his gun and warily walked to where Logan was saddling Matt's horse. "Craig Highsmith and Jimmy Antelope are bringing some horses from Ft. Laramie by the west route. They'll meet up with the Dorn brothers. You ride hell-for-election and meet up with them. The Dorns can take them the rest of the way to the ranch." He motioned for Matt, who stood weakly and shuffled to his big, stolen army horse.

Logan turned to Ed. "Find Craig and Jimmy and tell them we need them to pass that stolen herd off to the Dorn brothers, then come back thisaway. With two men down, we might need them."

"Need them where?"

"I'm thinking," Logan said and turned to Dutch. "What do you think? Will the stage lay over at Ft. Laramie?"

Dutch thought that over. Their horses surely must need changing. And passengers and Ira and that old, one-eyed driver must be exhausted by now. They'll need rest. That wounded man might need attention . . . "How bad was that farm boy hit?" he asked Ed.

"Bad."

"Bad enough he'd need to lay up for a while?"

101

"He was bleeding pretty bad," Ed said. "Damn Handy Johnson."

But Dutch noticed he didn't say it with much conviction. Almost as if it didn't happen the way he said it did. "A smart stage jehu would lay over until that farm boy mended up enough to travel. Or leave him for the next stage going north."

"Then we got us a little breathing room," Logan said. He held the stirrup for Matt and helped him into the saddle.

Matt slumped over before he caught himself and sat upright. "I'm all right. I can ride."

"Okay, Matt," Logan said, "you and me will take it slow. Ed, when you find Craig and Jimmy, tell them the stage will probably lay over for a day at Ft. Laramie. But I want them watching that stage route in case they leave the fort early."

"Sure, Logan. I gotta see a man about a horse, then I'll ride for 'em," Ed said and walked into the bushes.

"Think we can trust him?" Logan said as he looked after Ed.

Dutch shrugged. He walked to Ed's gray and lifted the flap on his saddlebags. Two full boxes of .44-40 pistol rounds sat in the bottom of one bag covered by a spare shirt. And under the shirt was a bundle of six scalps. Six Sioux scalps. Scalps that Miguel would never have given to Ed. So, Ed had fled the gunfight, letting Handy and Miguel shoot it out with Ira. Dutch thought about telling Logan, then paused. Perhaps he would hold that close to his vest. When he could confront the cowardly bastard at the least opportune moment for him. Something he should have done years ago, when he was fresh out from those murders in Colorado.

Dutch turned back when Ed grunted that he was finished and started walking back. "I don't much trust Ed either," Logan said. "But we have little choice. We're kinda running out of men."

The Canuck sat sipping tepid coffee all this time, oblivious to the rain dripping off his hat and into his cup, looking on as if everyone were speaking a different language. Nothing seemed to rile the big man, Dutch thought, as long as there was a fight of some kind at the end of the day.

Ed grabbed his rain slicker from his saddlebags. If he noticed someone had opened them, he didn't acknowledge it. He donned his slicker and had swung into the saddle when Logan stopped him. "Remember what I said: this time, Ed, if you or Craig or Jimmy harms one hair on any of their heads, I will personally see you are all dragged home by one of those cavalry mounts Jimmy and Craig are herding south."

Ed nodded. "I got ya'—we're just to shadow them if they leave the fort?"

"Shadow them and get word to us." Logan nodded to Matt. "We'll be travelling a little slower, but we'll set an ambush a few miles from that new bridge the army erected over the North Platte."

"And if they force gunplay?"

"They won't," Logan said, "if you stay out of sight."

"And if they leave all in a rush?" Ed asked.

Logan stepped closer to Ed. "Then do something to slow them down. Nothing else. And this time I mean it, Ed. If anyone on that stage is hurt, you and me will have a falling out when I see you again."

CHAPTER 12

Sally pushed the team harder than he would normally have. But these weren't normal times. Ira kept standing on the seat, looking around for any of Logan's men, but he saw none.

And that worried him.

As much as his failure to see Indians.

"Can we get any more speed?" Dauber said, leaning far out the window to plead with Sally. "Gordy here is in a bad way. Beth . . . Mrs. Warner . . . keeps the pressure on his leg wound, but he's lost a powerful amount of blood."

"Muddy road's bogging the horses down, or I'd be going faster." Sally spat tobacco the wind caught and slapped across his beard. He paid no mind as his whip snaked over the heads of the leaders.

"How long before we reach Ft. Laramie?" Beth asked, sticking her head out the window beside Dauber's, the wind whipping her blond curls over her delicate face. "Because Preacher here says the soldiers will escort us the rest of the way to the Black Hills."

Sally leaned over in the seat while he watched the road. The thunderstorm had passed, and the half showed where ruts were. He slowed whenever they were coming up to water-filled ruts big enough to swallow the stage. "Soldiers are sure to escort us when we tell them about Logan and his men."

"Don't give them false hope," Ira said when they had pulled their heads back in the coach. Sally cracked his whip over the heads of the swing team to pick up the pace. "With the Indian troubles lately, we're just as likely to be on our own."

"Just propping their spirits up after that last ambush," Sally said. He coiled his whip and rested it against his leg as he rode the brake down a hill. "Logan must be almighty sure one of the passengers killed his girl, or he wouldn't still be trying to stop us."

Ira ignored him, hoping that would shut the fat man up. It didn't.

"Which of the passengers you think killed his Cassie?"

"Not that again," Ira answered. "Like I said before, I doubt *anyone* on this stage killed her."

"Can't you go a mite faster?" Dauber yelled from inside the coach. "Gordy's wound opened, and he's talking real goofy."

"Tell Beth to do what she can," Ira said, and his hand went to his own bandage wrapping his stomach, and the piece of Beth's petticoat wrapped around his knife wound at the side of his neck. He had been surprised how easily the fancy lady had thrown off the mantle of aristocracy and helped the wounded. Under other circumstances, he'd wonder about more personal things about her. Ira leaned over the edge of the coach. "Tell Gordy to hang on until we get to Ft. Laramie and a doctor."

"*If* you had to guess, which passenger would you bet killed the girl?" Sally asked as he hauled back on the reins around a curve.

Ira ignored him and watched the steep cliffs on either side of the stage route. *Where the hell is Logan? 'Cause he sure wouldn't take it lightly that two of his men were killed, let alone thinking his daughter's killer is in the coach.* But had he found Handy and Miguel yet? They had little time to bury them proper, just deep enough to throw mud over their faces before they made a rush for Ft. Laramie. Ira hoped the rain had obliterated the stage's tracks. Hoped that would give them just enough time . . .

105

"I'd put my money on that Gordy feller." Sally only made it another hundred yards before opening his mouth again. "He was awfully set against taking off his gloves. You'd think a man who'd got shot wouldn't care if he died with gloves on or not."

"No more than you," Ira said. "Seems like you've been reluctant to show *your* hands. Perhaps *you* paid Logan's ranch a visit. Perhaps Cassie bit a chunk of *your* flesh off."

"That's a hell of thing to say to a man," Sally said just as the wind picked up and pelted them with sand and tiny rocks and tree leaves falling down Ira's collar and onto his sliced neck.

Ira closed his eyes until the wind passed. When he opened his eyes, it was as if a giant mirage loomed on the distant horizon. A mirage that looked exactly like Ft. Laramie. He pulled his hat low to the rising sun.

Sally yelled like he had just drawn a royal flush. "Fort's ahead!" His whip sang its tune over the horse's heads. He elbowed Ira, and the pain from his knife wound drove chills up his spine. "Change of horses and a hot meal, mate."

Sally slowed the lathered team as they approached the sprawling Ft. Laramie. The post was abuzz with activity this morning. A platoon of infantry drilled on the damp, green parade grounds, while a five-pound cannon pulled by a team of drays skirted the grounds on the way to meeting up with a company of cavalry already on the road. Another wagon piled high with loaves of bread from the bakery clomped in a leisurely manner toward the mess hall. Gordy would finally get proper medical attention, and Ira and the passengers would savor a hot meal.

As they entered the fort proper, Ira stood and looked around, but he saw no sentry. Ft. Laramie had never been successfully attacked—it was just too big, with too many soldiers garrisoned here. Yet the Lakota had sent probing war parties here enough times that Ira knew somewhere unseen sentries watched the stage, ever vigilant for another Indian attack. "Pull up to the hospital so's we can get Gordy to the post surgeon."

The post hospital was constructed of the same white grout other buildings here were but was whitewashed to give it the illusion of cleanliness. Ira had brought a Sioux boy of five or six he had found wandering the prairie some years ago to the fort. The boy had been cold and hungry and suffering from more chigger and insect bites than Ira could recall. He had looked over his shoulder as he sat the boy in front of him on his horse, expecting the whole Sioux nation to come riding down on him like a mean mama bear would if you took her cub. But no Lakota had come for the boy, and Ira wondered what happened to him after folks at the fort had sent him back East Pennsylvania way for a white man's education.

"And get patched up your ownself," Sally said.

Ira waved the suggestion away, but Sally pressed his point. "I need a shotgun messenger who is not bleeding all over my coach."

Ira had no argument for that, so he carefully climbed down from the seat when Sally stopped the coach in front of the post hospital. Sally and Dauber grabbed Gordy, the big farm boy, who was smiling and rattling off gibberish as they carried him into the hospital.

"Lay him on that table," a major ordered, slipping off his officer's tunic and donning a white jacket. "And you"—he nodded to Ira—"get in that room. You're bleeding all over my hospital."

"I don't need a doctor—"

"Sergeant Sean," the doctor yelled.

A uniformed man stooped to get through the doorway, and his shoulders rubbed the door jamb as he turned to squeeze through. "Yes, Major."

The doctor chin-pointed to Ira. "Show him a surgery room. Last thing I need is a civilian bleeding out here at my hospital.

107

Makes for bad press."

Sergeant Sean stroked a beard as red as a rusty pump jack handle. "You heard the major."

Even if Ira was in one piece, he wouldn't have tried the sergeant on for size, so he followed the sergeant into the surgical room next to the one where Gordy lay. The sergeant wore the lace-up boots of an infantry man—not the high cavalry boots—and Ira figured there wasn't a horse big enough for him to sit anyways.

"Stay here. You got a visitor, but do not leave that there table," said the sergeant.

Sally passed Sergeant Sean outside the room—looking like a leprechaun next to the army man—and poked his head in the room. "Come on down to the traders' store when you're sewed up. I've got to get me some tobacco and blue ointment."

"You're not staying at Brown's Hotel?" Ira asked.

"Not unless I can help it. We need to get on the road. We're late," Sally said. "But in case they need to keep you and Gordy and we *do* have to stay there, I'll have something to put on the bedbugs when the little critters bite."

Fatigue overcame Ira as he lay on the surgery table, and his eyes closed. But just for a moment, it seemed, because Gordy's screams reverberating through the quiet halls of the hospital woke him. Ira sat up on the bed. How long had he been out? He had swung his legs over the table when he felt a tight pulling on his stomach.

"Don't you dare get up just now," Sergeant Sean said, standing from a chair in one corner of the room. "Not until the doctor checks those stitches."

"What stitches . . . ?" Ira ran his hand across his abdomen. A fresh bandage encircled his stomach, and he faintly recalled the major patching him up. "What's with Gordy?" Ira said. "That farm kid next door."

As if on cue, Gordy screamed again. "Kid don't take pain well." The sergeant grinned. "Bullet nicked that big artery in his leg. Lost some blood, but he could have lost more." He jerked his thumb at the wall. "Took a few stitches the major is putting in right now."

Ira fell back onto the table, and his head hit the hard army pillow. "Then I'll just lie here until the good doctor tells me I can leave."

Ira walked slowly beside Gordy, who was hobbling along on the crutch the post surgeon had issued him. After stitching up the wound in Gordy's leg, the doctor came into Ira's room and pulled his bandages back. He'd been lucky: Miguel had been off by just enough that—if his knife had been an inch closer—Ira's stomach wound would have been fatal, and it would have been his guts spilling onto the stage route instead of the Mexican's. As it was, Miguel's knife had gone in only a fraction of an inch. Just deep enough to cause Ira trouble if he didn't take care of it.

The cuts on his neck and forearm were more a nuisance that anything else—more like deep scratches that would burn every time Ira sweated until they healed. Something to remind Ira that he'd lose no sleep over killing Miguel.

"I still think you should have taken the doctor's advice," Ira said. The major had tried to talk Gordy out of leaving the hospital.

"Son," the major had said, "you are awfully lucky to be alive with an injury like that. It nicked your femoral artery. Another hair's breadth and you'd have severed it completely and bled out right there. You should lie up at the hospital until that leg's mended."

Gordy grimaced with every step, but the kid was stubborn.

"If I'd waited here for a week like the doctor wanted, I'd miss out on some of that Deadwood gold."

"Gold will still be there a week from now."

"And how about you?" Gordy forced a grin. "Maybe you should have let the stage go on without you. Mend up like the sawbones suggested you do. Caught the next stage north."

"And be a week—or more—from finding Hickok?" Ira answered. "Not on your life."

Ira and Gordy walked past the long cavalry barracks of stone and adobe grout, past the post sutler's house with ornate trim work around the doors and bay window. The surgeon's wife and two other ladies sat on the porch of the doctor's house, eying Ira and Gordy shamble past like they were participants in a grotesque three-legged race. They bent their heads together and giggled as they watched them walking south past the officers' quarters.

"What'cha think Deadwood's like?" Gordy asked, like a kid asking what flavor candy he could buy for a penny. "Do you think it'll be easy pickin's, as folks claim?"

"Doubt it," Ira said and instantly regretted his words. He hadn't meant to diminish Gordy's enthusiasm, diminish his dream of overnight wealth. But Ira had been in Leadville when the silver boom hit Colorado and even thought about trying his hand at mining silver in Butte. The draw of silver was just not strong enough for him to break his back running a sluice. But gold . . . now that had an allure silver could never bring. He patted Gordy on the back. "I'm sure you'll make enough to live the good life."

They stopped for a minute to give Gordy a rest as they watched infantry march through their formations on the parade ground. Ira had been infantry at the start of the war. But they hadn't had to drill like these soldiers. He and the other blue coats had little time for drilling. They had to prepare for Johnny Reb.

"Looks like Sally's ready to leave or something." Gordy motioned to the stagecoach nearing them. It stopped at the edge of the parade grounds, and Sally set the brake.

"Thought you were handing the stage off to your relief," Ira asked.

Sally guffawed. "Relief—what's that?" It was the policy of the Cheyenne to Black Hills stage to swap out drivers and shotgun messengers at Ft. Laramie. Ira insisted he wanted to go all the way to Deadwood when he agreed in Cheyenne to ride shotgun. But he knew Sally didn't, and he was sure the man was feeling more than a little fatigued. "Seems like my relief driver went north with the last stage two weeks ago. Something about going to strike it rich in Deadwood Gulch," Sally said. "So you're stuck with me. Might as well climb aboard."

"Aren't we waiting for a cavalry escort?"

"Not today," Sally said. "Frank pissed off the OD when he fleeced some soldiers out of their monthly pay over a not-so-friendly game of poker."

Frank stuck his head out the door of the coach. "The soldier boys knew what the odds were when they decided to play five-card stud. But it wasn't so much me. It was Sally pissing off the officer of the day, is why he won't give us a cavalry escort."

"That right?" Ira asked. "You got under the OD's skin?"

Sally nodded. "Smart-assed kid. Seems like he took offense to my accent. Damned Irishman."

"More likely your attitude," Beth added.

Preacher got out of the coach and held the door. He propped Gordy's crutch against the side of the coach while he helped Gordy inside. "Made no difference what Sally said—if the army couldn't spare an escort, it mattered not a whit what kind of accent he has. Seems like Indians stole some horses from their

111

corrals yesterday, and a company of soldiers rode out to get them back."

Sally stuffed fresh tobacco into his cheek and slipped the rest of the plug inside his vest pocket. "The OD figures some Sioux passing by on their way to hunting grounds stole the horses. And some wagons west of here that didn't have the sense to circle up when they should have. Got most of those pilgrims killed, but a few made it here to the fort. Army sent patrols out west toward the Laramie Peaks looking for them. Snot-nosed captain says he don't have any men to spare to protect us from Indians, let alone from Logan's owl hoots."

"They won't find those Lakota," Ira said. He grabbed the edge of the seat. He held his stomach while he stepped up onto the coach beside Sally. "So, what's your plan?"

Sally lowered his voice. "I was going to talk that over with you, since you seem to know Logan Hatch as well as anyone here. The others want to lay over here at the fort until tomorrow morning, but I got a bad feeling about that. We've been here long enough that we might have given Logan a chance to catch up as it is."

Ira looked at the road leading out of the fort over the North Platte River bridge. Once they crossed that bridge, they would be in the leg of the trip where most of the Indian and road agent attacks had happened. "I think we ought to go with your gut feeling. My guess is Logan's men who ambushed us last night did so on their own, thinking they'd be in good standing with their boss. But we killed two, and by now Ed Mooney's rode back to report it to Logan. He'll figure we did just what the passengers wanted—lay over here. Rest up. If we leave now, we might just be way ahead of Logan when he realizes we didn't."

But more important for Ira: he needed to get to Deadwood. The thought of Hickok leaving before Ira arrived to challenge him caused the veins in Ira's head to throb. And only when he had drilled gaping holes into Hickok would Ira's internal ache be quelled.

Ira mulled over what Sally and he talked about. If they rode out now, it would indeed throw Logan's plans off, and he'd have to play catch-up. But eventually Logan *would* catch up. And, without an army patrol, their chances of making it to the Black Hills were fifty-fifty at best. Ira at least had to *try* to wrangle an army escort. "Take me over to the administrative building. I'm going to try to talk some sense into the OD."

"Won't do no good," Sally said. "The captain's in love with himself. But you can try if you want."

Sally drove the coach past the guardhouse, where a soldier hanging onto the bars inside yelled profanity at the stage; past the long infantry barracks with soldiers playing cards and dominoes on the deck; and they stopped in front of the admin building. Ira held his stomach and gingerly climbed down. He had stepped up onto the walkway toward the entrance when a private looking even younger than Gordy ordered, "Gots to leave your gun here, mister." If Ira stood so the sun was to the private's back, the slight fuzz of a mustache showed under the kid's nose. "Post orders."

Ira took off his belt and Bowie and draped them over a hook beside the main door before entering. Another private—Ira's age, old by army standards—sat behind a desk that looked too small for his bulky frame. The outline where a former sergeant's patch had adorned his shirt sleeve showed bright compared to the surrounding faded cloth. He looked up only long enough to take in Ira before dropping his head back to his newspaper. "What you want, sonny?"

"I'd like to see the officer of the day."

"People in hell want ice water."

"Let me rephrase that: I demand to see the officer of the day."

"Regarding?"

"Indians," Ira said. "And outlaws."

The private made no attempt to leave the comfort of his chair. "Captain Kramer is very busy—"

"Too busy to come out of his office and pick up pieces of his nasty old private from the floor?"

The private put down his newspaper and stood. He gave Ira a longer once-over. "This a veiled threat?"

"Nothing veiled about it," Ira said and exaggerated a broad smile. "It's just important when folks sight Indians hereabouts." He nodded to the private's chevron. "Looks like you made another bad mistake at one time. Don't repeat it. But"—Ira shrugged—"if I got to go *through* you to report, it don't make no difference to me . . ."

"Maybe I ought to use *you* for a broom. Drag your ass across the floor—"

"But not today you won't."

The private hesitated for a moment before his shoulders slumped slightly, and Ira breathed in relief. He really hadn't wanted to wind up in the post stockade. Or back in the hospital when his stitches broke.

"I'll see if Captain Kramer is busy."

The private disappeared into a side office, and Ira walked around the room, stopping at photographs of the Indian wars, and those of Ft. Laramie. One photo showed the signing ceremony, where members of the Lakota Nation and the Arapaho gathered here to sign the treaty in 1868 assuring them of continued ownership of hunting grounds from the Powder River to their sacred Black Hills. Without white encroachment. *Now look what the hell's happening,* Ira thought. White men flock into the hills unencumbered by the army, and the army was reduced to hunting renegade warriors from the Red Cloud and Spotted Tail Agencies, or escorting gold shipments from the Hills to Cheyenne and banks back East. All in violation of that treaty.

Ira looked at other pictures hanging on the wall, many, perhaps, taken not so long ago, and his face sagged with a sadness. Many of the Indians in these photos probably were no longer alive, perhaps killed by Crook at the Battle of the Rosebud, perhaps at the Greasy Grass when they fought Custer a week later. Ira knew no Indians, except the hangers-around-the-forts who came for their annuities.

And those he saw over the sights of his Winchester.

But he recognized a way of life that was fast disappearing for the Indian. And he was a part of that, as surely as the gold miners who had trespassed into their Black Hills.

"Private Arnett said you threatened him," a deep voice said. Captain Kramer emerged from his office and walked across the room. By Sally's description, the captain should have been younger. But he was Ira's age, perhaps older. But then—Ira reasoned—most people looked young to Sally.

Captain Kramer stood eye level with Ira—six foot and a little change—but heavier in the arms and shoulders. A farmer's arms and shoulders? And Ira placed his accent as New York. Connecticut perhaps. "We don't hold with civilians' threats . . ."

Ira stepped closer, and Kramer backed away. Perhaps he was unsure of the dusty and disheveled civilian with mud caked to his clothing who came into the admin building, demanding things. "I didn't threaten him." Ira nodded to Private Arnett. "I just wanted him to fetch the OD."

"Well, he's fetched," Kramer said, motioning Ira into his office. "What is it you need, Mister—"

"Ira Drang," he said, not offering his hand. "I'm riding shotgun on that stage out front."

"You're wasting your time." Kramer smiled. "That smelly old

115

driver already petitioned me for an escort. Something about a gang of outlaws after you."

"More than Logan Hatch and his bunch," Ira said. "Indians have dogged us for the last thirty miles."

"Sioux or Arapaho?"

Ira shrugged. "Too far away to tell the few times I've spotted them."

Kramer bent to the desk and grabbed a cigar from a cedar humidor. He closed the lid without offering Ira a smoke. "Still doesn't answer what you want the army to do exactly."

"They're Indians," Ira said, fighting to keep his voice low, before he flew off the handle and landed in the guardhouse. "That is what you do here, is it not? Find and fight Indians?"

Kramer drew out cutting the tip of his cigar, stalling, before he lit a match. He looked at it before shaking it out. "I cannot spare even one man. I had to send out Companies C and D to the field looking for the Sioux who stole our mounts yesterday. Probably the same war party that attacked and wiped out the stage returning from Deadwood." He blew smoke rings toward the ceiling. "And those civilian wagons foolish enough to try to make it to the Shining Mountains. I would have told that fat smelly driver all this, if he hadn't stormed out of here."

"Tell me about the stage that was attacked."

Kramer inhaled deeply. "Two days ago, the stage returning to Cheyenne was overdue, and I sent out a patrol. They found the coach overturned, and three people—including the shotgun messenger—dead." He grinned at Ira. "That might be you if you insist on continuing north."

"How about those troopers drilling at the parade grounds? I'd say finding the Sioux is a whole lot more important than looking pretty."

Kramer walked to the window and pointed with his cigar. "Those men—boys—are raw recruits. It will be months before we can get them shaped up enough so they'll have the discipline to face the Lakota. Ever since Colonel Custer and his 7th got themselves wiped out, I've had standing orders not to take chances. To bide our time."

"And when the time's right?"

"When the time is right the 7th's massacre will be avenged." He faced Ira. "Now, if there's nothing else you want—"

"That returning stage," Ira asked, "was it carrying mail?"

"I don't know." Kramer turned to Arnett. "Private?"

Private Arnett shuffled through papers on his desk and grabbed one. "Patrol sergeant's report says the mail was scattered about, but most was still there by the stage. The sergeant gathered the mail and stowed it in back of the guardhouse for the next stage coming through to Cheyenne."

"You're sure it was Indians?" Ira asked.

Kramer nodded to Arnett, who flipped a page and read the field report. " 'All passengers scalped. Horses stolen.' " Arnett spat into a spittoon, but his aim was off. Tobacco juice hit the edge of the brass pot and caromed off to *splat* against the wall. "Of course it was Indians."

"Tell me," Ira said, "was there any certified mail found?"

Arnett looked to Kramer, who shrugged. "Was there?"

"As a matter of fact," Arnett, said, "there was no certified mail recovered. At least nothing the patrol reported."

"What the hell's that got to do with anything?" Kramer asked.

"Every stage has *some* registered mail leaving Deadwood for Cheyenne. It's how many of the miners send their money—certified bank draft."

"So?"

"So what Indian would have use for a bank draft?" Ira said. "None. And there were none found. I'd wager road agents took down that stage. Scalped the crew and passengers to make it look like an Indian attack."

"Doesn't change anything," Kramer said. "And I will tell you, like I told that British lout who came in here pleading for an escort, report this to the civilian authorities when you arrive in Deadwood."

"*If* we arrive in Deadwood."

CHAPTER 13

They stopped beside a meadow ripe with buffalo grass and sunflowers overlooking Government Farm, fourteen miles out of Ft. Laramie. Or what used to be Government Farm before the government abandoned the crop experiments here. Sally stood in the seat and stretched. "Go off in that bunch of trees and take a leak if you have to," he told the passengers.

"That any way to talk around a lady?"

"Sorry I offended you," Sally yelled at Dauber and tipped his hat toward Beth. "I should have said you folks can go off and take a piss."

Dauber took Beth's hand and helped her out of the coach. She stumbled, massaging her forehead, and joined her husband, who was walking off into the trees.

Dauber looked at her for long moments before he turned and helped Gordy out of the coach. "Careful," Dauber said. Gordy grimaced as his feet hit the ground. Dauber grabbed Gordy's crutch and took hold of one arm. Gordy shrugged it off and hobbled toward the trees.

"Well, go help him," Ira said.

"He don't want my help!" Dauber snapped and walked off toward the grama grass meadow.

"Folks are getting a little testy," Sally said as he adjusted the tree attached to the harness's whiffletree just ahead of the coach. He patted the rump of one of the wheelers, a large roan more than fifteen hands tall and built to pull a stage. The crupper situated under the tail had split, and Sally took the strap off.

"Of course, they're testy," Ira said. "They thought there'd at least be some hot coffee here. Maybe some johnny cakes to take along."

Sally waved his hand around. "The army hadn't had a thing at this place for years. And when we get to Rawhide Buttes station, they'll shit when they find there's nothing there, either."

"I thought there was a swing station at the Buttes."

"There was, up till about a week before Crook got his butt kicked at the Rosebud." Sally reached in a bag under the seat and grabbed a new crupper. "It's like the Indians' smoke signals reached all the way from Montana to those Sioux on the agencies." He spat a string of tobacco juice that barely missed Ira. "Sioux burned the station house and some wagons in the corral. Stage line figured it wouldn't stay if they rebuilt it, so they never did. There's nothing there except charred timbers."

Ira walked off a ways and looked over the road they had just ridden. Last night's rain had already soaked into the parched dirt, yet the stage ruts made for easy tracking. But then, where else would a stage go but north on the road?

Ira scanned the area. Logan was out there somewhere, but Ira was sure he had been caught off guard by expecting the stage to lay over. He'd play catch-up, and Ira knew Logan and his men could make far better time than the stage. Before the stage pulled into Custer City on the way to Deadwood, Logan would catch them.

"What are you looking at, Mr. Drang?"

Ira spun around. If he hadn't been so exhausted, Beth would never have been able to walk up behind him like she had. "Just looking at the road is all."

"Afraid Mr. Hatch will find us?"

Ira remained silent.

"It's all right to tell us the truth," she said, and her legs buckled. Ira caught her and eased her onto a rock beside the meadow. "I guess I've just been worried about that boy . . . Gordy. He's lost so much blood . . . well, the worry and tending to him along with the rough ride, it's given me such a powerful headache, I think I might pass out."

Ira walked into the meadow and stooped to some dogweed plants, their yellow flowers fluttering in the breeze as if they were inviting people to pluck them. But most people living on the prairie avoided the smelly plant. Until they needed it.

He pulled leaves off the stem as he walked back to Beth. He grabbed a rock and crushed the leaves with the butt of his Bowie before handing the rock to Beth.

She backed away. "That smells awful."

"Put it under your nose and take deep breaths.

"I will not—"

"Trust me."

Beth looked sideways at Ira before she did as he asked. Her nose scrunched up as she breathed in. Within seconds, her nose began to bleed, and Ira handed her his bandana. "That was a mean trick . . ." She looked at Ira and smiled. "My headache is gone. What—"

"Indians use that trick when they have a raging headache. Your nose will stop bleeding in a moment."

She dabbed the blood under her nose until it stopped and handed Ira his bandana. "Where did you learn that?"

Ira stuck his bandana in his pocket and looked to the west. "Over thataway and to the north is Crow country. I was foolish enough to have two buffalo run me down four years ago when I was hunting them. Busted me up plenty. Hadn't been for the Indians, I'd have died." He remembered the good times when he was in the Crow camp, one of those times in his life when he'd been truly happy. But one of those times in his life when he also knew he didn't belong. Like Beth. She didn't belong, yet here she was, following her husband across the frontier, just so he could fleece miners out of their money.

"And you, Mrs. Warner—what's your story?"

Her smile faded, and she looked away. "What's to tell? Frank is a gambler, so we go where the money is." She looked up at Ira. "But I get *so* tired of picking up and moving on whenever he sees fit." She looked at Frank, but he was busy showing Gordy a card trick. "*Whenever* Frank sees fit." She laid her hand on Ira's arm. "What I wouldn't give to go see that Crow country you speak of." She smiled at him. "Maybe we could go there, you and me?"

Ira thought back to women he'd known. Whores mostly, only because he never had time to develop any decent, long-term relationship. Sure, he and Beth could go to Crow country. *If* Frank wasn't in the picture. But as importantly, *if* Beth was a woman of the trail. She just seemed so out of place here. She wouldn't last a week, living in the back country.

"We all heard about your brother . . . hanging himself." She laid her hand on his arm, but Ira didn't jerk his arm away. "Must be hard to lose someone so close."

"You have no idea. Jamie was such a gentle soul. He was my folks' late child, and he was fifteen years younger than me."

"But Mr. Sally said he . . . acted even younger?"

"My brother was not quite . . . all there. He was like a little child, yet he worked *so* hard to be a man." Ira felt his eyes water, and he looked away. "Most important thing you need to know about Jamie was that he was such a good person."

Beth leaned close to him. "It's all right to cry," she whispered. "I *could* be there for you—"

"Need your help!" Sally hollered to Ira.

He stood abruptly. "Got to help Sally with the horses."

"Perhaps we'll have this conversation another time," Beth said.

Ira shook his head. "I do not think that would be appropri-ate, Mrs. Warner," he said and walked to where Sally dug under the seat of the coach.

Sally opened the tin of axle grease and took off a glove. He scooped a finger-full of grease and motioned to Ira to step closer. Sally stood on his tiptoes and looked at Ira's face. "You need to duck when a man throws a punch." He smeared a dol-lop of Frazer's across a skin abrasion that spanned one cheek and part of Ira's forehead.

Sally looked around Ira as Beth joined the others. "It looked like you needed some rescuing," he said.

"Thanks. I did," Ira said. "That woman's making some invit-ing suggestions."

"Like suggestions she's made to Dauber and Gordy different times about leaving Frank?"

"Not quite so blunt, but that was the gist of it."

"If I was young, I'd damn sure take her up on her offer," Sally said.

"Even with Frank in the picture?"

"That is a little problem I would have to deal with."

"Well, I won't have to deal with it," Ira said. "All I want to do is get to Deadwood."

"So, we're going to have to go how far until we can get a hot bath and a hot meal?" Beth asked, sashaying toward them. "Maybe a nice cup of tea?"

"Shouldn't you be helping Gordy?" Ira snapped and recog-nized a hint of jealousy in his voice. "I mean, you've been help-ing the kid. I think he's begun to expect your help."

Beth glanced at Dauber, walking beside Gordy shuffling back to the stage dragging his crutch. Dauber held the door and helped Gordy inside the coach. "Dauber is doing just fine," she said. When Gordy was safely inside, Dauber walked to the front of the stage and sidled up to Beth. "I heard you wanted some tea, Mrs. Beth," he said. "I could boil some water—"

"We don't have time for tea," Ira said.

Dauber glared at him.

"We've got to get on down the trail. Help Sally lead the horses over to that buffalo grass. Sooner they're fed, the sooner we'll get out of here."

Sally looked sideways at Ira and nodded imperceptibly. He and Dauber led the horses away from the stage and hobbled them at the edge of the meadow.

"Did you get rid of the kid because of me?" Beth stepped closer to Ira and licked her lips. "I thought it was just a matter of time before you'd want to be alone with me—"

"What's your game, Mrs. Warner?"

Beth stepped back. "I don't understand."

"Of course you do. You've come on to Gordy, and when all he wanted was to make it to the gold fields, you started stringing that young cowboy along—"

"Dauber can make his own decisions."

"And now you're coming on to me."

Beth shrugged.

"And when your husband finds out you're . . ."

"Flirting?" Beth smiled. "Because that is *all* I have been doing." She batted her long eyelashes. "It keeps me . . . sharp."

"Let's hope your flirting doesn't get between your husband and either of those ranch boys."

"You *are* a little jealous." she said softly.

"Not hardly."

"Can you deny you aren't a little . . . *excited* when I smile at you?"

Ira felt his face warm, and he looked at Dauber and Sally tending to the horses. He looked at the meadow's edge, where Frank lay under the shade of a cottonwood. He looked at Preacher sipping his medicine in back of the coach. He looked anywhere but at Beth. "It doesn't matter whether you excite me or not. The thing that does concern me is what happens when your husband realizes you've come on to every man on the stage."

"Like I said before, I'm just flirting." She exaggerated a smile before turning and walking toward the horses. She glanced back, and her eyes met Ira's before she lay in the meadow beside Frank.

"Dangerous, isn't she?" Preacher approached Ira. He filled his pipe from a pouch and lit a lucifer on the side of his seat. "I overheard what you told her."

"She *is* dangerous," Ira said. "If she keeps coming on to those boys, she might just force Frank's hand."

"Can't argue there," Preacher said. "Frank strikes me as someone who flies off the handle at the drop of a stick. Last thing we need is fighting among us."

"Especially with Indians on our trail."

Preacher jerked the pipe from the corner of his mouth and looked frantically around. "Where—"

"I caught a glimpse of one warrior two miles back. But just a fleeting glimpse. Couldn't tell if he was Sioux or Arapaho, but you can be sure he wasn't alone." Ira kicked a dirt clod, and it flew against the side of a wagon wheel. "Figured this would happen—the Indians are bound to be on the move with the cavalry flushing them out."

"Think he spotted us?"

Ira looked at the others getting comfortable during the brief respite. "I have to assume he did."

"So, it's just a matter of time before they attack us?" Preacher said. "Dammit, just when *were* you going to tell us?"

"Sally already knows. We'll gather the others around, and I'll tell them what I saw."

Ira called Frank and Beth over and waved to Dauber to join

everyone at the coach. Beth leaned inside the coach and propped Gordy's leg on the center seat. Preacher leaned against the coach, and Frank squatted beside it. "Now what the hell kind of surprise you have for us?"

When Ira told them they should assume the Indians had spotted the stage—and would probably set an ambush—Frank slapped his hand against his leg.

"That's just sweet, isn't it? And us with only one rifle." He glared at Sally as he joined the others. "Dammit, old man, why the hell didn't you get the army to give us an escort?" He stepped toward Sally, who stood smiling at Frank, waiting for him to throw the first punch. Frank had him by twenty years and six inches, but Sally had Frank by twenty pounds and a lifetime of dealing with rough men and even rougher stock. If the jehu could handle a six team of horses, he could sure handle a fancy gambler. "You should have told us."

"Bugger off," Sally said.

Ira stepped between the two men. He would have liked to see Sally tangle with the fancy man, but Ira also knew now was not the time. If Indians were close, they needed everyone sharp. Ready. "Captain Kramer refused an escort," Ira said. "The stage returning to Cheyenne was attacked in the last few days, and patrols are out looking for Indians. Probably stole army mounts, too. With those patrols out, that left him thin at the fort. We could have stayed at Ft. Laramie, but we"—he nodded to Sally—"thought we'd make a run for it before Logan realizes we left the fort."

"Why didn't you ask us," Dauber said, "before you made a decision like that?"

"Would you have wanted to remain at the fort for a couple days? A week maybe before the patrols came back and were available?"

"*I* sure as hell don't want to waste any time getting to

Deadwood," Frank said.

"Me, either," Dauber said. "Me and Gordy need to get there before all the gulch is claimed." He scanned the high hills as if he expected an ambush at any time. "What's our chances?"

Ira thought that over. With one rifle and Gordy out of commission, their chances were looking slimmer by the mile. "Not good. But Sally says the horses can make good time if need be."

"All we have to do is make it the fifteen miles to Rawhide Buttes," Sally added. "There's natural shelter where we could make a stand. As least as good as can be, under the circumstances."

Preacher pointed to the horses. "Those critters look plumb worn out. They can't be pushed too hard, or they'll drop in the traces."

"If I pace the team," Sally said, "and save their pull in case we have to make a run for it—we might just have a chance."

Ira looked at the passengers. "This here's no democracy, but I'm asking each one of you what you want to do."

Dauber stepped forward, and his hand brushed Beth's arm. "I'm for going on. But I'd say we take it slow. I'd hate for Gordy's wound to open up."

"What're you yapping about out there?" Gordy called from inside the coach.

"Taking a vote if'n we outta' make a run for it or make a stand here," Dauber said.

"Well, I vote for going on," Gordy said, and Ira turned to Beth and Frank.

"If you ask us," Beth said, "we're for getting to Deadwood as quick as possible."

"Preacher?"

Preacher coughed into his hand and rubbed the blood off on his bandana. "You're right—this is no democracy. I'm just along for the ride. We make a fight here or a fight at Rawhide Buttes, makes me no mind. Like I said"—he winked at Ira—"I'm already dead."

"I'm with you folks," Ira said. "Sooner we get to Deadwood, the sooner I can talk to Wild Bill in my own way."

North of Government Farm, the route crossed buffalo grass, grama grass, tall switchgrass dried and crackling in the drought, past clumps of cactus and soapweed, cottonwood that spewed their cottony flowers like a mini blizzard when the wind kicked up. The stage passed an enormous prairie dog town spanning hundreds of yards. Sentries chirped a warming, and a thousand dogs scurried down their holes. Did the dogs alert their townsfolk to the stage, or did something else spook them? "I saw it, too," Sally told Ira. "We was far enough from that dog town, I'd have thought they wouldn't pay us no mind."

"But they did." Ira stood in the seat and looked up at the tall butte ahead of them. He saw nothing that might have alerted the prairie dogs, and he sat back onto the seat. "What I'd give for a few more rifles."

"I tried, but the post trader wouldn't sell me any," Sally said, easing the stage around a large mud hole in the road. "But the sutler, he just rambled on and on about how the commanding officer would hang him if he got caught selling arms to civilians. Something about being worried about them falling into the hands of the Indians."

"Or someone like Logan Hatch," Ira said.

Sally gave the leaders more slack in the lines, and the coach lurched ahead. "At least we gave Logan the slip."

Ira turned his back to the wind and began rolling a smoke. The coach rocked and jarred over ruts and rocks as more loose tobacco fell onto his shirt front than on the rolling paper. "I'd never count Logan out. We might have gotten a few miles ahead of him by hightailing it out of Ft. Laramie, but you can damn well bet he's already working out some place where he can spring an ambush."

"That's if the Indians don't beat him to it," Sally said.

Dauber stuck his head out a window. "Can you slow a mite? Ol' Gordy's leg's taking a beating against the seat. Beth . . . Mrs. Warner . . . used her shawl for padding, but he's complaining it's hurting him mighty bad. How far until we get to Rawhide Buttes?"

Sally slowed the coach as it entered a curve in the road. Lizards sunning themselves scampered away, barely missing the stage wheels. "Not more'n two miles till we get to Rawhide Buttes—"

An arrow—with the feathering of a Lakota—*thumped* into the side of the stage. Two more arrows flew at them, and one pierced the corner of Ira's hat before it sailed over the heads of the horses.

Two Indians burst from around a boulder big enough to hide the coach. They rode hard at them, clinging to the sides of their ponies, bare legs hooked over the shoulders of their horses, making themselves a smaller target. One clutched a Henry, bright brass tacks imbedded in the stock glistening in the afternoon sun, and he shot and levered on the run.

Three more Indians appeared from trees on the opposite side of the road. The lead Lakota levered shots with his rifle that hit the corner of the back boot. Leather flew past Ira as he snapped a shot that hit the warrior's pony. Horse and rider went down, but a passing Lakota grabbed onto his fallen comrade and hoisted him on back of his mount in one smooth motion as they gained on the coach.

Sally cracked his whip over the heads of the leaders, over the heads of the swing team, and the coach picked up speed. "I need you up here, Dauber," Ira yelled, levering rounds into his Winchester, firing as fast as he was able, fumbling in his vest pocket for more cartridges.

An Indian reached the back boot and was scrambling for a hold when Preacher leaned out the window and shot him in the face with his black-powder Colt. Smoke spewed from the bullet wound as the Indian fell off and another pony trampled over him.

The three Lakota who had attacked from the lee side had almost reached the stage when Frank's gambler's guns opened up, knocking one man off his horse. The other two Indians held back.

Dauber lay on top of the coach and fired as fast as he could. He ran out of ammunition, and Ira handed him his own Colt.

Hot, desperate firing caused the Indians to pause, and Ira squeezed a shot off that knocked one Indian off his pony. Those beside him dropped back as Sally urged his team on to more speed. Just before they disappeared around a sharp curve in the route, Ira saw the Indians give up. They had dismounted and bent to their dead and wounded lying in the road.

"We were lucky," Sally said, looking back at the Indians hunkered over their dead. "Almost makes a body wish for Logan and his bunch."

"Almost," Ira said as he scanned the high hills for the next ambush.

CHAPTER 14

The dapple gray snorted and shied from the tree line. Dutch reined the horse at the edge of the road and glanced over at the trees. He saw no reason the horse should have balked. But there *was* a reason. He and the gray had ridden enough trails together that Dutch knew that if the horse told him something was amiss, it was.

He dismounted and tied the gray to a boulder. He slipped the loop off the hammer of his Colt before he began walking the tree line, checking tracks. Something was here . . .

A smell assailed his nostrils. A smell he was all too familiar with. But where?

When he had gone twenty yards off the road, he saw what had alerted the gray and what had alerted him: a shallow grave with an arm—minus the hand—sticking out of the ground. He walked a wide circle around it, studying the ground. Tracks showed where it had been looted by coyotes, and a large lion, tracks telling Dutch where they had feasted on the body.

He walked back to his horse and grabbed his stub of a shovel from his saddle. He had dug enough graves—and dug up enough—to know the shovel would serve him well. As it always had.

The dirt had been tossed loosely over the body—a hasty grave, one that protected the dead very little from the ravages of the animals. If Ed Mooney was right, Dutch would find Handy Johnson and Miguel DeJesus here, dead by Ira's gun. Dutch could have ridden by, taking Ed's version of what happened as gospel. But he didn't trust Ed.

When he had excavated a dozen shovels-full of the dirt, the shovel struck something hard. A belt buckle or bone perhaps? He knelt beside the makeshift grave and tugged on the arm, ragged where the animals had been feeding on it. Dirt fell away, and Dutch recognized the checkered shirt Handy had worn the last time he was in camp. Dutch chuckled. *At least Handy won't be so lopsided now.*

He scraped more dirt away from the body and grabbed the handless arm. He pulled hard, and Handy reluctantly came out of the ground. Dried blood coated Handy's shirt where Ira's bullet had struck him. He dragged the body away from the hole. He began moving dirt from the body under where Handy had lain. Miguel's sombrero had been tossed onto his chest, and Dutch laid it aside. When he did, he saw the gaping wound to Miguel's chest. Certainly not from a bullet. Dutch squatted beside the grave. He tore Miguel's shirt away from his chest, the fabric having been sliced from his belly button nearly to his chest; dried guts spilled out of the wound into the hasty grave.

Dutch turned Miguel's face—frozen from his last terrible pain—away from him and examined the back of his head. The Mexican's shiny black hair lay disheveled, but no blood stained it. "Can't ever trust that sneaky son of a bitch to tell us the truth," he said. "Looks like Ira *didn't* shoot you in the back of the head, unarmed, like Ed claimed." He stood and stretched. "Looks like you got what you gave so many others—death at the hands of a sharp blade."

Dutch dragged Handy's body back to the grave and rolled it on top of Miguel's corpse. He shoveled dirt back over the shallow grave. It wouldn't stop the scavengers from digging up the bodies, but it made Dutch feel human, knowing he'd done what he could for them.

He would bury them proper if he had the time. He needed to catch up with the stage. That was even more important now, as Ed would be leading Craig Highsmith and Jimmy Antelope to catch up with it. The last thing Dutch wanted was for Ed to spring an ambush and kill the passengers. Logan was killing-mad *this* time. He'd for sure run over anyone who would kill Cassie's murderer. Logan had other plans for the killer.

The gray's lathered flanks twitched. He needed a rest, yet Dutch needed to catch up to the stage before Ed led Jimmy Antelope and Craig Highsmith to attack it. Logan'd had second thoughts after he'd sent Ed to meet up with the Indian and Craig. "That might have been the dumbest thing I done lately," Logan said, "trusting that sneaky bastard to just *watch* the stage."

"You want me to catch up with Ed? Make sure he don't hurt the passengers?"

Logan watched Matt huddled, shivering, close to the campfire, wrapped in a blanket. Blood had soaked through the bandanas Miguel had wrapped over his bullet wound. "I'd go myself . . ."

"Understood," Dutch said, and he did understand. Or he thought he did. With Cassie dead, Logan treated Matt more like the child he'd had before her brutal death.

Logan gave him strict orders—as if Dutch *needed* orders from his old friend—that Dutch was to prevent the three men from harming anyone on the stage. Harming Cassie's killer. Dutch would kill them if it came to that, though he really didn't want to. Finding thieves with their skills was a difficult task. Especially with the gold fields just to the north sucking all the talent away. Dutch had thought more than a few times about pulling up stakes and joining the miners up Deadwood way. And he would have, too, if Logan didn't need him.

Dutch stopped beside a stream trickling next to the road and grabbed his canteen. He walked to the bank, parted bulrushes, three-foot goldenrod, and moss off the water's surface before he filled it.

Dutch ran his hand over ruts where the stage had passed this way and aged them as mere hours old. He stood and looked to where the ruts appeared to have joined into one as the stage disappeared over a rise a quarter mile north. He wondered how much Ed was to be believed. They had hit one of the passengers—he claimed—when they had attacked the stage, but had they shot more people? Dutch could see Ed lying to Logan so he wouldn't get ventilated.

"Guess that's what we get for working with scum like Ed," Dutch said as he poured water into his hat and held it for the horse. More often than not recently, Dutch enjoyed talking with his horse more than he did cunning people like Ed and most others who worked for Logan. "Wouldn't be the first time I had to kill a man when I didn't want to," he told the gray, who ignored him as he lapped up water. If Ed did as Logan ordered—keep watch on the stage with Jimmy and Craig and wait for the others to catch up—Dutch wouldn't have to harm a hair on any of them. If not . . . well, Dutch would just have to prevent that. He had never taken to either Craig Highsmith or Pawnee Jimmy, but they were adept at stealing horses. Sneaks. He'd never taken kindly to sneaks, either, but they were necessary if the army was to lose mounts. He'd take your garden variety back-shooter any day over a sneak thief.

But Ed was different. Dutch had always been lukewarm to the killer from Colorado. He'd never trusted him, but he rarely gave the man more than a passing thought.

Until now. The grave showed that Ed had lied about Ira murdering Miguel, whom he'd always taken a shine to. The young Mexican had been amiable to everyone he came across. Except those he *had* to kill. Dutch reasoned that was why he had admired, and was a little envious of, Miguel—that he killed with a certain amount of remorse, something Dutch could never feel.

The gray finished lapping the water, and Dutch put his hat on, threads of cool water flowing down his dusty face. As he took hold of the reins, the gelding jerked away as distant gunfire resonated off the high buttes.

Dutch swung into the saddle and spurred the horse ahead as the gunfire intensified. Rifle fire. "Son of a bitch, Ed—you must have ridden your horse to death to catch up with Jimmy and Craig just to ambush the stage. I'm going to have to kill you now," he said to the gray as he bent over the saddle, running hard in the direction of the gunfire.

He'd galloped the better part of a mile when he pulled up short and dropped his hat over the gray's eyes to quiet him. Flashes of a painted pony running headlong through the trees caused him to head for cover of the tree line. Indians sat among the trees, watching the stage route below. Eight hardened warriors—more than a match for most white men in a stand-up fight. Dutch didn't intend on getting into such a lopsided battle with those Lakota.

The gray snorted, and Dutch leaned over in the saddle. He stroked the horse's neck as he said soothingly, "Shush now, or those Indians will know we're here. I can get a passel of them before they kill us, but there are just too many."

An Indian—sitting tall on his pony's back—looked in Dutch's direction. His eyes, blackened with war paint, scanned the area, while the lightning flashes painted on his pony's withers twitched with anticipation.

"Shush." Dutch soothed the gray, bending lower in the saddle, making himself a frozen statue on the back of the horse. "He *thinks* someone is here," he whispered to the gelding. "He just hasn't convinced himself of it enough that he wants to tell

135

the others and risk their joking."

After several tense moments, the Indian looked away. He said something to the others, and they made their way down the game trail onto the road rutted by stagecoach wheels.

Dutch eased the gray ahead until he could see through the trees. Two Sioux lay dead on the road, along with a finely marked Indian pony. Dutch cursed under his breath. That pony would have brought fifty dollars from one of the Texas buyers. "So Ira pulled a fast one," he said to his horse. "Didn't lay over at Ft. Laramie like we figured." There was no other explanation: someone from the stage had killed the Indians. But at least he knew the stage was not far ahead. He could catch up with it within a few miles; he was certain. And he should do just that. But he needed to warn Logan, Matt, and the Canuck that hostiles were close. He couldn't do both.

So, as he watched the Indians dismount beside their fallen friends, Dutch stopped.

Only when the Indians finished their death song over their dead and moved on would he leave the safety of the trees. And as much as he wanted to catch up to the stage—make certain he was there when Ed, Jimmy Antelope, and Craig Highsmith found it—he needed to warn Logan even more. And he hoped Ed and the other two peckerwoods did what Logan had ordered them to do: just keep watch on the stage.

CHAPTER 15

Sally slowed the stage, the lathered and spent horses offering little protest. He stopped the coach next to a tall butte to protect their backside, sloped hills offering protection from two other sides. In a field to the east the charred remains of the stage station were a reminder that the Sioux could appear any time.

So far, Sally and the coach passengers had been lucky—the Indians who had attacked the stage had not pursued them. As if they were licking their wounds and mourning their dead comrades. With any luck, the Indians would figure the cost of attacking this stage was too high and would continue to their hunting grounds on the Powder River.

Ira stood on top of the coach and looked back the way they had just come. "Gimme your spyglass."

Sally handed Ira the telescope before he turned to his horses, running his gloved hands over the animals, their muscles still twitching from the effort of the hard run. "We gotta give the horses a rest. Some water. If we don't, they might not go on much farther."

Ira glassed the road in back of them for Indians. Nothing. He bent and said into the coach, "Dauber, help Sally unhitch the team." Ira handed Sally his spyglass. "And lead the horses to Rawhide Creek."

"Dauber's got other things to do right now," Frank said when he'd climbed out of the coach. "He's going to have to bury his Gordy."

Ira jumped to the ground and looked inside the coach. Dauber sat on the center seat holding Gordy's head. Beth sat beside Dauber, rubbing his neck, whispering to him. Her blood-soaked shawl had fallen onto the floor of the coach. Dauber looked up at Ira and swiped a hand across his eyes. "Guess that last ride opened up the wound in his leg. We tried to stop the bleeding, but we couldn't. We are going to bury him proper, ain't we?"

Ira thought that over. With Indians nearby, he would have told Sally to make a run for it and bury Gordy later. But Sally needed time to feed and water the horses anyway. "Bury Gordy. But by the time the team gets fed and watered, the burying better be done. Frank," Ira said, "help Dauber bury the kid."

"The hell I will," Frank said. "I paid good money to ride this stage, and the only thing I've gotten out of it is being attacked by Indians and Logan Hatch's men. Let Preacher help with the burying. He can say some sweet verse over the body once it's in the ground."

Ira took off his hat and ran his fingers through hair soaked with sweat. "Preacher's going to help Sally and me with the horses. That leaves you to help Dauber—"

"I say otherwise." Frank squared up to Ira. His hands were poised by his shoulder holster. He glared up at Ira standing atop the coach.

"You won't get a shot off," Ira said. "But go for it—we'll leave your body for Logan Hatch. Pin a note on your leaking chest that you were the one who killed his Cassie."

"Enough!" Beth stepped from the coach and stood in front of Frank. "If I read Mr. Drang right, we need everyone to pitch in if we're going to get out of this alive. Even if we are passengers."

"Listen to your wife," Ira said. "And we all might make it out of this with our scalps on our heads."

"Can one of you take Gordy's legs?" Dauber asked as he struggled with his big friend's body.

Frank glared at Ira, his hand poised over his gun butt once more, before he turned to the coach and grabbed Gordy's legs.

"That was good advice you gave your husband," Ira said to Beth when he'd stepped down from the top of the stage. "I meant what I said—I would have ventilated him and left his corpse for Logan."

Beth looked up at Ira and smiled. "Then I thank you for sparing him. He needed to pitch in and help. We all need to."

"I'm glad you feel that way," Ira said, "because in the boot is some bacon and a fry pan. Build a fire and fix us some food."

"You mean cook on a crude open fire?"

"You do know how to cook, don't you?"

"People cook *for* me, Mr. Drang," she sputtered. "I haven't had to cook since I was a little girl."

"Then it's high time you remembered how to do it. And Beth"—Ira smiled back at her—"grab that sack of corn dodgers in the boot as well. Might be the last meal we get for a long time."

Ira adjusted the throat latch around one of the leader horses. "Take care of him," Sally pleaded. "He damn near run himself to ground back there. Like the rest of the team."

"I just need to take a look-see up over those buttes." Ira cinched the nose band tighter and swung a leg over the gelding. "Save me a corn dodger and a piece of bacon." He patted the gelding's neck. "We'll be back and get this guy in the traces before you know it."

"I hope you're right," Sally said.

Sally looked after his horses like they were his own, and he'd had second thoughts when Ira told him he needed one to scout the area high overhead. Places where an ambush was likely.

"Too bad Ed Mooney took Handy and Miguel's horses."

It was too bad. After Ira had killed Miguel, he'd looked the area over, finally spotting where Ed had ridden his own horse away, leading his dead comrades' mounts.

Ira leaned down and handed Sally his Winchester. "Just in case I'm not back in a couple hours, you go on without me." He patted the brown's chest. "And without this guy here."

"Understood," Sally said as he palmed the extra rifle rounds Ira handed him.

Ira headed out, eying the cliffs above him. He had been to this part of the territory five winters ago when he was wolfing, before the price of pelts in the East fell through. As he rode bareback on the stage horse, he fought to recall where the trail was that wound to the top of the buttes. All he remembered right off was that it went back the way they had come, toward Government Farm. The trail meandered up a gentle slope, rising for a quarter mile until it petered out at the top of the buttes.

He stopped and cocked his head. Another seven or eight miles back this way was where the Indian attack had happened. Had the Indians buried their fallen and ridden this way to avenge their dead? Or were they licking their wounds, as he hoped?

And then he saw the break in the trees where the trail ascended the buttes. Ira guided the horse with the halter and the pressure of his legs up the winding trail. He rode between stands of pine trees and brushed past thickets bearing the lavender flowers of horsemint as he picked his way to the top. He needed to get to the high ground to see if the Lakota had followed the coach. He needed to know if the stage ought to stay at the buttes and make a stand or try making it to the station at Running Water. But he doubted the horses could run the eighteen miles to the next station.

Halfway up the trail, the gelding turned and tried nipping at Ira, but he jerked the halter. The horse was used to the traces, used to being hitched to a singletree. He wasn't used to a man riding atop him. But Ira figured he wouldn't be riding the gelding any longer than he had to.

When he reached the top of the butte, he saw the stage below in the distance, looking mighty small. Beth squatted at a fire, stirring bacon in a pan with a spoon, while her husband worked the business end of a shovel helping Dauber bury Gordy. Sally and Preacher were taking off feed bags for the horses, and Ira almost felt bad that he'd had to take this one away from his supper. Almost.

He rode slowly, watching the ground, looking into the sun, looking for anything that gave him an indication of whether the Indians had skirted the rim to attack from above. He rode the last mile to where he could look at where the attack had played out, but fallen warriors were nowhere to be seen. That didn't surprise him—Indians only left their dead behind when they had to.

He cursed Captain Kramer, even though he knew the cavalry was thinned out and looking for Indians. Even if he refused to send a patrol escort, he could have given an indication where his troopers were, where they thought the Indians who killed the stage crew and passengers from Deadwood *might* be. But the Indians had probably melted into the countryside as effortlessly as those who had just attacked the stage. If it *was* Indians who attacked the south-bound stage. It wouldn't be the first time that a stage was robbed, drivers and messenger killed to make it appear as if the Sioux had attacked.

He turned west and started cutting sign, keeping the setting sun between himself and the ground when . . . he pulled up short and dismounted, picking a twig out of a distinct track. Shod horses had crossed here. It was hard to age the tracks in this mud, but his best guess was that they'd been made here within the last hour. Logan? Ira could think of no one else. And Logan would see the tracks of Ira's horse and work his way back to where the stage—and passengers—were all but helpless against Logan's hired killers.

Ira mounted and slowly rode into the trees away from where he'd spotted the tracks, winding his way among thick spruce and scrub juniper, laying obvious tracks for Logan to follow. He rode a wide circle, intending to lay tracks over the ones he'd just made. Ira knew that, even if his tracks confused Logan and his men, they wouldn't confound Dutch for long. But all Ira needed was to get back to the stage before the sun set.

When he'd laid sufficient tracks, he started back in the direction of Rawhide Buttes. He heard the snort of a horse, and another followed—an impatient snort.

He pulled up short, the gelding sensing something was not right. It crowhopped, then bucked again. Ira quickly covered the horse's face with his bandana as he strained to hear the other horses. He turned his head and cupped his ear: the sound came from the other side of a thick grove of willow and quaking aspen, across a shallow clearing rimmed with chokecherry bushes.

Then he saw a flash of white through the trees, then another, and Logan emerged, leading the wounded cowboy, followed by the Canuck. They rode single file. But not Ed Mooney. And not Dutch. And they worried Ira.

The Canuck rode slowly behind Logan, who held the reins of another gelding. The horse thief, Matt Ales, clung to the saddle horn, riding half bent over, blood seeping through his shirt. But why were they not on the road where the stage would have to be? Why were they here? Ira couldn't answer that, but he did know they would soon pick up the circle of tracks he'd laid. With any luck, that would keep them occupied long enough for him to ride back to the stage.

The riders once again disappeared behind the thick trees, and Ira took his bandana from his horse's eyes. He grabbed a dead branch from a fallen spruce and had begun the slow process of covering his back trail while he made his way back to Rawhide Buttes when . . .

. . . a shot from a heavy bore rifle erupted. Ira felt the bullet enter the gelding's chest and come out the other side. Blood splattered Ira's leg, and he kicked himself free of the horse as it collapsed.

Ira had drawn his Colt, frantically searching for the shooter, when another shot kicked up dirt inches in front of him. He looked uphill to the west and finally spotted Dutch aiming his heavy Rolling Block at Ira from a hundred yards away.

"Even I wouldn't dream of taking on Dutch when he's got that rifle of his pointing my way." Logan rode toward Ira from the trees, his gun holstered, smiling, for he didn't need to draw his weapon—Dutch could hand Logan Ira's head any time he wanted to. "Why not just drop that hogleg."

Ira dropped his pistol.

The Canuck rode to Ira and dismounted. He watched Ira warily as he bent and grabbed the Colt.

"I'd say mount up, but I'm afraid Dutch had to put that horse down. Shame."

"Shame that you didn't get a chance to steal it?"

Logan shrugged. The Canuck laughed.

Dutch started slowly down the hill, his Remington .50 cradled under one arm. He stopped a dozen yards from Ira. "It *was* a shame. But shooting that horse was the only way I could be sure to capture you without killing you. Not that I'd mind that, either." He motioned with his rifle. "Shuck that Bowie, too. I seen what damage you can do with it."

"So you found Handy and the Mex," Ira taunted, stalling for

time in order to figure out how to save himself from this mess. "He wasn't as adept with a blade as any old Indian I've ever met."

"I ought to kill you right now—"

Logan pushed Dutch's rifle barrel down. "We don't want him dead."

"You're going to kill me anyway," Ira said. What he wouldn't give to have his pistol in his hand once again. Now all he had left was a chipped-bladed Barlow knife folded in his pocket. Against these killers, it was no weapon at all. "Why not just kill me now?"

"Because we need you," Logan answered.

"I'm all about folks needing me."

"Cut the smart-assed attitude," Logan said. "Dutch saw where the Indians attacked the stage— where's it at now?"

"On the road somewhere, of course. Safe by now."

"If you would have laid over at Ft. Laramie, like you ought to have after those Lakota attacked you—"

"You see that?"

"Not exactly." Dutch put his rifle in the saddle scabbard and began rolling a smoke. "I just worked out what happened from the tracks."

"There you have it," Ira said, looking over the men surrounding him, any one of whom would have enjoyed killing him. "But we *didn't* lay over at Ft. Laramie, and the stage is probably crossing Old Woman Creek by now."

Logan dismounted and approached Ira. He stood several inches shorter than Ira but had him by twenty hard pounds. "You telling me the stage is forty miles down the route?"

"I am."

Logan lashed out and slapped Ira hard on the side of the face. Ira staggered back, fighting to remain erect. "I don't abide liars—"

"But you do abide thieves and killers—"

"I don't abide *liars*. The stage couldn't have made that good a time with only five horses." He nodded to the dead gelding. "And the stage attack by Sioux slowed it up."

"And if you worked out the Indians' tracks," Ira said, "you know Sioux are still in the area."

Logan looked away.

"That's what you were doing here, trying to spot the Indians."

Logan nodded. "A man would be a fool not to want to know where the Sioux are and act accordingly. Now, where's the stage?"

"I told you where it was about now—"

Logan hit Ira on the chin. The blow caught him by surprise. He staggered back and nearly lost his balance. "Now I'll ask you one more time: how far did the stage get?"

"Why the hell you still think your girl's killer is on the stage?"

Logan's face flushed, and he grabbed Ira by the front of his vest. "You can walk away clean if you tell me who the killer is—"

"How the hell should I know?"

"Cassie bit her killer," Logan said. "I told you that. Now who on that stage has a chunk out of his hand? And where *is* that stage now?"

"I can get him to talk." The Canuck tied his roan to a chokecherry bush, and the horse seemed to breathe a grateful sigh of relief that the big man was off its back. "I have . . . persuasive abilities."

Logan shoved Ira across the clearing and into the Canuck's grasp. He hit Ira deep in the stomach, and Ira doubled over in time to get a knee to his face. Ira's nose flattened, blood spurting from it, and he dropped to the ground. He struggled to breathe with his broken nose, but it was his stomach wound that worried him. The stitches had pulled loose, and warm, sticky blood flowed down his belly, down his leg.

The Canuck lifted Ira effortlessly off the ground, holding him with one hand, the other cocked when Ira waved the air. "All right. All right. Let me catch my air, and I'll talk."

The Canuck looked at Logan. Logan nodded, and the big man let Ira fall to the ground.

Logan bent to Ira and lifted his head off the ground by his hair. "All right, here's your chance to live through this. Talk."

"That big farm boy—Gordy—his glove slipped off once." Ira coughed, trying to regain his breath. "He had a nasty wound on his hand," Ira lied. If he could convince Logan his daughter's killer was still alive, it might give Ira time to try to get out of this mess. "When the Indians attacked, we were camped at Government Farm. An axle broke. Sally rode back to Ft. Laramie to get another."

"So this Gordy feller is stranded by Government Farm?"

"We buried him at Government Farm," Ira lied again. "When your men ambushed us, Gordy caught a bullet in the leg. Sawbones at Ft. Laramie sewed him up, but the wound opened up, and he bled out. We buried him proper as we had time for—before the stage driver returned to Ft. Laramie for a new axle."

"I rode past Government Farm," Dutch said. "I didn't see any coach laid up."

Ira wiped blood from his nose with the back of his glove. "Sally will have arrived at the coach with a new axle long before now and repaired it. They're miles away by now."

"That don't explain why you're this far away from them."

Ira picked up his hat and brushed dust off it. He breathed heavily through his mouth, his nose splayed across his cheek. Useless. "I wanted to know just where the Sioux were. Same as you. I was working my way back to Government Farm when you put the grab on me. And now you're just going to kill me without a fair chance."

"I'm not going to kill you unless what you said was a lie."

Logan stepped away and grabbed Matt's reins. The Canuck had started to mount when Logan stopped him. "Stay here and watch Ira," Logan ordered.

The Canuck drew his pistol and pointed it at Ira's head.

Ira caught a glance between Logan and the Canuck that told Ira they had no intention of allowing him to live. He just hoped his lies would give the coach a chance to put distance between them and Logan.

When Logan and Matt and Dutch disappeared into the trees, the Canuck motioned with his gun. "Take off your boots."

"What?"

"Your boots. Take them off. I do not want you running away." He laughed and patted his belly. "As you can see, I am not built for running."

"Does it matter if you shoot me with my boots on or not?"

"I am not going to shoot you." The Canuck tipped his head back and laughed. "You must think we Canadians are . . . brutes. Now take off your boots."

Ira crowhopped around on one foot while he took a boot off. "For a man who's not going to shoot me, your pistol says otherwise."

"This?" the Canuck said. As Ira got his other boot off, the Canuck grinned and holstered. He took off his gun belt and tossed it aside. "I have no intention of letting you die quick. These"—he held his fists up—"will give you the fair chance you want."

The Canuck stood several inches taller than Ira and was forty hard pounds heavier. With a nose that had been flayed to one side of his face a time or two, and a busted cheek that had not healed right and remained deformed, the big man looked to Ira like he'd been hit by a mad bull. And lived to kill the bull.

"I wouldn't call a fight with you a fair chance," Ira said.

147

"It is the hand you drew today. You ever seen a man beat to death, eh?"

"Does Logan know what you are about to do?"

The Canuck smiled wide, and Ira could count the number of teeth left in his mouth on the fingers of one hand. "If he were here, I am certain he would enjoy the entertainment." He stepped toward Ira—quick for such a big man—and flicked out a jab that felt more like a hard right when it connected with Ira's already-broken nose. Ira was staggering back, struggling for his footing, when the Canuck lashed out with a left hook that landed flush on Ira's cheek. He fell to the ground and felt his eye quickly swelling shut. And his hand brushed against the Barlow knife in his pocket.

"Get up, little man. We are not finished dancing yet, you and me."

Ira struggled to stand, and—when he gained his footing—the Canuck threw two quick jabs and a right cross that felled Ira again. He rolled on the ground and lay on his side. The side where the Barlow rested in his pocket.

Ira worked the knife out of his pocket through his trousers, careful that the big man didn't see what he was about to do.

"If you don't get up," the Canuck said, "I'll kick you to death right where you lie."

Ira waved the air. "Give me a moment." He gathered one leg under him as his knife cleared his pocket. He thought back to Gordy, who had nearly bled out when the artery in his leg was nicked. If Ira could just get close enough . . .

"That's it," the Canuck said and reared back with a boot. Ira sucked in his stomach and half caught the boot. His stitches broke loose. Blood oozed from his stomach wound as he rolled across the clearing. He lay on his stomach, hiding his knife as he fumbled to open the blade.

If I can get in close, he thought. "I can't get up," Ira said as he held the small knife concealed beside his leg.

"Then you'll die where you lie," the Canuck said as he moved in for the kill. Ira palmed his knife, and, when the Canuck reared back to deliver another kick, Ira threw himself at the incoming leg.

He wrapped one arm around the Canuck's thick leg.

With the other hand, he pushed the blade hard against the Canuck's dungarees and ripped it across the inside of the big man's thigh. Ira rolled away as the Canuck froze, looking down at his dungarees, which were quickly soaking with blood. He held his hand tight against his leg, blood seeping through his fingers, a look of shock crossing his face a heartbeat before he howled like a cougar and rushed Ira.

Ira sidestepped the Canuck and put all his weight behind a right cross. *If I can keep out of his reach for another couple minutes,* Ira thought and felt the big man's cheek shatter. The Canuck fell to the ground, his leg forgotten. He howled again, fighting to stand, fighting to gain his balance.

Ira placed his hand across his stomach, aware all the stitches the army surgeon had sewn in had opened. All he needed was to keep his flesh together long enough for the Canuck to drop from blood loss . . .

The Canuck rushed in. Ira stepped aside. The big man countered and threw himself at Ira.

Hands wrapped around Ira's throat and lifted him off the ground as the Canuck roared with a rage Ira hadn't seen since he wounded a bear on the Yellowstone.

The Canuck cut Ira's airway off . . .

. . . his throat collapsing . . .

. . . his temples throbbing with pain.

He felt himself lose consciousness. He lashed out as his legs flailed the air, and he hit the Canadian's face, his head, his throat, but the blows had little effect.

Ira grabbed the Canuck's hands.

He felt a thumb snap and a finger break as he pried the man's hands from his neck. But the Canuck showed only an intense rage that slowly . . . diminished.

Pressure on Ira's throat eased. He sucked in a needed breath.

The Canuck's hands began to relax until . . .

. . . he let Ira go, and both men fell to the ground. The Canuck fought to stand as his eyes began to glaze over. One hand went to his leg and came up bloody, and he looked at Ira lying in the mud beside him. The Canuck's lips moved, but nothing came out.

A moment later he fell face down in the dirt.

Chapter 16

The stirrups of the Canuck's saddle were over-long for Ira, and he sat lower in the saddle than he was used to. He'd adjust them when he had time so that his legs could take up some of his weight, but for now he was thankful for *any* horse and saddle under him. Ira had taken the Canuck's spare shirt from his saddle and wrapped it around his stomach as he urged the horse toward where he remembered the trail down to the bottom of Rawhide Buttes to be. The mile took longer than Ira recalled any such ride taking, and he arrived at the summit of the Buttes.

But he forgot where the trail leading down was. And without the trail, he wouldn't be able to reach help. Wouldn't be able to reach anyone who could wrap his stomach. He had already lost too much blood. Delaying help any more might prove fatal.

Ira looked over the side of the buttes, but the stage would not be where he had left it. It had been hours since he told Sally he would return, and he was certain the stage had gone on without him. Ira dug spurs into the Canuck's horse. He needed to find the stage quickly, because Logan would soon realize the stage— and his daughter's killer—was not by Government Farm as Ira had told him. When Logan returned and found the Canuck dead and his horse gone, he'd know Ira had lied.

He urged the roan—a Morgan and mustang cross used to carrying much heavier weight—along the rim of the buttes while Ira tried making out the descending trail in the dusk. The horse seemed to enjoy stepping out lightly, and Ira spurred it along, stopping only long enough to examine each game trail, until . . .

. . . shod hoofprints showed in the soft dirt, hooves that seemed to lead directly over the rim of the cliff—hoof prints of the now-dead stagecoach horse Ira had ridden up that path.

Ira eased the Canuck's roan along the game trail descending down into the floor of the canyon. The animal faltered, and Ira prepared to throw himself free if the horse lost his balance. The thought of plunging over the face of the butte with a thousand-pound horse rolling on him was a chilling one. But the horse kept its footing, and twenty minutes later horse and Ira had arrived where he had last left the stage.

But the stage was not there.

Thankfully.

Sally had wisely made a run for the next station, and Ira figured the stage was nearing Running Water station by now.

Ira dismounted and tied the horse to a willow at the edge of the clearing while he bent over to examine the tracks. Closer to the butte, a dirty Stetson fluttered in the wind atop a make-shift cross: Gordy's grave. Logan would eventually come across it, but by then, Ira hoped to be in Custer City. Perhaps Deadwood, if things went well.

The camp fire had been doused with water, and Ira could almost smell the bacon and corn dodger he was so looking forward to. He ran his hand over the stagecoach tracks—Sally had gone on to the next stage station one horse short.

For a moment, Ira thought about riding straight for Deadwood. He had a fit horse. He had his gun and the Canuck's rifle, plus a double eagle the Canuck had carried in his pocket. He could make it to the Black Hills in a couple of days and be closer to dropping Hickok.

He almost took that route.

But he'd made an agreement with the stage line to protect stage and its passengers all the way to the Black Hills. Even if he had to force himself to honor that agreement.

Ira took a moment to adjust the stirrups before he swung a leg over the Canuck's roan. He gave the horse its head and rode as fast as the animal was capable on the road toward Running Water station.

Ira caught up with the stage only five miles out of Running Water station. Sally saw him and pulled the team up short. He gave Ira time to tie the roan to the back boot before he and the passengers attacked him with questions. "We had to start," Sally said. "I just figured the Lakota caught you, and your pecker was some brave's tobacco pouch."

"Thanks for the confidence," Ira said and laid his hand on Sally's shoulder. "But you did the right thing." He turned to Beth. "You have any of those corn dodgers left?"

"They're all gone. I would have saved you a few and some bacon." Beth shrugged. "But we just put our money on the Sioux." She motioned to his shirt. "But before you eat we best get fresh bandages on that stomach wound of yours."

Preacher climbed out of the coach and walked back to the Canuck's horse. "This looks like that big bas—man's roan what rode with Logan."

"It is." Ira sat on a front wheel, catching his breath, holding his stomach, which leaked blood over his hand.

"What the hell?" Frank said. "You stole his horse, and now he's going to be able to track you right back here."

Ira felt his anger rise. "I could have ridden straight to Deadwood—"

Beth put her hand on Ira's arm. "Please tell us what happened, Mr. Drang. As soon as I clean you up."

She led him to the back boot, and he sat as she dipped a bandana in water and wiped the crusted blood off his cheek before nodding to his shirt. "Take it off, Mr. Drang."

Ira peeled his shirt off and looked at his stomach. The stitches had indeed opened up. *Miguel's revenge.*

Beth looked at his stomach and told Dauber, "Open my travelling bag and grab my extra petticoat."

Dauber's face flushed red, and he was speechless as he grabbed her travelling bag. "As soon as we get time, you need to get your nose set straight." She winked at Ira. "Or else you'll have to work twice as hard to get a lady to hang on your arm." She looked over her shoulder at Frank leaning against the front of the coach. "But *I* wouldn't mind if you're damaged goods."

Ira grabbed her hand and pulled it away from his face. "In case you haven't noticed, you're a married woman," he whispered.

Beth shrugged and had started for the water bucket on the opposite side of the coach when she paused and looked back at Ira.

"Told you she was dangerous," Preacher said. "But don't feel lonely—she's been coming on to every man on this stage wearing pants."

"Everyone wears pants."

"That's my point. I don't know what her game is, but I'd be mighty careful, were I you." Preacher turned his back and lowered his voice. "Odd thing is, her damned husband doesn't even seem to mind."

"Maybe he's too dense to know what she's up to," Ira said.

"He knows, all right," Sally said. He squatted in the dirt beside Preacher and Ira. "He was right there when Beth flirted with Dauber strong enough, I thought she'd hump him right there."

"We don't need any more problems on this trip," Ira said.

Beth returned with fresh water just as Dauber handed her the petticoat. She winked at him and tore the fabric into wide strips. She dipped a strip into water and started washing Ira's face, but he stopped her. "What I need most, ma'am, is this fixed." He pointed to his stomach. "Stitches pulled out."

"I saw that. I don't have any thread, but I plan to wrap it with my undergarment."

"That's as close as I plan to get to your undergarments," Ira said and turned to Sally. "We need to get to Running Water and fresh horses." Ira watched Beth tear a long strip from her petticoat. "It won't take Logan long to figure out I snookered him, and then he'll ride like hell to catch up with us."

"You never did say how you got away from Logan."

Ira explained how Logan was so anxious for news about where the stage was that he let himself fall for Ira's lies. "Soon as I told him Gordy had a big chunk of meat bit off his hand—and all he needed to prove he killed Cassie was dig up Gordy's grave—Logan's eyes got kinda glassy, and he and Dutch rode off, leaving that big Canuck to batter me to death."

"Gordy didn't have any meat bit out of his hand," Sally said, looking over at Dauber, who eyed Beth as she wrapped her petticoat around Ira. "When we buried him, we took his gloves off—"

"You stole his gloves?" Ira said.

"Not exactly stealing," Sally answered. "You know how hard good gloves are to get in this part of the country. We . . . I just figured ol' Gordy wouldn't be needing them any time soon."

"You just wanted to see if Gordy was Cassie's killer."

Sally shrugged. "I'm guilty."

Ira thought back to Logan. He despised what the man was doing—chasing after the stage so he could find his daughter's killer—but he admired the man as well. If it had been Ira's kin murdered like Cassie'd been, he would be doing the same thing—running the killer into hell if need be.

Ira recalled a man in Ohio, a neighbor next to the Drang farm, who one day staggered into town crying how a passing bum had killed his son. Incensed neighbors, hell-bent on finding the man, went on the hunt, only to learn the reporting father had killed his son himself in a fit of rage. Was that what Logan was doing now—making so much noise because he killed his own daughter? He thought back to what he knew about Cassie Hatch: a looker, by all cowboys' accounts. And a flirt, much like Beth, but in an inexperienced package. Perhaps her flirts had gone too far. Perhaps *Logan* had gone too far in disciplining the girl and killed his own daughter.

One way to find out was for the passengers to expose their hands. "I think we all ought to show one another our hands," Ira said.

"What do you mean? "Dauber asked.

"Ira means he's beginning to believe Logan and thinks his daughter's killer is among us, Ain't that right?" Sally asked.

"You're the one who first thought her killer was one of us," Ira said. "Besides, I just think we need to know where we all stand." He yelled for Frank to join them.

Ira waited until Frank joined them before standing. Beth tied off the fresh bandage around his stomach, and Ira pulled down his shirt. He took off his gloves and held out his hands so everyone could see them. "They're dirty and scarred, but I have no meat bit out of them like Logan claimed." He turned to Frank. "Now it's your turn."

Frank took off one glove, leaving the other on as he rolled a cigarette. "You think I killed Cassie Hatch? And if I take off my other glove, and there's a nasty wound where she bit me, what are you going to do then? Turn me over to Logan?"

Preacher stepped closer to Frank. "There some reason you don't want to show your other hand? Maybe you *do* have just such a wound. Maybe we'll leave you trussed up for Logan to find."

Frank took a step back and bladed himself. His gloved hand

inched closer to his gun butt.

"That's enough!" Beth stepped in front of Frank and stood with her hands on her hips as she glared at each man. "You are all doing what Logan wants. Again—scratching at each other's throats. Is that what you want?"

Ira looked at Sally, who looked at Preacher, who looked away. Dauber kicked a stone with the toe of his boot and peered up at the sky.

"She's right," Ira said at last. "Logan *would* love nothing more than for us to be clawing at each other's throats." *Damn you, Logan,* he thought. *I made the mistake of believing you for a minute, and I might have just made things worse.* "I think we'd all better work together and make sure we get to Deadwood in one piece."

"Then let's get to the horses," Sally said.

They had begun walking away when Frank stopped them. "Just so you know," he said and took off his other glove. He held out his hands to the others: soft hands, gambler's hands. "For the record, I wear gloves like any other man does—to protect my hands. If these get injured, I might just lose what little money I do have."

CHAPTER 17

Right after the stage crossed the Running Water—the Niobrara River—leading to what used to be a stage station, Ira caught a brief glimpse of a rider a thousand yards out beside Cardinal's Chair. Ira shielded his eyes but could not make out who the rider sitting near the eroded stone formation was. "Give me your spyglass," he said. But by the time Sally dug it out of his possibles bag and handed it over, the rider had disappeared.

"See somethin'?"

"Rider watching us by Cardinal's Chair."

Sally pulled back the reins to slow the stage as it dipped over the lip of a hill. "Logan or Indian?" he asked.

"Has to be Indian," Ira answered. "Logan couldn't have come this far by now, not with Matt Ales slowing him up. My guess is they've just made it to the buttes about now."

"I'd like to see his face when he digs up Gordy and realizes you snookered him." Sally chuckled. "As long as we can get us fresh horses at Hat Creek, we might just outrun Logan."

"But we'll never outrun the Sioux." Ira handed the spyglass back.

"I've outrun them so far," Sally said, singing his whip over the heads of the horses. "I hardly make a run that I don't encounter some braves hell-bent on doing the stage harm."

"Be my guess is—if that was an Indian—he's weighing if it'd be worth him and his warriors attacking."

Sally chuckled. "Could be he's part of that last bunch. We

158

peppered 'em, so they might think twice before ambushing us again." He expertly maneuvered the stage along the road, making the twelve miles to the Hat Creek station with the team a horse short—and the rest of the horses all but exhausted—faster than Ira would have imagined. He had suggested they hitch the Canuck's horse beside the other leader, but Sally had disagreed.

"It'd take longer to break that critter to the traces than we got. That big ol' roan would just throw off the other horses."

As the stage pulled through the shallow valley and within eyesight of the station, Dauber let out a whoop from inside the coach. "Can't blame him," Sally said, the lines loose in his hands. "This will be the first real stop since Ft. Laramie."

The large log station was a welcome sight. The complex hosted its own telegraph, post office, brewery, and bakery to go with the blacksmith shop. And, just in case the Indians attacked, it had an underground tunnel to Sage Creek, so folks holed up inside could still get water if they were under siege.

Chesty, the station master, ambled out of the stable like he had no other plans for today. He carried a Spencer rifle slung over one thin shoulder. Sally stopped the stage beside the log station, and Chesty stopped to scrutinize the team. He scratched his bald head. "Don't you know you ought to run with six horses, not five?"

"Of course I do, you damned fool," Sally shot back. "We got one of the leaders shot, but that's a story for another day." He nodded to Chesty's rifle. "Expecting trouble?"

"Indians. Or haven't you heard? They attack at the damnedest times," he said, taking the lines from Sally. He stuck his head inside the coach. "Hot meal inside. Best take advantage of it."

"And Chesty," Sally whispered to the station master, "we got us a woman passenger, so leave your shirt on."

"Will do," Chesty said and nodded knowingly.

"What's with making him keep his shirt on?" Ira asked when the last passenger had disappeared inside the station. "Seems like he ought to go bare if'n he's got a mind to. Especially as hot as it is."

"Ever seen Chesty bare?"

"Can't say as I've ever seen him at all. The last time I stopped through here, his missus said Chesty had ate something that disagreed with him. Said he was pert' near living in the outhouse."

The last time. Last summer. He and Jamie had stopped here on their way west, where Jamie wanted to hunt buffalo in the worst way. And when it came time to kill the shaggy beast, Jamie just never had the heart to pull the trigger. The last time through here.

"Well, Chesty's got 'im a habit of stripping to the waist," Sally explained, "and he's got him a set of breasts any upstairs girl would be proud of. We sure don't want Mrs. Warner to see that."

"Hell," Ira said, "*I* don't want to see that."

He slapped dust off his dungarees and headed for the water trough. "How's about you take the first watch?" Sally said. "Soon's I'm done feeding my pie hole, I'll telegraph Ft. Laramie and tell 'em we were attacked by Indians. Then I'll spot you, and you can grab some victuals."

Ira walked to the water trough and pumped the handle. Cool, clear water gushed out, and he filled his hat with it. When he put the hat on his head, pure heaven cascaded down his face and neck. Water got into his neck wound and trickled over the abrasion on his forehead and cheek where the Canuck had hit him, but he didn't even mind. It was a luxury to have cool water running over his parched head.

Ira took off his hat and ran his fingers through his wet hair as he surveyed the terrain that would take them out of the valley north toward Deadwood. The road climbed steadily out of a natural basin away from the stage station. The basin afforded the station a ready supply of good water for the horses. But it also rose high enough that Indians would be able to look down on the station and plan an attack.

Sally walked from the small telegraph building and had started into the station house when Ira stopped him. "What did the army say about the Indians that attacked us?"

"How the hell should I know?" Sally said. "Telegraph line's been cut here, too."

While Sally joined the others inside, Ira leaned against the water trough and built a smoke. Considering the Indian attacks and Logan's men ambushing them, they had been lucky to lose only Gordy, though he doubted Gordy would feel the same way if he were here. They were a day behind schedule, but the other passengers were alive, if frightened.

Sometime during Ira's second cigarette, Chesty emerged from the corrals. "I'll take the watch." He walked to one side of Ira and squinted. "That's some nose you got there. And your eyes are all black, like a raccoon. Somebody bust you?"

"More like some horse kicked me," Ira answered, gingerly feeling his swollen nose where Sally had set it.

"Well, you go in and help yourself, young fella. I'm sure you're hungry."

"Starved," Ira said as he snubbed out his cigarette butt. "What's for lunch?"

"Beans."

"Beans and what?"

"Beans and more beans," Chesty answered. "Enjoy."

Seemed like the last time he was here, Chesty's missus had made beans. Guess that answered the question of why he was practically living in the crapper last time Ira and Jamie came through. That, and the fact that the stage company paid Chesty a flat rate daily for passengers' meals. He and his missus would turn a profit if they served beans and little else.

Ira walked to the station house, the shouts from inside becoming louder the closer he got. When he stepped inside, Sally was hollering over the other passengers' voices. Dauber was nose-to-nose with Sally—soon to be nose-to-flattened nose, if he get any closer to the Brit. Preacher stood in back of Dauber like he was waiting his turn to yell at the driver. Only Frank and Beth remained calm as they seemed to enjoy the argument. Ira walked past them and grabbed a plate beside the cook stove. He dished himself up some beans and sat across from Frank and Beth. "What're those guys yelling about?" Ira said at last. "You ought to be stuffing your faces. Won't be long before fresh horses are hitched, and we'll be outta here."

Dauber wisely backed away from Sally. "This . . . old man has demanded that we take our gloves off for him. Show him our hands. But I say to hell with him, if he don't trust us."

"Dauber's right," Preacher said. "Sally didn't believe us when we said we never stopped and paid Cassie Hatch a visit."

"That so?" Ira asked Sally. He broke off a corner of his corn bread—which was as hard as the cedar table—and soaked it in his beans. "Thought we just had a discussion back on the road earlier."

"We just can't keep wondering when the Indians *and* Logan will attack. We find the killer, and Logan's one thing we don't have to worry about."

"So if Dauber or Preacher is the killer, you're going to turn him over to Logan?" Ira looked across the table at Beth. "Or turn *her* over?"

Frank stood abruptly, his hands poised close to his vest holster. "You accusing my wife?"

"We've already been through that," Sally said to Frank. "You wouldn't be able to skin that gun in time."

Frank hesitated for a moment, when Beth laid her hand on his arm. "Mr. Drang is right, you know. I should not be excluded from proving myself like everyone else."

Frank shook off Beth's hand. "It just rattles me when someone accuses my wife of something she didn't do. Look around the room—*everyone* here is wearing gloves."

Sally refilled his coffee cup and sat the pot back on the top of the stove. "We already have one man dead because the killer might be on the stage—"

"Maybe *you* killed the girl," Dauber taunted. "Maybe we ought to hand *you* over to Logan."

"Me?" Sally looked around the room for friends, but there were none to come to his defense. "I'd be the last one to have the opportunity to kill her. When Cassie was being murdered, I was getting ready for this run."

"I saw how you were getting ready," Preacher said. "In the saloon working calluses on your elbows. Belting down shots of liquid breakfast Sunday morning. Who's to say *you* didn't kill the girl? You had time to make it back to town and start drinking by the time she was found."

Sally stood and advanced on Preacher. Though about the same height, Sally had Preacher by thirty pounds. Still, the preacher remained calm as Sally neared.

Ira stood from the bench and stepped between the two men. He jabbed the air with his fork. "Next man starts trouble will get a fork in his eye. Now, all of you just back off! We're not turning *anyone* over to Logan Hatch. I know him—if somehow we did ferret out who the killer was and handed him over to Logan, he would *still* kill us. Maybe you forget we've killed three of his men. He ain't gonna' let that pass."

"But Preacher there . . . he rode with Quantrill," Sally said. "Who better to kill a helpless girl than the likes of him?"

Preacher held up his gloved hands as if taunting Sally. "Every man is worthy of redemption. Even me. Even you. And, by the way, what was that offense in England that drove you to flee the hangman's rope?" He grabbed Sally's arm and jerked his shirtsleeve up over his forearm. "Anyone sporting numbers like that is a suspect in Cassie's killing."

A faded number was tattooed on Sally's arm, and he jerked his sleeve back down. "So I served some time at Her Majesty's pleasure. I paid my dues—"

"Murder?" Dauber taunted.

Sally shook his head. "Stealin'. But that was when I was a young lad." Spittle flew from his mouth. "Maybe it was you."

"You cannot accuse *Dauber* of anything," Beth said and laid a hand on Dauber's arm. "He's just a boy."

"A boy Logan knew by name," Sally said.

"Of course, he knows me. I told you: I delivered a bull to him this spring."

"And got almighty friendly with his budding daughter." Preacher coughed into his bandana. "Though in my younger, sinful days, I might have done the same thing."

"Enough!" Ira shouted. "Logan is dividing us, and he don't even know it. How the hell we gonna make it to the Black Hills if we can't trust one another?"

Dauber walked to the stove with his bowl. "It's just that I take offense to anyone accusing me of something I ain't done."

"I take no offense," Preacher said and smiled at Sally. "It's just I'm not takin' off my gloves for him or anyone else, just on principle. Like you said before, Logan Hatch can take his suspicions to the territorial marshal if he thinks he knows who Cassie's killer is."

"I've had enough of this bickering," Ira said. "I'd better check how Chesty's getting along."

Ira had started for the door when Beth stopped him. "Just

one little thing . . . since we know about each other, we don't know anything about who is protecting us. Just what is *your* story?"

"If you think I could kill the girl, forget it. And in case you don't know already, it's not neighborly to ask a man about his past out here."

"Normally," Frank said. "But maybe my . . . wife's got a point—we don't know what kind of man you are. All we've seen is you killing Logan's men. And a couple Indians."

Ira turned and faced them. "Not much to tell. Lied about my age and sneaked into the Ohio infantry during the war. Out at twenty when the war ended, and I knocked around Tennessee for a bit—"

"That's right," Frank snapped his fingers. "Logan seemed to know you. Intimately."

A smile crept over Ira's face as he recalled how he knew Logan and Dutch. "They were paid to track me down and bring me before a tribunal of Nashville's neat and elite. They dogged me for a couple years before the reward went away."

"And maybe you took some revenge for them hounding you," Frank said. "Maybe you're the one who stopped by Logan's ranch last Sunday."

Ira breathed deeply, getting a handle on his rising temper. "I figured I didn't intend getting my neck stretched for killing a man in a fair fight, so I fled Tennessee. With Logan and Dutch only a half step behind. Pissed them off to no end when they lost me. A few years later, the family rescinded the reward, and I stayed clear of both of them. Until now." He looked at each of them. "And I've since all but forgot about it. Satisfied?"

When no one spoke, Ira turned on his heels and walked out the door. *Maybe Chesty will be better company,* he thought.

Ira walked outside to the porch. And froze. Something was wrong. He *felt* it more than *knew* it. Even the mild breeze they'd experienced the last couple of hours had stopped entirely.

Chesty emerged from the corral leading fresh horses hitched to the stage. The team stood, anxious, in their traces, their muscles twitching with the anticipation of running, but Ira felt no such enthusiasm.

Chesty stopped the stage at the station house and tied the team off at the post. "Critters all set for ya'," he hollered to Sally.

Sally stepped from the station house brushing beans from his beard. "Climb aboard," he told the passengers.

Ira watched the horses as the passengers climbed inside the coach. Both wheelers showed the whites of their eyes, like frightened broncs. Something had spooked them, too, but what? He knew a horse was every bit as savvy a guard as a dog, and he followed the horses' gaze. Dozens of scenarios drifted through Ira's mind, but the one he settled on was that Lakota were concealed somewhere in the rain-washed ravine fifty yards to the west, a coulee deep enough to hide a man and horse. He shielded his eyes from the sun and looked about. "I need to check on something," he told Sally.

Sally waved over his shoulder at Ira and went back to separating the lines in his hands.

Ira slipped the thong from around the hammer of his pistol as he walked slowly toward the ravine. When he got to the edge, he peered over.

Nothing.

He moved so that the sun was between him and the coulee, and he walked the ground slowly. There *was* something amiss here. He just hadn't spotted it.

Until he bent lower to the ground. He saw moccasin prints, and he squatted beside them. Not moccasin—he finally realized—but boot prints, a squared-off toe digging into the hard earth. Beside the boot print and a few feet out was dried tobacco juice. Someone had crouched here within sight of the station house and watched for some time.

The boot prints went down the ravine, and Ira followed them as the man walked straight for a scrub oak bowed over by years of fighting the wind. Ira bent and ran his hand over the ridges made by the man as he walked. He had met up with two other men at the tree before they separated, and Ira aged the tracks.

Recent.

Within the last hour, perhaps when . . .

"I think you ought to stand up real slow like," a voice behind Ira commanded.

He cursed himself—the man had worked his way around to get the drop on him. Ira hadn't even noticed, he was so busy looking at the boot prints.

"Turn around, pard, 'cause I don't shoot men in the back."

CHAPTER 18

Ira turned and faced a man ten years younger and thirty pounds lighter than he. The man's pearl-handled Colt pointed at Ira's midsection. The man's hat was set at a rakish angle, matching his grin, and the jinglebobs on his Spanish rowels tinkled when he stepped closer. He stopped. Fifteen yards separated the gunny from Ira. Fifteen yards that might as well have been fifteen miles.

There was no way Ira could cover that distance before the man drilled a hole in him. If he could get the cowboy talking, perhaps his first shot would be off . . . "Logan always send a boy to do his dirty work?"

"Boy?"

"Sure. Boy." Ira spat the word out, taunting, his gaze roving over the ravine. The kid had two other men with him. But where were they? "You can't be more 'n twenty. Just done sucking the teat'd be my guess." He forced a laugh. "A hind teat, at that."

"I'm twenty-two and have killed four men." The man's face flushed. "You'll be the fifth."

"And your friends—will they help you kill me? Without giving me a chance?"

"What friends?"

Ira nodded to the tracks. "You met up with two others."

The kid grinned. "Soon's I shoot your ass, that'll be the signal for them to take the stage."

Ira didn't recognize the man, but he recognized his kind. Up from Texas, at one time seeking work, landing on Logan's doorstep. Did he work cattle and horses, or was he hired because of what he could do with that Colt? The man was missing a thumb, probably when he'd caught it under his dally just before the cow—or horse—jerked the rope tight. "Looks like you tried your hand at cowboying, but it weren't in you, huh? You're just another one of Logan's back-shooting killers. Texan, if I got your accent right, and those spurs."

The man nodded.

"Why not just kill me now?"

The man smiled. "And spoil things? Besides, Ed would have my ass if I alerted the stage before it's time. You'll live until Ed starts the party."

"At least you can tell me the man's name who's killing me."

"Fair enough. I am Craig Highsmith, and I'm up from Amarillo."

Ira wished he had a view of the stage. If Highsmith was right, his two *compadres* would ambush the stage as the passengers were boarding, and they'd be caught out in the open. "I hear all Texans can shoot well," Ira said, keeping the man talking as his own hand inched closer to the butt of his gun. "Dead shots."

"That's why Mr. Hatch hired me."

"And you're a good man with a horse?"

The man puffed out his chest slightly. "The best. I ride most anything Mr. Hatch puts a bridle on—"

Ira dropped to one knee and drew his Colt in one smooth, practiced motion.

The Texan shot. Creased Ira's hat. Thumbed the hammer for another shot with his off hand . . .

But he was a heartbeat too slow.

Ira's bullet slammed into Highsmith's gut, his second bullet entering just above the man's eye, and he was dead before he hit the ground.

Ira had little time to load fresh cartridges into his pistol before gunshots erupted over the berm. He clawed his way up the side of the ravine and peered over the edge. An Indian—Piute, Pawnee perhaps—crouched behind four heavy iron water barrels in front of the stables, heat shimmering off the hot rifle barrel, distorting his face.

Forty yards on the opposite side of the barrels, Ed Mooney fired from under the corral, while the passengers hid behind the coach as well as they could. Ira's gunfight with Highsmith must have come too soon for Ed and the Indian to spring the ambush, and Sally and the others had made it safely behind the stage. But for how long? None of them had a rifle, and Frank and Dauber's shots fell far short of Ed and the Indian. Preacher's .36 fared little better.

The closest man to Ira was the Indian, fifty yards away. Fifty yards of open ground. If Ira ran that ground, Ed would spot him coming up on the Indian's back. But it was his only chance.

Pistol shots from the stage and puffs of black smoke drifted up and were caught by the breeze. Preacher. He finally had the range, but his round balls impacting the barrels the Indian used for cover did not penetrate. If Ira could distract the Indian, lure him away from the barrels, perhaps Preacher might catch a break.

"Shoot for the Indian!" he hollered over the gunfire.

Frank's tiny guns winged rounds toward where the man crouched behind his cover, and Dauber's shots fell twenty yards short, but still close enough to the Indian to keep his head down.

Ira steadied the butt of his pistol over the bank and took up slack on the trigger. His first shot fell ten yards short, but he quickly followed with two more. They struck the ground a few feet beside the Indian.

He had turned, trying to see where the shots had come from,

when Ira fired again. The bullet plowed a furrow in the ground a foot in front of the man. One more, and Ira would have the range.

The Indian pivoted—exposing himself. He spotted Ira, and he half stood while the muzzle of his rifle turned on Ira. The Indian shouldered his rifle, and was taking careful aim, when two quick shots—two quick puffs of black smoke—came from the stage. Preacher's .36. It grazed the Indian's neck, and he dove behind cover just as a large caliber rifle fired over the noise of the pistols. The muzzle of Chesty's Spencer poked out of a gun port of the station house. His second shot found the Indian. He took a stumbling step away from the barrels before he slumped over atop his rifle, the back of his head gone.

Before Ed Mooney could react to the Indian's death, Ira ran, zigzagging toward the barrels. Ed turned and levered his rifle, firing, his bullets a step behind Ira. Ira threw himself on the ground behind the barrels. He peeked around them as he reloaded.

He made out the brim of Ed's hat. The corral post protected him. As did the forty yards separating him from Ira.

Ira needed a rifle. The Indian's rifle.

He gathered his legs beneath him and—when Ed paused to load fresh cartridges into his Winchester—darted from the safety of the barrels and threw himself on the ground beside the dead Indian. The rifle lay under the man, and Ira grabbed the stock. He tugged hard, and the rifle came free just as Ed started winging rounds his way. Ira ran to the barrels and dived behind them, the *pinging* of Ed's bullets caroming off the metal.

Ira checked the Indian's rifle: one round in the chamber, none in the magazine. And Ira had no ammunition for the Henry. "Anybody hit?" he called out to the stage, then ducked his head back behind the barrels.

"A bullet grazed Dauber's arm, but we're all in one piece,"

Preacher yelled back.

Ira chanced another look around the barrels. If Sally and the passengers could keep Ed busy for just a moment, Ira saw where he would have a straight line to a pile of firewood where he'd be in a position to hit Ed. "Preacher!"

"Yeah?"

"Count five, then you and Frank and Dauber open up with everything you got."

"But he's too far away."

"He won't be for me if I can get a bee line on him. Count now!"

Ira gathered his legs under him and held the rifle tight. When the shooting erupted from the stage, Ira ran.

He dropped to the ground behind the wood pile and steadied the rifle. When the shooting stopped—the passengers out of ammunition—Ed rolled out from the fence and levered rounds at the stage. Too late he spotted Ira, and Ed swung his rifle. Ira touched off the round, but the bullet went lower than he wanted. It struck the butt stock of Ed's rifle. Wood shattered, driving splinters into Ed's cheek. He howled in pain and dropped his rifle.

Ira stood and sprinted toward Ed as he clawed at the wood embedded in his cheek. He looked up and saw Ira had closed the distance to pistol range. Ed's hand dropped to his gun butt.

"Please," Ira said.

"Please, what?"

"Please draw that pistol."

Ira became aware that the passengers had crawled out from under the stage. They stood looking over the backs of the horses at Ira and Ed. "Kill him!" Frank yelled.

Ed's hand twitched, and his jaw tightened. Ira spread his feet, his hand poised over his own gun.

Ed seemed to ponder his chances, then raised his hands

slowly overhead. "You wouldn't murder a man."

"I'd do the same for you as you were happy to do to the passengers a moment ago."

Blood wept from a half-dozen pieces of wood sticking out of Ed's face. "Now take just one hand and shuck that Colt over thisaway," Ira ordered.

Ed carefully grabbed the butt of his pistol by two fingers and tossed it toward Ira. "Now what?"

Ira didn't answer him as he crossed the last few yards and stopped in front of Ed. Ira holstered and quickly drove a fist into Ed's stomach. He doubled over, and Ira hit him in the back of his neck. Ed fell to the ground and rolled over in pain, clutching his stomach. "That's for damn near killing the passengers."

Preacher and Frank walked over to peer down at Ed writhing on the ground in pain.

"I think we ought to string him up," Frank said.

"I vote we do, too," Dauber said. He held his hand high to stop the bleeding. He had taken off his glove and ripped his shirt for a pressure dressing to stop the bleeding.

Preacher held up his hand. "Even the likes of him deserves a second chance."

"You weren't giving him a second chance a moment ago," Frank said, cocking his gun and pointing it at Ed's head. "I say we shoot him now."

"What do you say, Ed?" Ira asked. "You think we ought to string you up, or just kill you outright?"

Ed coughed violently. He struggled to stand but remained kneeling in front of his tormentors. He ran his fingers through his scraggly hair, the gray in the middle standing in contrast to the rest of his coal-colored hair. "I ought to—"

"What?" Ira asked. "You ought to kill me for that? How's about I give your gun back, and we'll see who walks away."

Ed flicked a piece of wood from his face and wiped the blood off his cheek with his bandana. "What's your play now?"

"You want to live to see tomorrow's sun rise?"

Ed nodded and picked another imbedded sliver out.

"Then you tell us just where Logan and Dutch are about now."

Ed remained silent, and Dauber kicked him in the side. He fell onto his back. Dauber reached down and grabbed Ed's bandana from his hand. Dauber was awkwardly trying to wrap his injured hand with the neckerchief when Beth walked up beside him and took his hand in hers. She smiled at him while she tied off the bandana.

"That was for Gordy," Dauber said and was cocking his leg to kick him again when Ed held up his hands.

"All right. All right," Ed said. "I'll tell you."

Ira waited until Ed stood. He half bent over as he held his gut. "By now Logan's found that big, dumb farm boy—"

Dauber cocked his fist, but Ira pulled him back. "Let him talk."

Dauber jerked his hand free. "All right, but Gordy weren't dumb."

Ira turned his back on Dauber and faced Ed. "So, he's probably found Gordy, but. where's Logan at now?"

Ed shrugged. "I dunno." He smiled. "But he's bound to be within a few miles of this stage station."

"And he sent you three owl hoots to kill us?" Ira asked. "That's out of character for Logan. He'd rather kill us himself."

Ed looked away.

Ira lashed out and slapped him on the back of the head. "He didn't want you three fools to kill us, did he?"

The smile faded from Ed's face. "He wanted us just to keep track of you."

"But when you saw us, you figured we looked like easy marks?"

Ed shrugged. "We figured if we killed some of you, the others would help us find Cassie's killer."

Ira looked over the hills above the stage station. *How close was Logan?* "What do you think Logan will do to you, now that your men are dead and the only thing you did was to warn us?"

Ed started trembling. And it was a hundred degrees out.

"Logan's going to kill you," Ira said at last. "Maybe he'll turn you over to Dutch to have some fun."

"Not if you let me go."

Preacher laughed. "What would that do?"

"I'd give you my word I'd not ride to Logan." He looked north, as if he were able to see the gold fields of Deadwood Gulch. "Always wanted to try my hand with the pan."

"Let's just kill him here and now," Dauber said. The bandana on his hand had soaked with blood that seeped through the fabric. "He don't deserve to live, not with what he tried."

"I vote with them," Sally said. He looped the lines around the brake and walked around the team. "If we let him go, he'll just go running to Logan."

"I vote we dust him," Frank said.

"This is not a democracy," Ira said. "I'd as soon drill him where he stands, too, but . . ."

"But there's still a smidgen of conscience in you?" Preacher smiled. "The Lord *has* touched you, it appears."

"Lord's got nothing to do with it," Ira answered. "It's just not right to kill a man outright. And if we bring him along to turn over to the law, he'd just find some way to kill one or all of us. Wouldn't you?"

Ed nodded. "Same thing as you'd do if you were given the chance."

Beth stepped between Ed and the other passengers. "Mr.

Drang is right—you can't just murder him. That'd make you no better than Logan Hatch."

Ira turned to Ed. "Where's your horse?"

"Back in that ravine a couple hundred yards."

"Then I'd suggest you get to it and make a run for Deadwood."

Ed's shoulders slumped. "Thanks." He held out his hand. "My gun."

Ira looked at the Colt and tucked it in his waistband.

"You're not going to send me out there"—Ed waved his hand around the stage station—"without a gun?"

"It's the hand you drew."

"But there's Indians nearby!" Ed shouted. "I won't have a chance if I'm not armed."

"Go grab your rifle."

"It's busted," Ed said. "I can't use it—"

"You would have done the same to us," Frank said.

Ed grabbed Ira by the arm. "You can't—"

Ira shook Ed's hand off his arm. "Better get a move on before Logan or the Indians catch you. Or before these folks change my mind."

Ira watched Ed stumble toward the ravine. When he dropped over the rim of the coulee, Ira told Sally, "Get ready to head out soon's I get back."

"You gonna' kill him after all?" Preacher asked.

"I'd enjoy it, but no. I figure the attack on the stage to Cheyenne yesterday that the Indians got blamed for was Ed and those two's doing. I'm going to grab the mail before he rides out."

Ira caught up with Ed at the bottom of the gully, and he stopped. "Now what?"

Ira shoved him. "Just get to your horse."

"You are going to kill me?"

"I ought to. Take off your gloves."

"What?"

"Your gloves," Ira repeated. "Take the damned things off, and show me your hands."

Ed smiled and pulled on the fingers of his gloves. "If you think Cassie's killer is one of us, you're crazy." He pocketed his gloves and showed Ira his hands. "Uninjured, like a baby's." He put his gloves back on. "The girl's killer is one of your passengers. And Logan's gonna find out who it is before you get to Deadwood."

Ira shoved Ed again, and they walked fifty yards before climbing out of the gully on a narrow trail. Ed's gelding was hobbled next to a rangy mustang and a mare with one torn ear. "Step aside," Ira said, and he stopped at the gray. He opened the thong of Ed's saddlebag and found mail stuffed inside. Ira took the bag off and draped it over his shoulder.

"That stage robbery was Highsmith and Jimmy Antelope's doing."

"Then you won't mind if I take this and see it gets returned to the stage company."

Ira looked the three horses over. The mare and Ed's gray looked game, but the mustang held one foreleg like it bothered him. Ira ran his hand over the horse, and he jerked back when Ira's hand massaged the leg.

"You can *have* that one," Ed said. "That was Jimmy's—some bangtail he . . . found up around Indian creek when he was running some stock down to Logan. Take him and that mare, too."

"That's mighty generous of you." Ira took the hobbles off Ed's horse and the mare and slapped their rumps. Within moments they had disappeared over a hill toward the prairie to the west.

"What the hell—"

177

"This mustang will get you to the gold fields, if that's where you want to go. Or to Logan, if you want to chance telling him what you and those other two did."

"But he's all but lame."

"Would you rather walk?" Ira said. "Now get going."

Ed spat tobacco juice that hit Ira's boot. "You son of a bitch— I'll be waiting for you when you get to Deadwood—"

Ira started back to the stage. "Then we'll meet up in Deadwood after I'm finished with Hickok," he called over his shoulder. "I'm looking forward to it, back shooter."

CHAPTER 19

Logan watched the Harding ranch stage station through the telescope. The station master—Chesty—wore a bandana over his nose as he dug his shovel into the hard ground again. Logan snapped the spyglass shut and handed it back to Dutch. "Looks like they're burying someone out back of the station."

"Indians?" Matt asked. His bloody shoulder dipped as he canted in the saddle.

Dutch leaned over and straightened him before he fell. The kid was holding them back. Slowing them down. If it had been just him and Logan—like in the old days—they'd have caught the stage and dealt out their kind of justice. They'd have Cassie's killer by the *cojones*. But Logan looked after Matt, doted on him, and had even favored him among the hired hands before Cassie's murder. Perhaps—Dutch often thought—Matt reminded Logan of the daughter he no longer had.

"Maybe that war party we tracked a few miles back attacked the station and bit off more than they could chew," Logan said. "That station house is as secure as most forts."

"Not likely," Dutch said. "Last time I was through here, that old man and his missus were the only ones besides the blacksmith and telegraph operator. Those tracks we just came across showed more'n ten warriors. If they'd attacked the station, things would be burning."

"I suppose you're right," Logan said. "They might have lasted the first assault, maybe even the second. But eventually the

Indians would torch the place. Let's go have a look-see and get a meal while we're here."

Logan led the way down the hillside toward the Harding ranch station. As they passed the blacksmith shop, Chesty shuffled from in back of the station where he had been shoveling. He was shirtless and sweat dripped off his sagging chest and shoulders. He swiped a hand across his eyes and took the shovel off his shoulder. "Howdy."

"Howdy to you," Logan said. He motioned to the pathway leading to the grave. "Looks like you've been busy."

"Have been." Chesty walked to the water trough and dunked his head in the water. "You fellers might as well come inside," he said when he came up for air. "The missus promised fresh pie for when I got done burying those fellers."

"What fellers?" Matt asked, but Chesty didn't hear him and walked into the station house.

A large, raw-boned woman Logan remembered as Chesty's missus came from in back of the kitchen and bent to a pie safe in one corner of the room. The odor of freshly baked peaches wafted past Dutch's nose, and he watched her bring the pie to the table. "Sit," she commanded and turned to a cook stove. She put cups in front of each man and poured fresh coffee.

"Not you," she said to Matt. "Looks like you got a wound opened up. Come in the next room, and I'll put a clean dressing on you."

Dutch walked to the door, looking out into the yard. The stables were three, maybe four rods from the house, and the house itself sported shutters one could drop in the event of an Indian attack. Gun ports spaced every few yards would afford anyone inside good protection while they returned fire to anyone foolish enough to attack. Still, defending against ten or more hardened Sioux—most likely fresh off the Crook and Custer fights—would prove daunting for the station masters.

Matt emerged from the next room with a fresh bandage under his clean shirt. He looked more presentable, in the muslin shirt and patched dungarees. But the color still hadn't returned to his face, and Dutch knew it was a matter of time before he'd drop if he didn't get to a doctor.

"That's all I can do for him," the woman said. "But that boy needs a doctor."

"I do not . . ." and Matt had one of the coughing fits he often had the last few days.

Chesty grabbed a pie knife and was reaching across the table when his woman smacked him on the head with a spatula. "Where's your manners?" she said. "Guests first." She took the knife from him and cut into the pie. She passed cut pieces around for each man before serving Chesty, who still rubbed his head. He had picked up a fork when she smacked him again. "*Now* what's that for?"

"You put a shirt on before you sit at the supper table. These men don't want to see your droopy boobs while they eat."

Chesty shook his head and walked to a deer-horn coat rack beside the door.

Dutch looked after him. His woman was right—they really didn't want to see a sixty-year-old sagging chest with more hair than your average grizzly.

Dutch took a small bite, the gooey peach and syrup staying on his tongue long enough to slide down his throat. It wasn't like his mother's pie, but then, fresh peaches had been plentiful in Georgia before the war.

Logan blew on the hot coffee and said to Chesty, "You been burying someone, by the look of it."

Chesty grabbed a shirt hanging from the coat hooks beside the front door and put it on. "Now?" he asked sheepishly.

"Now," his missus said, and he sat back down and dug into his pie. "In answer to your question, I've been burying a few someones." Chesty winced as he wiped a piece of hot peach that had dropped onto his arm. "We had us a little excitement earlier, and I buried some fellers."

"Friends?"

Chesty guffawed. "They weren't no friends of mine."

Logan stood and grabbed the coffee pot. He walked around the table and refilled cups. "Someone from the stage, then?" He sat back at the long table. " 'Cause I'd hate for any passenger to come up harmed."

Chesty wiped his mouth and eyed the pie plate for another piece. "I was expecting the stage folks to get drilled. They were sitting ducks when those three fellers opened up on them."

Logan and Dutch exchanged looks. "So, those were passengers you buried?" Dutch asked.

"Nope," Chesty said and took a sip of coffee.

Dutch was quickly losing his patience with the old man. "Just tell us who the hell you just buried."

Chesty backed away and squinted at Dutch. "Just why do you need to know?"

Dutch leaned across the table, his face inches from Chesty's. "I don't need a reason."

"All right." Chesty put up his hands as if to ward Dutch off. "It was two fellers that attacked the stage."

"Thought you said there were three?" Logan said.

"There were, but only two got kilt. The young 'un and the Indian—"

"Sioux?"

"Pawnee," Chesty answered.

"Jimmy Antelope," Dutch said. "Describe the other one—the kid."

"Short. Pistol strapped down like he fancied himself a gunny." Chesty stood and stepped away from the table. "If'n you're family, I can give you their guns."

Logan waved the air. "I don't give a damn about their belongings. Who the hell killed them?"

"Ira Drang kilt one," Chesty said. "And he sat right at that table like you folks are just before he got into that gunfight." Chesty grinned wide. "And I drilled the Indian when I got a clean shot. I seen it all from the window—" Chesty shook his head. "Ira Drang—he was sure sumpin'."

"So the stage went on its way?" Matt said, rubbing his shoulder. "With no one on the stage killed?"

"None were the worse for wear, 'cept one young feller got hit in the hand by that third man I was telling you about."

Dutch rubbed his forehead. "You ain't told us nothing about that third man. Who was he?"

"Never seen him before."

Logan drew his pistol and pointed it at Chesty. "We don't have time to beat around the bush. You tell us what you know and tell it now!"

Chesty held up his hands again. "Sorry, friend. Just making conversation." He wiped the sweat from his forehead. "That Ira Drang, he shot this third man's rifle and disarmed him. Ed something-or-other. Ira led this Ed feller off towards a ravine where his horse was and came back to the stage station in a short time. Then the stage left."

"And what became of Ed?"

Chesty waved the air towards the north. "Sally—that's the jehu on this run—said he rode off, headed to the gold fields."

"Looks like they got a couple hours' start on us," Matt said. "Maybe I ought to ride back to the ranch. I'm just slowing you down."

"You trying to catch that stage?" Chesty asked.

Logan nodded.

"If you're going to rob it, I'd say there ain't nothing worth robbing with them folks."

"We're not robbing it," Logan asked. "The killer of my little girl's on that stage."

Chesty whistled. "In that case, you might just catch them sooner than you figured."

"How so?" Logan asked, holstering his pistol.

"When the shootin' started," Chesty explained, "two of the horses was hit. I'm doctoring them now. But the stage had to continue with a four-horse team. It'll take them a mite longer."

Logan stood, and Dutch and Matt followed suit. "One last thing: did you get a look at the feller who got shot in the hand?"

"Mabel!" Chesty yelled, and his missus walked into the room. "Mabel doctored that young feller." He faced his wife. "Tell him about that cowboy what got hisself shot."

Mabel shrugged. "Not much to tell. Bullet hit his arm and travelled to his left hand. Blew off the last two fingers—"

"Did he have any previous injuries to his hands?"

"Not the hand that got shot. The other one was covered by his glove," Mabel said, "and I'd know 'cause I patched him up. Why?"

"Let's just say we're closer to finding my Cassie's killer."

"I have a feeling about Dauber," Logan said as they mounted their horses and started out of Hat Creek station. "The way he looked at Cassie the day he delivered the bull—"

"Mabel never saw his other hand." Dutch cinched his rifle scabbard tighter. "Could be one of the others."

"Don't much matter at this point," Logan said. "We could kill them all, and it'd make little difference to me."

"But it'd bring the army down on us," Dutch said as they started across Sage Creek. The creek was barely a trickle in this drought, the recent rain having added little. "Last I heard Captain Egan and his company of Grays were still garrisoned there."

"We won't have any problem with the cavalry. Not if we set it up so the Indians get the blame."

Dutch smiled. "I like the way you think." But did he? Logan's obsession with finding Cassie's killer had taken several dangerous turns for them thus far. Dutch looked to the north and thought how the gold fields would be so much safer—and more profitable—than running down a murderer. Even if it was the murderer of his friend's daughter.

Dutch turned in the saddle and watched Matt. The ride had reopened the bleeding in his shoulder, yet the young cowboy complained not at all. Dutch knew Logan would be hard pressed to find a horseman as adept as Matt, who could curry the kinks out of the rangiest mustang. Logan's loss would be great once Matt finally died. "You sure you're up to ride?"

Matt grimaced. "I'll keep up."

"There's no shame if you can't ride farther," Logan said. "We can leave you here and pick you up on the way back."

But Dutch knew—as Logan did—that if Matt were left to himself, he'd not make the next sunrise. Either he'd bleed to death, or the marauding Indians would find him. "We're fixing to get into Red Ranch country, and God knows how rugged that is," Logan said, as if convincing Matt to lay up here.

"I'll be all right," Matt said. "At least I won't run out on you like Ed did."

"Ed always was a coward," Logan said. "Only reason I kept him around was there was no one better when I needed someone back-hot. If I catch up with the son of a bitch, he'll rue the day he disobeyed me."

"Important thing now," Dutch said, "is catching that stage away from the cavalry. And the Indians. We sure don't want to ride this road. Out in the open, we'll be easy picking for the Sioux. We don't have as many guns as the stage does."

"They only got one rifle among them."

"Indians don't know that," Dutch said.

"The stage is headed for the Harding ranch. If we're lucky, they'll be pulling in about now. They can't ride as fast or as far with only four horses. Not with Red Canyon up ahead."

Dutch rolled a cigarette and thought hard. He hadn't liked Ed Mooney, any more than he liked the other thieves working for Logan Hatch. When Logan and Dutch came west some years ago, they handled the business with the help of a couple stock boys to tend the horses until a buyer could be found. But that was when they ran only a few head of stolen horses now and again, not a rustling operation that spanned three states.

Then Logan got greedy. Started taking on people like Ed Mooney. Handy Johnson. Miguel DeJesus. The brutal Canuck. Men who would rather slit another man's throat in the night than face him in a fight. Dutch flicked his ash away from his dapple gray. He had no trouble killing men. He had ambushed more than his share in his lifetime. But when someone like Ira Drang needed killing, a man in Dutch's line of work just *had* to have some standards. He'd face Ira alone. A man like Ira deserved to have a stand-up chance, even if he really had no chance at all against Dutch.

But first, he had to make sure the stage didn't make it to Deadwood. If they ferreted out Cassie's killer, that was fine, too. But it really made no difference to Dutch. All he wanted was a fair fight with Ira. Dutch looked at Matt's heavy eyelids as he sat the saddle and motioned Logan aside. "Matt is slowing us down," he said as he flicked his butt away.

"We can't leave him—"

"A moment ago you would have."

"Dammit, I was just frustrated." He looked at Matt. "I'm not leaving him." Logan turned his horse to face Dutch. "You got something on your mind?"

"The stage ain't been quick, but it's got a big enough start on us that they'll reach Deadwood if we don't do something." Dutch motioned north along the stage route. "I can ride faster alone. Slow them up at Red Canyon. That'd give you time to catch up."

Logan stood in the stirrups and stretched his legs. "Shit! As always, you make a good point." He looked over at Matt. Logan had wrapped two more bandanas around the boy's shoulder, but still the blood seeped through. "Go on ahead. Me and Matt will join you. Soon's Matt rests up a bit."

CHAPTER 20

Sally stopped the stage on the hill overlooking the Harding Ranch station and grabbed his spyglass.

"What are we stopping for?" Frank called out from inside the coach. "I'm about starved—"

"Shut up!" Sally said as he scanned the station. "Damn," he breathed and handed Ira the spyglass. "Something's wrong."

Ira steadied the glass and looked the station over. Clay bluffs surrounded the station, which had been dug into the side of one of the hills surrounding the house. The grass-thatched roof fluttered in the wind, and Ira saw two arrows stuck in a log in front of the station. A rifle barrel stuck out of a gun port. "Looks like they had company," Ira said and handed Sally the telescope back. "And it looks like they're expecting more."

"I'm just hoping Mel Lind's alive on the other end of that rifle barrel."

Sally released the brake and eased the coach down the steep hill.

"Look alive," Ira called to the passengers. "The place has been attacked, but we got no way of knowing if Indians are inside the station waiting for us or if it's the station master."

Ira studied the terrain around the station as they neared. The house led to a fort, logs covering the roof and two sides, the clay bank another. There was no sign of life. If Indians were waiting, they'd hidden themselves well. But then, Indians did that better than any white man. "Telegraph line's been cut," Ira motioned to a wire dangling from a telegraph pole.

"And I don't see any horses in the stable," Sally said. "Shit!"

Preacher opened the coach door and climbed atop. He drew his Colt .36 and held it tightly. "What do you make of it?"

"Never saw the station so . . . dead," Sally said. "Every other time I been through here, there's been folks out—Mel tending to his horses, maybe his missus milking the cow. Telegraph office taking bills. But now . . ."

As the stage neared the station, the rifle barrel tracked them. When the coach was thirty yards from the house, the rifle barrel disappeared, and an old man burst from inside. He held a beat-to-hell Spencer rifle in one hand and a pistol shoved into his waistband as he shuffled toward the stage. "Sally. Thank God you're all right."

Sally stopped the stage and set the brake. "What happened here?" Sally pointed to the arrows. "And where are my fresh horses?"

Mel propped his rifle against the water trough and took a tobacco pouch from his vest pocket. He filled his pipe and tamped it down with a bone poker. "They raided at daybreak yesterday. Some of American Horse's Miniconjou Lakota. Killed my hostler and telegraph operator. I was the only one that made it into the fort." He motioned to the corrals. "I killed four of the bastards, but they managed to run the stock off." He lit his pipe with a lucifer. "They tried to smoke me out, but I had enough ammunition stocked up from the last time."

Ira looked over the wide field of fire. If Mel was any kind of shot, the Indians would have been foolish to attack the fort. That none of the dead Sioux remained where Mel shot them was no surprise—Indians most often took their dead with them. "Thought there was a company of cavalry stationed here?"

"Out chasing Indians," Mel said. "They rendezvoused with the 4th Infantry out of the Red Canyon station. Besides ranches being raided all along the Cheyenne River, the stage to Cheyenne got attacked—"

"Wasn't Indians," Ira said. "It was some of Logan Hatch's men. Made it look like the Sioux."

Mel glanced at the trail leading to the station and grabbed his rifle. "Logan Hatch? Don't tell me he's been seen around here."

"We don't know *exactly* where he is right now," Preacher said. He climbed down from the stage and offered to help Beth, but Dauber beat him to it. "Logan don't give up. And right about now, I'd wager he's breathing down our necks."

"What's he want with your stage?" Mel asked. "You ain't carrying nothin' 'cept passengers."

"He thinks his daughter's killer is on board," Sally said. While the passengers walked the stiffness out of their legs and visited the outhouse out back, Sally explained that Logan insisted Cassie's murderer rode the stage. Insisted Cassie bit her attacker before she died.

"Easy fix," Mel said when Sally finished. "Order everyone to take off their gloves, and turn the bastard over to Logan."

"That's just what I thought," Sally said. "But if I ordered folks to take off their gloves, there'd be a riot. Folks take exception to not being trusted." He took the lines from around the brake. He had begun to lead the coach to the stables when he paused. "We'll have to lay up for a while, not that I look forward to doing that with Logan close. But this team's been run to ground. They need a rest bad, and so do we."

"You got victuals?" Ira asked. "And room enough that we can grab a little sleep?"

Mel motioned to the fort. "Can't hole up in the station house—not with the Sioux still close—"

"Maybe the cavalry caught up with them already," Frank said.

Mel chuckled. "Not if the Sioux don't wannabe found. They'd as soon lead the army away from here only to double back and attack again." He watched Sally take off the rigging before turning the horses out into the stables. "Not much reason to attack again if I'm the only one here."

Ira helped Sally set the collars over a fence post. "We'll be gone soon's the horses rest up."

Mel hesitated. "Long as you're gone by sunup."

"Tell the others to get inside the fort," Ira told Preacher when he came from the outhouse buttoning his trousers. "We need to be out of here by sunup."

"I'll rustle up some victuals," Mel said.

Ira walked to where Sally was untangling the lines. "Mel wants us out by sunup. He figures with us gone, the Indians have little to gain by attacking again."

"Can't blame him," Sally said. He shut the gate and leaned over, watching the horses feed on hay piled in one corner of the corral. "I'm not so sure these guys can get us to Red Canyon station. They've done their best, and they're beat. Like us." A stalk of hay twitched from one corner of Sally's mouth as he spoke. "Mel's right, just like I'm right—if we turned Cassie's killer over to Logan, the only thing we'd have to worry about is the Indians."

"And you were also right when you told Mel there'd be a donnybrook if you ordered Preacher and Dauber to take off their gloves."

Ira watched Beth walk close beside Dauber as they disappeared inside the fort. "I know Logan. At this point, it would make no difference if he had the killer in front of him or not. We've killed some of his men, and he won't let that lie."

"Still, it's worth a shot." Sally tossed the stalk of hay aside. "You saw how Dauber kept his other glove on the hand that wasn't shot. Who the hell walks around with just one glove?"

"Let it lie," Ira said. "We'll talk to the law once we get to Deadwood."

Ira walked to the coach and untied the rear boot. He grabbed the mail he had taken from Ed Mooney's saddlebags and followed Sally into the station. The height of the roof was just right for Sally. Ira had to duck his head in order to get through the low door. Dirt sifted down from the thatched roof, thick enough that no Indian arrow or lance could get through.

The passengers had already started to eat. They sat around a rough-hewn table chewing on biscuits and meat. Beth helped Dauber cut some tough deer meat, while Frank paid no attention to his wife's attention to the cowboy. Preacher sat in one corner wolfing down beans and venison, while Mel refilled their coffee cups. Ira handed Mel Ed's saddlebags filled with the south-bound mail. "Pass this along to the next stage headed to Cheyenne. It's a lot safer with you than it is with us."

"Might be awhile. Won't be any stage until the army can round up the Indians."

"How long we going to be holed up in here?" Frank asked between bites. "The longer we wait to get up to Deadwood, the more our chances of running into Logan are."

"Look here," Ira said when he'd gotten their attention. "Sally figures the horses will need at least six hours to rest up."

Dauber started to interrupt, but Ira talked over him. "I'm not happy about it either. But we got Red Canyon up ahead, and— with two horses short—it'll be hard enough on them as it is. There's some steep pulls there. You all might as well get as much rest as you can."

"And I'd suggest you folks visit the outhouse in pairs," Mel added. "Indians might still be lurking around."

Mel took the first watch and woke Ira when it was his turn. Ira stood, hunched over inside the low fort, and took up a position behind one of the gun ports looking out into the yard. With the setting of the sun, and with the thatched and sod roof, Ira appreciated the coolness after baking in the intense heat of the last few days.

He thought about Sally's argument. How easy it would be to force everyone on the stage to show their hands. Turn Cassie's killer over to Logan. *If* the killer were among them. Ira still thought the girl's murderer could be among Logan's own men.

Preacher stood from the floor and tossed his blanket aside. "Got to see a man about a horse."

Ira let his rifle lie in the gun port and hitched his trousers up. "I've gotta' go myself."

Preacher followed Ira outside, and they had started walking to the outhouse when Ira stopped.

"What is it?"

Ira slowly turned his head.

Nothing.

"What do you hear?" Ira said.

Preacher looked about and shook his head. "I don't hear anything. It's as quiet as confession on a Saturday night. Why?"

"That's my point. There's no crickets, no night hawks or owls. There's just . . ." He squinted and picked up movement in the stables. "Indians at the horses—" An arrow sliced the air, whizzing past Ira's head. "Get to the stables!"

They ran across the open ground, drawing their pistols as they ran.

A warrior popped up from the inside the corral, and let fly another arrow that barely missed Ira, flying just over his back.

And stuck Preacher with a *thud*.

Preacher slumped to his knees, clutching his arm. The arrow had penetrated his shoulder, the trade point sticking out his back. Ira fired two quick shots when another Sioux stood from a shallow ravine. He had notched an arrow when Ira's bullet tore into his face, and he dropped where he'd crouched.

"Get the hell up!" Ira wrapped his arm around Preacher. He had hauled him erect when another arrow broke the night and stuck in Preacher's chest. He groaned once, blood pumping out his wound. "Don't go now . . ." but Preacher slumped, dead, in Ira's arms.

He laid Preacher gently on the ground and was faintly aware that the others inside the fort were firing wildly. He dropped beside Preacher and took his Colt. He emptied the pistol, black smoke hanging over him as he squinted to see the Indians.

Two Sioux fought the team. They had slipped braided hackamores over the heads of the horses, but they jerked away, frightened, the whites of their eyes showing in the moonlight. Ira hip shot an Indian, and—when the other one let go of the horses—Ira shot him as well.

Dauber and Sally burst from the fort, firing as they ran, while Frank and Mel fired rounds from the gun ports.

Ira stopped long enough to reload, crouching, looking for other targets, seeing faint forms disappear in the night. Dauber skidded in the dirt beside Ira, pointing his pistol at nothing.

As suddenly as the attack began, it ended. The surviving Indians had melted back into the night.

"They might try another attack," Ira said. "Stay here." He ran bent over to the corral and climbed over the gate. The horses clustered around the far side of the corrals, snorting, shying away from the dead men. They had surely smelled fresh blood, and they shied away from Ira as well. He bent to each warrior, checking them, making certain they were dead.

"Preacher's gone, ain't he?"

Ira nodded to Dauber. He had climbed into the corral and stood, holding his bloody hand, as he peered down at the dead warriors.

"Guess I wasn't much help. Can't hardly shoot with my left hand."

"Wouldn't have made any difference," Mel said. He pulled the tube from the butt stock of his rifle to reload while he walked toward Ira. "If those brown bastards can put the sneak on an eagle, they damn sure can sneak in here and kill us. Or steal our stock." He chin-pointed to the horses. "But not tonight. What alerted you?"

"Can't say anything did," Ira answered. "Me and Preacher were walking to the outhouse when I saw Indians in the stables fixin' to steal the stock. Just that quick, they killed Preacher."

"Same as the missus two years ago," Mel said, his mouth drooping in sadness. "Killed her when she went for water. She weren't much to look at, but I sure do miss her cooking."

"What now?" Frank walked ahead of Beth as they emerged from the fort. "We'd better fort-up again in case they decide to come back."

"Not for a while they won't," Mel said. "Between the four I killed earlier and these, they're more'n likely off licking their wounds. Getting hoary-eyed drunk, mad that they couldn't carry their dead back with 'em." He turned to Sally. "If it were me, I'd get those horses in their traces and head out. The Indians will come back, but not for a few hours."

"Ira?" Sally asked.

Ira weighed the odds, and none were any better than he got in that crooked faro game with Nebraska Slim. "We need to leave, but maybe we *ought* to stay here. If they come back for another go and you're alone—"

"Don't fuss over me." Mel motioned to the fort. "They'll never get me in there."

"All right, then," Ira said. "Sooner we get the horses hitched and away from here, the less likely we'll run into them anytime soon." He motioned to Frank and Dauber. "I'll carry Preacher for burying. You guys carry the Indians out back—"

"What the hell for?"

"Last I looked, they were men, too. It won't be the burial they'd have wanted, but we got to do it."

Frank took a step toward Ira, but there must have been something in his eyes that caused Frank to stop mid-stride. His jaw muscles clenched, but he said nothing more as he followed Dauber to where the Indians lay dead in the corral. "I'll do it, but I don't like it. They'd have skinned us alive if they'd got the chance."

"Just do it," Beth said, taking Dauber's hand and examining it. "The sooner we bury them, the sooner we get to Deadwood."

CHAPTER 21

"We need to stop," Sally said. "These horses are plumb tuckered out. That couple hours of rest didn't do them any more good than it did us."

They had gone little more than five miles, still six miles from the Cheyenne River ranch station. Not that they'd get any fresh horses there, either. Mel said the army had left the Harding ranch station headed that way, intending to escort the Cheyenne River station master and his wife to a safe place. They would find the station empty. Probably burnt down, if Mel's assessment was correct. Ira pointed to a tall cliff face that would shield them on one side if an attack came. "Let's stop there."

Sally reined the team alongside two gigantic cottonwoods at the base of the cliff. He set the brake and climbed down before he lit a lamp and began checking the traces.

"How long we got?" Dauber said as he helped Beth from the coach with his good hand, the other one a bloody mess soaking through the bandage she'd wrapped around it.

"Not less than an hour. Just enough time for the horses to catch their wind and for me to unhitch the Canuck's roan. Damned thing's only slowing the others down." Sally ran his hand over the swing team, soon to be acting as leaders. Sally had hitched the Canuck's horse as a leader, but the critter balked and pawed the ground every chance it got.

Sally grabbed a water bucket and had started toward the slow-running river, when he motioned Ira along. He slid down the bank and dipped the bucket in the stagnant water. "You see Preacher when we buried him?" Sally whispered when the others had gone into the bushes to do their thing.

"I saw him when he got killed. Why?"

Sally looked around Ira, but no one was within earshot. "I took off his gloves. The man had no injuries to his hands. They were smooth as a baby's bottom. He couldn't have been that girl's killer."

"Didn't figure he was," Ira said. "You still on that—"

"Damn it, Ira, that means it's *gotta'* be Dauber. Frank already showed his hands, and I know it's not me." He backed away. "And I don't *think* it's you."

Ira shook his head. "Of course it's not me. And I don't think it's Dauber, either."

"He keeps that one glove on all the time."

"Well he damned sure can't get the other one on; his left hand's blown half away." Ira slapped Sally's hand. "You keep yours on all the time. Same's me. Don't make us murderers."

"I say we order Dauber to take that glove off."

"Then what?" Ira asked. "If his hand's been bit all to hell, do we tie him to a fence post so's Logan can find him? Listen to yourself. In case you haven't noticed, we're sucking the hind tit here. We're two horses down, and the ones left are about played out, with Red Canyon still ahead. And the only help we got to fight off Indians or Logan Hatch is a cowboy with one hand, a gambler and his wife with piss-ant little guns, and me."

"Don't I count?"

"You don't. You got the stage to worry about."

Ira let Sally tend to the team and walked up the bank to the coach. He surveyed the area where they had stopped, noting that the cliff would afford them excellent cover in an attack. Another time, they could hole up here and let the horses rest. But Ira needed to get to Deadwood; he *had* to get to Deadwood and look up Hickok. For his brother, Jamie. Besides, even if the army managed to put the run on the Indians, there was still Logan to worry about. And worse—Dutch.

"We *will* make it to Deadwood, won't we?"

Ira jumped at the sound of Beth coming up so easily behind him. He blamed his exhaustion for letting his guard down. Another time, another circumstance, if she sneaked up on him she might be dead. "We'll make it," Ira said over his shoulder.

Sally headed for the horses with the water bucket, and Ira had started walking toward him to help when Beth stopped him. She walked around Ira and stood looking up at him. Except for a layer of fine dust clinging to her skirt, her hair, her gloves, her knee-high boots, she *still* looked as if she were attending a formal ball. "You don't sound very confidant."

"Those Indians back at the Harding ranch were told by *someone* to steal the horses. I counted six Lakota back at the ranch, but that don't mean that's all there were. Or don't mean that another *tiospaye*—another clan—of Lakota won't attack."

"The army will find them."

Ira shook his head. "Most the army's going to do is get led away from the stage route."

Beth reached up and brushed dirt off Ira's cheek. "But you'll protect us, will you not, Mr. Drang?"

When he didn't answer, she stepped closer. "You will protect *me*." Ira backed away, but Beth pulled his face close to hers. "And when we get to Deadwood . . . perhaps we will become close, you and me."

Out of the corner of his eye, Ira saw Frank look their way, yet he did nothing in reaction to his wife's flirtations. Perhaps, Ira thought, he was as exhausted as Ira and didn't even care.

Ira backed away from Beth. "Best get back to your husband."

Beth smiled. "If that's what you *really* want?"

Another time, Ira *would* be interested. But the last thing he needed now was to cloud his mind with thoughts of spending time with someone like Beth. "It's what has to be."

She walked away, glancing back and smiling, before joining Frank, who was seated beside Dauber on a log.

Sally watched Beth walking back to Frank, and at Ira, joining him at the horses. Sally leaned over the back of a horse. "Seems like the closer we get to Deadwood, the bolder she becomes. Heard her come on to Dauber right in front of Frank. And now you."

"I want nothing to do with her—"

"Of course you don't." Sally smiled that ragged smile once again. "She's sure no slag. She's kinda exciting, isn't she?"

Ira shrugged. "If it keeps her busy and out of the way, I don't care. How long?"

Sally looked at the team slumped in their traces. "Those beasts need a long rest. They damned sure ain't going to spring to life any time soon, so any time's as good as the next."

"Let's just make it to Cheyenne River ranch. Might not be anything left of the station, but at least there'll be good grass and water for the horses."

Sally urged the tired team the last six miles to the mouth of Red Canyon. Ira had been through here last spring, when he drove a breeding pair of Morgans to a buyer in Custer City. It was the last time he and Jamie ever did it together. Jamie's face had lit up when Ira told him he could come along. "How long will it take to walk there?" Jamie had asked.

"I'll borrow a horse for you," Ira answered. "A nice, gentle one." It had been the only time the boy had been on horseback, and he giggled with delight nearly all the way as he was led along by Ira.

It was at the mouth of Red Canyon that he had his only encounter with the horse thief and murderer Persimmon Bill.

Ira knew Bill by reputation only. The slight man—suspected of the Metz Massacre and of killing Stuttering Henry Brown, route manager on this very stage line months earlier—opened fire on Ira and Jamie. The breeding mare they were delivering was struck and killed, and Ira barely managed to get the stallion—and Jamie—to safety. He had left Jamie at the stage station and worked his way in back of the thief. Ira got the drop on Bill and disarmed him, then took every dollar the thief had stashed in his money belt. Bill had threatened to hunt Ira down and kill him. Just as soon as he got loose from the tree Ira had lashed him to.

Sally stopped at the mouth of Red Canyon. A sign—littered with untold rifle and pistol bullet holes—warned: ABANDON HOPE ALL WHO ENTER HERE.

"Kind of chilling, ain't it?" Sally said, spitting a string of tobacco that plopped against the sign. "I read that thing every time I enter the canyon—"

"I didn't know you could read."

"Actually, I can't," Sally said. "But I memorized it. I recite it to remind me that the likes of Persimmon Bill could be lurking around the next blind spot in the road."

Ira craned his neck up at the high cliffs, which were becoming higher the farther into the canyon they went. "With Logan in the area, I doubt even Bill would want to buck him."

"All the same, I'll look forward to that new route the line's gonna' run." Sally—in his quest to be the noisiest stage driver on the line—told Ira more than a few times about the new route that would pass May's ranch and Robber's Roost on the way to Deadwood, a route offering fewer places for road agents and Indians to ambush the stage.

But this route was different. More stages were stopped and robbed along this stretch of the route than any other. Plus, it was smack in the middle of the Lakota's route travelling to hunting grounds in the Powder River and the Shining Mountains.

Ira grabbed the seat and leaned over the side of the coach. "We're entering Red Canyon," he told the passengers. "Look alive—there's bound to be Indians close. Or Logan."

Ira rested Sally's shotgun against the seat where the fat man could reach it. He fished three rifle rounds out of his pocket and held them in his hand. "Frank. Get up here."

Frank stuck his head out the window. "What the hell for?"

"I need another set of eyes—"

"I'll send Dauber up."

"Dauber can hardly hold his hand, let alone look for Indians. Now get up here!"

Frank opened the door and stepped on the window sill. He crawled up and glared at Ira.

"Might as well put that little gun away," Ira said. "We get shot at, bullets from that little thing won't even make it to the top."

"Then why do I need to come up there?"

"I need an extra set of eyes," Ira repeated. "Just keep watching that east rim. I got the west side." He nudged Sally. "Go slow."

"That's all we *can* do with these horses," Sally said and rode the brake.

Ira turned in the seat. He'd seen the glint of metal shining for the briefest time. He squinted at the top of the canyon rim but didn't see the shine again. "I saw it, too," Sally said. "Do we stop?"

"No," Ira said. "Let's try to get through as quick as we can. If we can make it to Cheyenne River station, we can hole up for a little while."

Sally cracked his whip, but the horses seemed not to pay attention as they plodded ahead.

Ira smelled the smoke a quarter mile before the Cheyenne River station came into view. The station house and telegraph office smoldered, embers showing bright in the night. The corrals had been set afire, the wind causing flecks of burnt hay to fly skyward. When the coach had travelled another eighth of a mile, Ira told Sally, "Hold up. I need to do some checking."

When Sally stopped the stage, Ira climbed down from the seat. The moon showing bright on a cloudless night cast its own shadows, and he walked bent over, studying the hoof prints that crossed the road: barefooted. Unshod ponies. "I'd say the Sioux torched the station within the last two hours, if I'm reading my sign right," he called up to Sally.

"I hope the army got the station master and the others out before the attack," Sally said. "He and his missus is nice folks, even though they are Irish."

Ira walked beside the stage as Sally eased it toward a field leading down to the Cheyenne River. He stopped the stage beside a grove of ash and pine a hundred yards from the station yard. "Do we go in?" Sally asked.

"Get the passengers out for a stretch," Ira said. "But be ready to pile back in and make a run for it." Ira walked the last hundred yards with his rifle cradled in the crook of one arm, thong off the hammer of his pistol, watching the high hills. And watching for any movement from the station.

A hawk sat on the telegraph pole, paying no mind to the cut line swinging in the wind, while a small herd of pronghorns grazed behind the telegraph office. They looked up at Ira walking slowly toward them, then bolted and disappeared through a field of rabbit brush and silverweed.

When he reached the station yard, he paused and tested the

wind. Charred timbers gave off a pungent odor, and hay that had been piled up for the horses still smoldered. But he didn't smell the terrible odor of burnt flesh as he'd feared, so he continued across the yard.

In the middle of the burned-out house the cookstove stack jutted skyward, as if the stove was giving Ira the middle finger. As if he could have done something if they had gotten here sooner. He picked his way among the ashes but, if there had been anything salvageable, the Indians had taken it.

The Sioux had knocked the pump jack over in case passers-by needed fresh water. Ira walked to the corrals. Hooves of a dozen horses trampling out of the corral wiped out all sign of Indians, but Ira spotted a partial moccasin print beside the gate.

He faced the stage where he knew Sally was watching him through his spyglass. He waved, indicating the stage should stay where it was.

On the way back to the stagecoach, Ira saw Beth helping Dauber out of the coach, their hands entwined for long moments. Ira wondered how long it would be before Frank finally got fed up with his wife's flirtations and exploded.

"How many you figure?" Sally asked when Ira arrived back.

Ira took a long pull from his canteen and slung the strap over the brake handle. "Hard to tell with all the horses wiping out tracks. But it's safe to say there were upwards of twenty raiders. My suggestion is to stay here for a few hours and hope they continue on to their hunting grounds."

"Then that's what we better do." Sally stepped down and tapped Frank on the shoulder. "Got bacon in the boot. Best tell your missus to fry some up. Might be the last meal we have for a while."

Ira waited until Frank had joined Beth and Dauber before leading Sally aside and asking, "What's your honest take on these critters? They gonna' make it to Deadwood?"

Sally pulled the pin on the singletrees and wrapped the lines around his hand. Ira walked beside Sally as he led the horses toward the free-flowing creek. "If the Indians haven't fired Red Canyon station, we'll be able to get a fresh team there. If not, these horses will never make it. Maybe if we had the time, we could hold over. But we *don't* really have the time, do we?"

"The Lakota could return. It's a toss-up."

"Then there's Logan," Sally said, running his hand over the ribs of one of the gaunt wheelers. Ira was horseman enough to tell when a critter was ready to drop in the traces. "Think he's still following us?"

Ira scanned the high hills. Logan—or one of his men—could be looking down on them even now. And they'd never know it. Another hour, when the sun started rising, they might see him, but now—here they could be shot like a crap shoot. "If I were a gambler like Frank, I'd put every cent I had on Logan still dogging us."

Chapter 22

Dutch tied his gray to a willow and crept closer to the edge of the cliff. He surveyed the area, looking for game trails that would put him closer to the stage, but there were none. He would work around that. He often killed from long range. And he actually enjoyed it more, if what he did was enjoyment, though there was something appealing about standing ten feet from your man in a stand-up fight and watching the life fade from his eyes.

He untied his bedroll from in back of his saddle and returned to the cliff's edge. He laid a box of ammunition beside the bedroll and looked down. The coach appeared small from up here, the people walking around even smaller. He wondered how close Logan and Matt were. If Logan was alone, he would have been here by now. But with Matt wounded and slowing him up, Dutch knew Logan might not get here until after the shooting started. Logan wanted Cassie's killer alive. He wanted to prolong the murderer's suffering before he finally allowed the man to die.

But it made little difference to Dutch. He just wanted Cassie's killer dead. He would tell Logan that Ira and the passengers had started the shooting. He'd claim he'd had no recourse but to return fire. Logan would fume and stomp the ground until he finally wound down. After he had vented like an old iron steam pot, Logan would find his Cassie's killer among the dead, and the fire would finally die out. Then he and

Dutch could return to selling the best horses the army—and whoever else was unlucky enough to pass their way—could provide.

He returned to his horse and slowly—almost lovingly—slipped the Rolling Block from the rifle scabbard. He blew dust from it before he grabbed the long, cylindrical canvas container. The rifle had served him well, hunting runaway slaves. Hunting men with a price on their heads. A brief moment of sadness overcame him. That was perhaps the happiest time of his life: hunting runaways with Logan. Logan had liberated Dutch from that Union prisoner of war camp, engineering a breakout that cost the Union twelve soldiers, and freeing up twice as many Confederates. All to free the man the Union said had killed more field officers at long range than anyone else. Dutch had never had a real friend in his life, but Logan was the closest. But a time like this—when Logan let an obsession come between them and business—was straining their friendship.

And the good times after the war. He and Logan had made a name for themselves as bounty hunters, Ira Drang being the only one who'd ever managed to stay two steps ahead of them. Their success had allowed them to move west, buy homestead land, run others off theirs, set up a successful ranch. They'd also built a thriving horse rustling business. These years had been good to both of them.

Until Cassie's murder.

Now Logan's fixation on finding and slowly making Cassie's killer pay was overriding his common sense. They had lost six men—seven, if Matt bled out, as it appeared he would. As Dutch lay down at the edge of the cliff, a sudden thought came to him: perhaps he would head to Deadwood himself after he killed those huddled around the stage. Miners would be easy pickings for a man like him, Dutch thought, and he felt his heart rate rise.

The notion of breaking it off with Logan seemed alien to him. Yet, here he was, thinking of going it alone after today. And that's just what he had decided, as surely as he had decided to throw in with Logan hunting slaves so many years ago.

Dutch began to second guess himself, to doubt his decision to go it alone. He and Logan had profited from the market on horses, even those with changed brands. But after the bodies of the passengers and Ira and the fat driver were discovered, the law would be out for blood. And they would follow the trail of clues right back to Logan.

Then Logan would have to defend himself, because Dutch would be far north, profiting from the gold fields. And, even if the miners weren't as easy to rob as he thought they'd be, Dutch could still work a sluice box or a pan.

He closed his eyes and calmed himself. He didn't want to think about what he would do after this day.—He needed to stay calm so that, when he walked away, no one down in the valley below would be left to tell what had happened.

He laid the blanket roll on the ground before resting the fore end of his rifle on it. He snapped out the spyglass and took in the scene below. Ira sat with his back against the coach, his rifle—still the only long gun in the bunch—rested across his lap. Dutch grinned. When the shooting started, Ira would try his best to hit Dutch. But he knew the .44-40 had little chance of reaching him this far away, this far up.

But Ira would try.

Dutch had to give him that, though he would prefer to kill Ira from a few feet away. Prefer to see the look in his eye as life left him.

Dutch set the rifle aside and grabbed the spyglass again. The fat Englishman held his team—what was left of it—as the horses drank from a creek trickling tepid water, while the fancy man cleaned his small gambler's guns—as if they would even things up once the shooting started.

Dutch swung his telescope to watch Dauber sitting beside the woman. Dutch would do his best not to hit the woman—after all, he still had *some* scruples—but Dauber was another matter. Logan had bet the farm that Dauber was the one who had killed his Cassie. "Don't you remember how he tried to get next to Cassie this spring?" Logan had argued.

Dutch did remember. He also remembered how he had to hold Logan back from chasing after the boy and killing him. "Bad for business," Dutch had argued. "He won't be back."

But when Logan saw Dauber on the stage, he suspected the cowboy was Cassie's killer.

Dutch wasn't so certain. As much as he liked his friend's daughter, she had sashayed around in frilly skirts with the tops tight and low and had flirted with everyone wearing trousers who crossed her path. Most any of the ranch hands Logan hired to tend cattle and horses could have killed the girl. After all, most men Logan hired were either accomplished horse thieves or gunmen. With those kinds of men, Dutch knew any one of them would be capable of attacking the girl. But the tracks that morning clearly showed the killer leaving the ranch in the buggy.

But where was Preacher? Dutch scanned the area, the trees shielding them on one side, and the open area where the horses were picketed. No Preacher.

That bothered him.

Dutch liked things to be neatly laid out for him, liked things to be in nice rows. Organized. But with Preacher loose someplace, Dutch became worried. He knew what the man was capable of. He didn't buy that Preacher had seen the Lord. Dutch believed the man was going to Deadwood for the same reason as he was—to fleece and rob miners of what gold they panned out of Deadwood Gulch. But where *was* he? Dutch felt the hairs on his neck rise. But at this point, he had no choice.

He'd have to go through with his plan while he kept an eye out for Preacher putting the sneak on him.

Dutch arranged his rifle rounds in front of him, then rolled a cigarette. He inhaled long and deeply, calming himself for what he was about to do as he watched the scene below. The woman had dished up food for the men, and they gathered around the campfire, their guard down. They'd soon be sleepy after their meal, exhaustion overtaking them. Dutch had been there more times than he could remember, tired beyond comprehension. But he was a predator. And predators couldn't afford to succumb to exhaustion.

Dutch set the spyglass aside and opened the cylinder. He slipped the long, telescopic sight out of the case and blew on the front and the rear glass before setting it atop the barrel. He lined up the dovetails and turned the scope to lock it in place, then tightened the metal claw mounts.

He looked down at the valley again: a cross wind—ten miles an hour perhaps—kicked up leaves and dust. He adjusted the telescopic sight to compensate for the wind and for the seven-hundred-yard distance, calculating the range with the sharp down-angle and shooting into a rising sun.

He snubbed the cigarette out and grabbed a piece of dried beef. Soon he would be done with the passengers. And with Ira Drang. He would leave the bodies for Logan to find. Leave them so the man could see which of the passengers was Cassie's killer. Dutch would head for the gold fields. Once again, the thought of being on his own excited him, and he breathed deeply.

He put the rifle's hammer to full cock and thumbed the rolling block away, exposing the chamber. He opened the cartridge box and took out one perfect round. He always paper-patched his bullets, so the lead never came in contact with the rifle's barrel. Never interfered with the accuracy of the rifle. Logan often chided him for rolling the paper patch over the lead bullets on those nights they sat around a campfire, talking, cutting the paper to an exact size.

He eased the cartridge into the chamber, snapped the rolling block closed, and the hammer fell to half-cock. As it should.

He ate the last of the dried beef before he brought the rifle to full cock and lay behind the stock onto the bedroll. He sighted into the scope.

But Ira was gone.

CHAPTER 23

Ira watched Beth rewrap Dauber's mangled hand with her torn petticoat, the colorful red and yellow Monkey Ward bandana he'd worn at the start of the trip gone. The wound had opened up when he had gathered firewood, and Beth had insisted on rewrapping the bandage. Beth sat close to Dauber, their shoulders touching, while Frank leaned against the coach and paid them no mind.

"I figure it's just a matter of time before Frank gets fed up with his wife flirting with Dauber." Sally sat on a log away from the campfire. "Then we'll have trouble."

"Don't you think Frank would have said something by now?" Ira shrugged. "I don't think he cares. But that's the least of our worries." He motioned to the horses hobbled at the edge of a small clump of grama grass beside the creek. "The thing we need to worry about is those horses holding up."

Sally nodded. "You ain't telling me something I don't already know. Soon's I rest up a little I'm going to start shucking weight. We'll never make it to Deadwood, but if we lighten the load, the horses may make it to Custer City. Dropping Beth's case alone ought to be good for forty pounds."

"That's a start . . ." Ira craned his neck upward. He shielded the sun with his hand as he scanned the cliff above.

"What is it?"

Ira swore he saw a glint of . . . steel. Perhaps some glass bottle, from the top of the cliff. He looked away and saw the glint again in his periphery. Someone *was* on the top of the cliff. Someone watched them. "You ever shoot a rifle much?"

"Not since I lost my eye," Sally answered. "But I can if I need to."

"You'll need to." Ira walked behind the coach, keeping it between him and the cliff. He looked around the coach at the cliff face. Trails wound upwards, narrow trails fine for mountain goats and deer, but not for men. Except one trail, wider than the others, going up the side of the rock. Ira followed it with his eye. If someone was up there, the trail would put him within fifty yards of where he last saw the sun reflecting off *something*.

He motioned to Sally to stand behind the coach and handed him the rifle. "This gun won't reach up there"—he pointed to the cliff top—"but it might keep someone guessing."

"Does someone need to be guessing about something?"

"I'm not sure if someone's up there or not. I gotta have a look-see."

Sally looked around the coach. "Don't see how you're going to get up there—"

"That game trail." Ira pointed it out. "It's the only chance I have to get close to whoever's up there." He laid his hat on the seat. "As easy as you can, tell the others to get behind the coach. If shooting starts, wing rounds up there."

Ira peered up, but he could not spot the glint he saw before. Perhaps he was just imagining things. He'd blame exhaustion later. Ira cinched up his boot strings, looking over the passengers a last time. Beth sat shoulder to shoulder with Dauber, while Frank lay on the ground with his hat over his eyes. Ira walked quickly away from the coach, glancing back. But the others paid him no mind as he disappeared into a ravine.

He ran bent over until he reached the cliff. The game trail—a natural shelf two feet wide—narrowed to no more than a foot halfway up the side of the cliff. He had started up the trail, walking over deer tracks, and a mountain lion's prints impressed over the deer when . . .

. . . the first shot rang out, echoing off the canyon walls.

Ira flattened himself against the rock face and looked down at the coach. Sally stumbled beside Frank, struggling to hold the gambler up by his belt. Frank's arm dangled, useless, at his side, blood dripping off his silk vest, when the second shot erupted. The bullet exited Frank's chest, and he shook violently before he slumped, lifeless, in Sally's arms.

Sally let Frank drop to the ground and ran for the coach as the shooter fired again. The round grazed Sally's leg, and he fell. Dauber was scrambling toward Sally when another round bounced off the confines of the canyon. Dauber fell, clutching his stomach. He screamed in pain as Sally grabbed his arm and dragged him behind the coach. Beth peeked around the back boot, her skirt fluttering in the wind.

Then silence.

Ira could imagine the shooter waiting for a target to appear from behind the coach. It was what Ira would do. And all the shooter had was time to wait until those below showed themselves.

"Damn!" Ira swore under his breath. He'd been so focused on Indians attacking them, he hadn't thought Logan could have caught up with them. Or maybe it was Dutch. Ira recognized Dutch's buffalo gun by the sound of the heavy charge. It had nearly killed him that one time Dutch had gotten close to Ira years ago.

Was Dutch alone, or was Logan with him?

Ira had no time to worry about that. He picked his way up the side of the cliff. Deer—sure-footed where Ira was not—had used this trail for generations, perhaps. As had mountain goats. More than likely the Sioux knew about it. But it would serve Ira's purpose well if it got him to within pistol range of Dutch.

Ira glanced up. He was within forty yards of the cliff summit when the shooter fired again. One of the horses went down—shot through the neck—and the shooter's next round killed the horse beside it.

Sally peeked from around the coach and started firing Ira's rifle. The rounds hit halfway up the cliff face. Ira counted the rounds. When Sally was empty, he broke from the safety of the coach and ran to his horses. The next shot tore into Sally's back, and he was dead before he hit the ground.

Twenty yards farther along, Ira thought, *twenty yards to the top*.

When he reached the top of the cliff overlooking the scene below, he lay for a moment on his back to catch his breath. The shooter had not fired since Sally went down, yet he knew Dutch would not leave until everyone down there was dead.

Yelling below caused Ira to look over the rim. Dauber, still holding his stomach, had swung over the back of one of the horses, and he held out a hand. Beth was running toward him when the next shot struck Dauber in the head and knocked him off the horse. The critter ran across the creek and disappeared over the hill while Beth dove back behind the coach.

Ira stood and picked out the way he would approach the shooter. Heavy timber would conceal him, but for how long?

CHAPTER 24

The shooting stopped as abruptly as it had started.

Ira cocked his head in the direction of the shots, but he heard nothing.

He picked his way through the trees, stopping every few feet to look around at the ground. Had he been wrong as to where Dutch had lain when he fired on the coach? Had Dutch fled? Ira thought not, for Dutch had the high ground. He could stay there all day behind the gun, waiting for another shot, waiting for Beth to make Dauber's mistake and expose herself.

Ira walked another ten yards and dropped to his knees when he reached a clearing. A rolled-up blanket lay at the edge of the cliff, empty rifle rounds neatly lined upon the ground beside the blanket.

But no Dutch.

Ira stepped from the trees and walked to the spent casings. He picked one up: .50-70. Heavy black powder-fouling showed the shooter had fired heavy bullets. Unburned paper lay close to the blanket. Paper-patched bullets meant only one thing—the shooter was a marksman, picky about his ammunition. Of course it was Dutch.

The thought caused Ira to shudder, when he heard a twig snap behind him. He whirled around and faced Dutch holding his Rolling Block rifle pointed at Ira's gut.

"I know *just* what you're thinking," Dutch said, a wide grin on his face, a piece of twig twitching between his teeth. "You're asking yourself if you can draw that pistol before ol' Dutch can drill you."

"Pretty heavy rifle," Ira said. "Perhaps that's just what I can do."

Dutch pulled the hammer to full cock. "If I killed those folks down in the valley that far away, don't you think I ought to be able to hit you from thirty feet? Now toss that Colt aside and we'll jaw a little before . . ."

"Before what?"

Dutch grinned again. "The gun . . ."

Ira tossed his pistol away. Dutch squatted on his heels and lowered his rifle a few inches. "You're the one that got away. Whenever me and Logan ran a man to ground after the war, we'd always wonder how it was that we missed Ira Drang."

"You missed me 'cause I'm a better trail hand than you." Stalling. Looking about for anything that might distract Dutch. "I eluded you both because I could always lay false trails to lure you away." Ira winked, seeing Dutch's face flush red. "You two missed me because I'm a whole lot smarter than you two are."

Dutch raised the rifle. "You son of a bitch—"

"And because I'm just that much faster with my Colt than you. Given a fair chance." He nodded to the Rolling Block. "That's all you got left—killing me outright so you brag to folks how you killed Ira Drang." Ira smiled. "But you'll never admit to them I was unarmed at the time. And you'll wake up every day wondering if you *could* have outdrawn me. Wondering if the *only* way you could have bested me was by getting the drop on me." Ira spat. "You're just a pathetic back-shooter. Always have been."

Dutch stepped closer. "On my worst day, I could beat the likes of you." He laughed, and Ira heard his nervousness. "Hell, that's why Hickok taunted your little brother—he knew you wouldn't dare look him up."

"I *will* look him up," Ira said, "once I'm done with you."

"You're mighty certain I'll put this here rifle away and face you in a stand-up fight."

"I am," Ira said, working the soreness and kinks out of his gun hand. "Because you want to prove to yourself that you're not like Logan. Not like that fool Handy Johnson or that Highsmith feller who thought he could earn a reputation by ambushing me. You want to go to sleep nights knowing you beat the man who could beat Hickok in a stand-up fight."

"Like I said, on my worst day you were never as fast as me. Unless"—he glanced around—"you have help. Where's Preacher?"

"Behind you."

"I'm not dumb enough to fall for that. Now where the hell is he?" Dutch asked and raised the rifle to center on Ira's head.

"Sioux drilled him with a couple arrows," Ira said, and Dutch breathed a visible sign of relief.

"A moment ago, you weren't sure you could take Preacher and me both. But you're still having doubts, and it's just me you're facing." Ira forced a smile. If he could get Dutch's ire up, he might just have a chance . . . "You're thinking you're a little too old to take on the likes of me."

"Bullshit—"

"You're kicking around in your head all the tales you've heard about Ira Drang. Wondering if the stories were true, or if they were exaggerations. And you *want* to know if you're as fast as me. You *need* to know if you can beat me."

Dutch's jaw muscles tightened, and his finger turned white on the rifle's trigger. "We'll see. With two fingers pick up that Colt and holster it."

Ira picked up his pistol and blew dust off it before carefully settling it in his holster. He squared up to Dutch, his hand hovering over his pistol butt as Dutch kept his rifle pointed at him.

"Before we start this little dance, tell me who Cassie's killer is."

Ira shrugged. "Haven't a clue."

"You've been around all those passengers. Every man on that stage wore gloves. Cassie bit her killer. Was it Dauber?"

"What difference does it make? Dauber's dead now anyways."

"It makes a difference to *me*. I want to know if our men getting killed was worth it."

"I guess you'd just have to go down and check yourself. But you won't make it through this little dance."

"Oh?" Dutch laid his rifle on the ground in front of him and slowly straightened. He moved the flowing duster away from his pistol. Ira had never seen Dutch draw against any man, but he'd heard stories. Was *he* having doubts? Ira knew better—he'd *always* had doubts he could ever beat Dutch McMasters. But if Ira could get Dutch talking, concentrating on explaining himself rather than drawing his gun . . . "Then you tell me: why did you start working with that cutthroat Logan Hatch?"

Dutch paused. "Because he sprung me from camp—"

Ira drew while he . . .

. . . stepped to one side.

Things slowed, then, his movements seeming to come inside a bubble. He . . .

. . . thumbed the hammer back as . . .

. . . Dutch's bullet sliced the air, tearing a hole in Ira's shirt a heartbeat before Ira's slug thudded into Dutch, center-chest. Dutch dropped to his knees, fumbling with his pistol, looking at it dangling from his trigger finger, unable to make his hand work.

Ira stepped to him and kicked it out of his hand.

Dutch fell on his back, a look of astonishment on his face.

Frothy blood spewed out of his mouth, and he struggled to speak. "How—"

Ira opened the loading gate and shucked out the spent round. He plucked another one from his belt loop and holstered. "How? Doubts crept into your thinking, doubts whether you could *really* beat me."

"How—"

"I told you—I was a lot smarter than you, that's how. When you were talking, you should have been drawing your gun."

Dutch struggled to sit up as he tried to talk, looking down with disbelief at the hole in his chest. Then he shuddered, and he fell back lifeless to the ground.

Ira's legs buckled, and he dropped to the ground beside Dutch. Damn, the man *had* been fast. He felt his side where the bullet had grazed him. Dutch's shot had gone true—but Ira just hadn't been *there* when he shot. *If* Dutch hadn't talked when he should have drawn his gun . . . And *if* Ira hadn't stepped aside those few inches . . . Thinking about the *if*s caused his hands to tremble, and he took out his bible and began rolling a smoke. Tobacco shook onto the ground and onto his shirt front, but Ira finally got enough into the paper to lick it and fish a lucifer out of his pocket.

When he'd smoked the cigarette, his heart had slowed, and Ira felt able to stand. On wobbly legs, he walked to Dutch's dapple gray and untied the flaps on the saddlebags. He tossed out a shirt—which would have been too small for Ira—and a pair of dungarees with the knees worn through and about a foot too long for him. In the bottom of one saddlebag was a Double Eagle. Ira pocketed it, along with the extra rounds for Dutch's buffalo rifle.

He returned to Dutch's body and felt his vest pocket. He came away with Dutch's bible and pocketed it. The least Dutch could do—Ira thought—was let him smoke a cigarette for all the trouble he'd put Ira and the others through.

CHAPTER 25

Dutch's gelding eyed Ira warily when he went to swing into the saddle—the whites of its eyes showing like a bronc about to be tested. Ira grabbed the cheek strap of the bridle and pulled it hard toward him. The gray's head turned, and Ira swung atop the horse. It began to buck, and Ira jerked the cheek strap harder. The horse turned its head sharply and nipped at Ira. He cheeked the animal even more forcefully, and it finally settled down.

Ira sat atop the gray, ready for the worst, but the horse remained calm. Ira adjusted the strap holding the long-range rifle safely to the saddle scabbard while he got a feel for the critter. The stirrups dropped too low, but that mattered little to Ira; he'd adjust them later. For now, he needed to reach the bottom of the valley and see if any passengers had lived through Dutch's attack.

It took Ira more than an hour to work his way down, and he broke from the rocks a hundred yards from where the coach sat like a scow listing to its death in a heavy wind. Even before he got close enough to identity the dead, the wind shifted and blood rotting putrid in the heat drifted past his nose. He thought back to Dutch. He had it made sitting on his perch on the cliff. The victims below had no chance of hitting him. But Dutch's over confidence with his handgun—and his underestimation of Ira's skill—had gotten him killed.

Now there were only Ira and Beth left. Sally lay where

Dutch's heavy slug had killed him, beside the horses he loved, while Beth sat on the ground holding Dauber's head in her lap. Not Frank's.

Ira dismounted and tied the horse to the coach. Beth cried, heavy makeup smudging her rouged cheeks, but Ira walked past her.

He bent to Sally, though he knew there was no reason to check. He was dead, and Ira—on a whim—slipped Sally's gloves off. He turned both hands over. They showed the rough and cracked hands of a working man, but no recent injury. Certainly none made by a biting Cassie Hatch.

Ira laid Sally's hands on his chest and closed his eyes, as he looked around at the carnage one shooter with a buffalo gun had wrought. The horses were dead, and the only one alive had run off, probably among some passing Indian's remuda by now. He and Beth were the only ones alive, and they would have to double up on Dutch's gray in order to get to Custer City.

He turned to the coach and looked down at Beth. "Shouldn't you be mourning your husband?" Ira asked, taking Dutch's bible from his pocket.

"Dauber was going to get me to Deadwood." Snot ran down Beth's nose, and she took the papers and tobacco from Ira and started rolling a smoke. "We *were* going to paint the town red."

"And leave your husband to fend for himself?"

Beth waved the air. "Frank was no good. Ever since we were little kids—"

"You're not making any sense."

Beth motioned to Frank's lifeless body. "Frank wasn't my husband—he was my brother."

"Well, ain't I the dumb ass. That's why he didn't care if you flirted with other men."

Beth chuckled. "He didn't care *anything* about me. When we came west from St. Louis, we decided it was easier if we went as husband and wife." She forced a grin. "We figured I'd have fewer men trying to get into my pantaloons if they thought I was already spoken for."

Ira sat on a log beside the campfire. "So that's why you hit on everyone on the stage—so *someone* would take you to Deadwood if something happened to Frank." Ira shook his head. "I'm still confused. I thought that's what Frank was doing—taking you to Deadwood—"

"I figured that damned fool would probably just wind up dead before we got to the Black Hills." She swiped a gloved hand across her eyes. "Although I thought Frank would get himself shot when he was caught cheating at some poker game." She blew her nose on the bandana Ira handed her. "Either way, I needed a plan if he got killed." She laid Dauber's head gently on the ground. "And Dauber was the feller among all you who was . . ."

"Easiest to manipulate," Ira finished for her.

"He was." She shrugged. "I could always tell which ones were easy. But you can't fault me for hedging my bet."

"Can't say as I do," Ira said, reaching under the coach. He came away with a shovel and handed it to Beth.

"What am I going to do with *that*?"

"Dig graves."

She tossed the shovel at Ira's feet. "I will not!"

"Suit yourself," Ira said. "But if I have to bury these men myself, you can damned sure walk to Custer City on your own."

"Custer City? I need to get to Deadwood."

"We'll be *lucky* if we make it to Custer. Now you want to walk?"

Her face flushed redder than the rouge she wore, and she picked up the shovel. "Where do we bury them?"

Ira motioned to a grassy area at the base of the cliff. He waited until Beth sank her first shovel into the ground before he started dragging corpses to her. He dragged Frank and Sally by the legs and dropped them beside the hole Beth was digging. Before he dragged Dauber's body to the grave, he took the glove off his uninjured hand. Like Sally, Dauber's hand showed no indication of recent injury. Ira had been right from the start.

Cassie Hatch's killer had *not* been on the stage.

Beth dug until she was exhausted, then Ira took over, digging a hole deep enough for three men. He knew they'd stay buried for just so long, what with the wolves and coyotes and cougars roaming the area for an easy meal. They'd smell the bloating horses first, and easily find where the men were buried.

"Fry up some beans while I finish up," Ira said.

When Ira had filled the hole with the three men, he stood and arched his back, stretching. He wiped the sweat from his forehead as he walked to the creek and dipped his hat in the water. He tipped it up over his head, and tepid water washed thick dust from his head and face. But he knew, in this heat, he would soon be as hot as he'd been a moment ago.

He walked to the fire and squatted across from Beth. She handed him a plate of beans and bacon and sat back on a log. Gone was the defiant woman looking to manipulate *any* man to take her to Deadwood, replaced by the woman who knew how to use her perceived innocence on a man.

"We will make it to Deadwood, won't we?" She smiled, her voice turning soft. Alluring. Any other time in his life, Ira would have succumbed to her charms. But not today.

"I don't know about you, but *I'll* make it."

"I don't understand—"

"I told you, I'll get you to Custer City. From there you can find some lonely cowboy to take you the rest of the way to Deadwood."

"So you're not taking me with you to Deadwood?"

Ira shook his head. "No offense, but you'll just slow me down. I've wasted enough time. I need to find Hickok before he leaves for some other boom town. Now if you've finished eating, pack a few things you need, and we'll get going before it gets dark."

Ira finished the meal and walked to the creek. He swished his plate around and waved it in the air to dry before joining Beth. She struggled to carry her bag to where Dutch's gray was tied, glaring at Ira with each step. "Can you at least help me tie this bag across the saddle?"

Ira set the bag on the ground and opened it.

"What're you doing—"

"Seeing what you need that's actually necessary." He tossed out undergarments and skirts and bustles until all that was inside the bag was one change of clothes. "The rest of your stuff we'll leave for the Indians."

"You wouldn't dare."

Ira smiled. "Remember that threat of walking to Custer City by your lonesome?"

Beth backed away. Her fists clenched and unclenched, like she intended to slug Ira.

"You can buy more clothes when you get to a town," Ira said as he bent down and closed her bag.

"You'll just slow *me* down," Beth said. "Now step away from the horse."

Ira turned to face Beth's tiny derringer. She waved the gun until Ira stepped away from the horse.

"It looks small, but I assure you it is .41 caliber of lead ball that will open up a hole in your heart as quick as the gun on your hip. Take it off, and hand it to me."

Ira unstrapped his pistol and handed it to her. Beth draped it over the saddle horn.

"You'd leave me out here with no gun? No horse?"

Beth smiled. "You had your chance. I'd have preferred to

ride to Deadwood and spend time with you rather than that fool Dauber. Now, about a gun—those men we just buried had guns. Dig them up. But I'd do it quick before Indians find you on foot."

Ira backed away when Beth untied the reins of Dutch's horse from the coach. "I'd like to say I feel sorry for you, but I don't," Ira said.

"Sorry about what?"

Ira kept silent, waiting for justice to erupt.

Which it did as soon as Beth stepped into the saddle. The gray sunfished hard before bucking high and coming straight down on all fours. Beth flew off the horse, her gun flying in the opposite direction. And, as Ira grabbed onto the reins, all he could see was her petticoat and bustle up around her bare belly.

They rode slowly, the dapple gray unused to someone as heavy as Ira on its back; certainly not used to the extra weight of Beth and her travelling bag. The sun had set an hour ago, yet Ira made no plans to stop any time soon. A three-quarter moon offered enough light to see where they rode, and he wanted to put as much distance between them and the stage as Dutch's tired gelding would allow.

"You knew the horse would buck me off."

"Guess I'm guilty there." Ira laughed. "But don't feel too bad—he was a little randy with me, too. I had to cheek the hell out of him the first time I threw a leg over him. Guess he was just used to 'ol Dutch."

"All right," Beth said. "But there's no reason not to untie me."

Beth wiggled against the leather strap Ira had tied her with. "So you can grab for my gun? No chance."

"What's to grab while I'm sitting in front of you? And can't we at least take a little rest?" Beth pleaded. "My back is killing me."

"Not just yet," he said. "By now Indians have found the stagecoach, and Logan has found Dutch's body. Neither will give up until they've run us to ground. If we're lucky, we just might make it to Custer. Then you're on your own."

CHAPTER 26

When they arrived at Spring-on-Hill, Ira stopped. The wind caught the odor of charred wood and grass, and he cautiously coaxed the gray forward. It snorted and stopped, refusing to go farther, so Ira dismounted. He helped Beth down before he tied the horse to an aspen at the edge of the forest surrounding the stage station. "Wait here."

She grabbed his arm. "Where are you going? You're not leaving me here, tied up like I am—"

Ira clamped his hand over Beth's mouth, and she bit down, much—he suspected—as had Cassie the day her killer visited her. But unlike Cassie's killer, Ira wore gloves. "Quiet," he whispered, taking his hand from her mouth. "I can't tell from here when that barn and house was torched. Looks like the Sioux have been all up and down the stage route, burning and killing. Sit quiet now. I'll make it back soon's I go for a look-see."

Ira took his Winchester from the scabbard and skirted the tree line, bringing him closer to the house. When he'd come to within thirty yards of the stage station, he paused. When the moon peeked from the clouds, Ira saw what he'd expected to see: the station master's house and the barns and corrals had all been burned. He approached, feeling no heat emanating off the charred house, guessing the fire had happened yesterday sometime. Perhaps the day before.

He walked to the house and through what used to be a fine

home for the station master and his missus. Something caught the moonlight, and Ira followed the glint: an arrow lying on the ground. Probably fell from the quiver of a raiding Indian. He held the arrow to the moonlight: Arapaho. Allies of the Lakota at the Red Cloud Agency. The two tribes shared many things. Including burning and killing anything connected with the white man.

Ira walked a wide circle around the house, checking tracks, until he saw where unshod ponies had ridden over prints of shod horses. "At least the station master made it out before the Indians attacked," he said to himself. Perhaps escorted by the cavalry searching for those same Indians. He couldn't discern exactly how many Arapaho had been in the raid, but it would be more than he cared to fight by himself.

He used the same tree line circling the house to return to where he'd tied Beth and the horse.

But she was gone.

He squinted as he bent and studied the tracks. A struggle had occurred here, he saw, in the brief time he was gone.

He studied the prints in the loose dirt and picked out the distinct impression of a boot. He had slipped the thong off the hammer of his pistol when a gun cocked to one side of him. "You want this little lady dead?"

Ira stood stock still. "That you, Logan?"

"Who the hell else would it be? Now answer my question: you want her dead? Look over here, dammit," Logan commanded.

Ira craned his neck around. Logan held Beth tight, with one hand over her mouth, his other hand holding his pistol to her head.

"She means nothing to me," Ira said.

"She means nothing to me, either. Difference between us is you'll lose sleep if I splatter her brains all over the ground; I won't. Now, real slow-like, toss that Winchester aside and shuck your pistol."

Ira thought it over for a brief moment. Beth really *did* mean nothing to him. But an innocent person getting killed because of Logan's obsession was something that would live long with Ira. He tossed his rifle aside and slowly took the pistol from his holster and lobbed it to lie beside the Winchester.

Logan shoved Beth hard, and she stumbled a few steps before falling at Ira's feet. "I tried to warn you—"

"I'm sure you did," Ira said. He picked up Beth, and they faced Logan. "What now—you just going to kill us?"

"Maybe if I find out who killed my little girl, I'll let you live."

Ira shook his head. "Everyone you thought might be the killer is dead. Every passenger—and Sally—died because you thought one of them might have murdered your daughter."

"One of them *was* her killer—"

"I looked at every one of their hands," Ira said. "And not a man among them showed any sign of injury." Ira took a step toward Logan. "You damn fool. Men are dead because you were wrong about the people on this stage. And now you're going to kill us even though you know by now we had nothing to do with Cassie's murder?"

"I'm going to kill you because of Matt Ales," Logan said, and his mouth turned down. "I loved . . . liked that boy. But he died in the saddle not five miles back. Bled out, he did. He didn't deserve to get shot—"

"He tried sneaking around to kill us that first time you stopped the stage. Or have you forgotten?"

"I haven't forgotten."

"And now, with your men dead . . . the passengers and the fat man dead, you're going to carve another couple scallops on your Colt?"

"That wasn't my intention when we started out," Logan said.

"I just needed to find my Cassie's killer." His sadness was quickly replaced by anger in his eyes. "As much as I needed all my men, I could go to the grave without *any* of them. Except Dutch. When you murdered—"

"There was no murder to it," Ira said. "Man got bested in a fair fight, is all."

A murder of crows took flight from the trees to the west, and Logan swung his gun in that direction.

Ira stepped closer, but Logan swung his gun back. Logan was just too far away for Ira to rush him. "I ought to kill you slow—"

"You touch off a round now, and the whole Sioux nation will be down our collars in seconds."

"What the hell you rambling on about?" Logan asked.

Ira nodded in the direction of the trees. "I picked up tracks of six—maybe eight—it was hard to decipher—warriors a few miles back."

"You're just stalling. Prolonging the inevitable."

"Am I?" Ira said as he looked around for a place, any place, where he and Beth could hide once the Indians realized white men were close. "This is prime country for Lakota passing through on their way to their hunting grounds. You know that. If I know my markings right, they've got some of their Cheyenne friends with them. And my guess is they've worked out our trail by now, and it's just a matter of time before they find us."

Logan looked over at the tree line and seemed to be mulling over his options.

"They're going to bust through those trees in a matter of minutes." Ira pressed his point as a coyote burst from the trees running ahead of . . . Indians? "And, when they spot us, it's Katie bar the door."

Another murder of crows suddenly took flight.

"Make up your mind," Ira said. "In about half a minute you're going need me."

A horse behind them snorted.

A gopher scurried across the road.

"Shit," Logan breathed. "Get the hell behind those rocks."

Ira snatched his rifle and pistol on the run and grabbed Beth's hand as he rushed past her. They dove behind a large boulder as a rifle round careened off it mere inches from their heads.

Logan—firing from the safety of another boulder—snapped a round that knocked the lead Lakota off his pony.

Two Indians behind him reined in their horses and dove for the trees as Ira and Logan fired as one. "How many?" Ira yelled.

"I count ten. Nine now that I killed one."

Ira swore under his breath. In a stand-up fight, Ira feared no man. Including Hickok. But in a setting where they'd as likely sneak up behind you and slit your throat, the Lakota had few rivals. It was something Ira admired. As if he had the luxury to admire them just then.

"I think I saw two of them Indians working their way around back," Logan said, ducking his head back as a volley of arrows flew his way.

Ira drew Beth close to him. "You sit here with your back against this rock," he ordered her. "If one of those Lakota sticks his around a tree, empty your little gun at him." Ira fished her garter gun from his vest pocket and handed it to her. "Just don't point it my direction again."

She grabbed his arm when he turned to leave. "Don't leave me—"

Ira jerked his arm away. "Do as I tell you."

He was running bent over for the trees when an arrow whizzed past his ear. When he dove behind a pine tree, another one stuck in the tree inches from his face. He levered a round into his rifle and looked around the tree.

But the Indians were gone.

Across the clearing, Logan's rifle fire kept up a steady pace, and Ira strained to hear where *his* Indians had gone.

A game trail cut through the pine trees on the way up the slope. Ira sat on the ground and propped the rifle's fore-end on a rock. He had a clear field of fire for any Lakota putting the sneak on him through the trees. But he was certain they'd take the easy path, down the game trail, away from the six-inch needles that jabbed a man like a thousand pin pricks when . . .

. . . he caught a momentary glimpse of something brown waving in the breeze, and a moment later two Indians crept down the trail, carefully putting their moccasined feet down with each step. Quiet. Concentrating.

But not on where Ira sat.

He sighted down the Winchester on the first Lakota, now within fifty yards, and tickled the trigger.

The bullet caught the warrior under the chin, and Ira had levered another round before the man hit the ground. The other Indian was running for the trees when Ira's bullet dropped him.

Ira fumbled in his pocket for more rounds, loading as he scanned the trees. After half a minute, he had stood up, intending to help Logan, when he caught movement out of his periphery. He swung the rifle around at a running Indian, just as the warrior dove on him. His weight knocked Ira's rifle aside, and he fell sprawling to the ground. He rolled over and was clawing at his pistol when the warrior's knife slashed down at him. He jerked his head to one side, and the blade cut off a piece of his ear before sticking in the ground.

Ira drove his knee into the man's groin, and he rolled off, clutching himself.

Ira drew his gun, but another figure leapt on him from behind a boulder, and they rolled across the clearing. The man's forearm came across Ira's throat, the full weight of the Indian behind it.

Ira's head felt as if it would explode.

Precious air. He. Needed it. He saw . . .

. . . visions of the Canuck choking him yesterday . . .

. . . feeling himself black out, when . . .

. . . his hand found his gun. He drew it.

He jammed the barrel into the Indian's side. Pulled the trigger.

The man's grin disappeared as Ira rolled him to one side. He gathered his feet under him. The other warrior kicked Ira's gun from his hand and swung an axe at Ira's head. He jerked up, catching the Indian's arm, pulling the man down with him. Ira drew his foot up into the man's stomach and flung him off. He ran at Ira, both men diving for the Colt, when a shot behind them startled Ira. The Indian jerked erect as a second bullet struck his head, and he dropped.

Beth stood holding her small gun in front of her like a divining rod.

Ira held up his hands. "They're gone," he said, as soothingly as he could. Her glove clutching her gun had ripped open, remnants of a red and yellow bandana jutting from the leather. Dauber's bandana. Her gun hand went limp beside her, and her legs buckled. She fell to the ground, shaking uncontrollably. "You could have been killed. I could have been killed . . ."

Ira picked up his Colt. He blew dust off it before holstering it and helping her stand.

"You all right?"

She nodded, and Ira realized that Logan's firing had stopped, too. "Stay here."

"You're not leaving me this time," Beth said and followed Ira around the boulder field just as Logan reloaded and holstered. Three Lakota lay dead within striking distance of him.

"Never liked that sneaky bastard Ed, anyhow," Logan said, pointing to a fresh scalp hanging from one of the Indians' belts. The scalp looked like a skunk, with its gray stripe running down the middle. Logan looked past Ira, and he nodded to Beth. "Your glove's been torn."

Beth looked down at her hand and put it behind her back. "That sharp rock I stumbled past must have ripped it open."

"Let me see your hand."

Beth remained quiet.

"Your hand!" Logan said and stepped toward Beth.

Ira raised his gun, and Logan stopped. "I don't know what the hell's gotten into you—" Ira said.

"Her hand," Logan yelled. "Look at it, man!"

Ira moved so he could keep Logan in sight while he faced Beth. The bandana trailed from the cut in her glove, and dried blood looked as if it had been crusted for days. "What's wrong with your hand?"

"I told you," Beth said, her eyes darting from Logan to Ira. "I cut it on that rock—"

"Bullshit!" Logan bellowed and stepped closer. Ira leveled his Colt at Logan's head. "I'd hate to kill you just now. Later maybe."

"Her hand," Logan said. "Look at her hand. It's been injured for some days. And it looks just like someone bit her."

"Let's see your hand—"

"Ira," Beth said, looking up at him, her eyes soft. "Let's just go to Deadwood. Make a new start for ourselves—"

Ira grabbed Beth's hand from in back of her and looked at it. He jerked the tattered glove off. Days-old infection had set into a nasty wound clearly made by teeth. "When did you get this? It didn't happen on the stage."

"It happened at my ranch," Logan said. "Only explanation. I told you Dutch tracked the killer to that surrey Hap Johnson hired."

"And Old Zip Coon said Hap was paid by someone to buy a ticket on the stage," Ira said. "Never said two tickets." He grabbed Beth's face. "Look at me: did you kill Cassie?"

Beth slapped Ira's hand away. "Well *I* damned sure didn't kill that little wretch! She bit me, but *I* didn't kill her."

Ira backed away from Beth. "You *were* at Logan's ranch—"

"It was Frank's idea," she said, wrapping her hand up with the bandana. "That one-armed hired gun of Logan's went around the saloons bragging how much money his boss had stashed in his house. And how Logan always went to church on Sundays with his precious little girl."

"So, you saw a chance to make yourselves rich?" Ira said.

"But they didn't get rich," Logan said. "My money box was never disturbed."

"Not 'cause we didn't try. Damn Frank." Beth tied off the bandana and sat on a rock holding her hand. "When we went into the house, Cassie surprised us. She wasn't supposed to be there—"

"She was sick." Logan seemed to be pleading. "She had to stay home."

"Her bad luck," Beth said, "and ours. While I looked for the money, Frank watched Cassie." Beth tossed a rock across the clearing. "Damn her, she wasn't supposed to be there."

"But why not just do your looking and ride off?" Logan asked. "She didn't know you."

Beth shook her head. "That was *exactly* my thinking at the time. But my brother—he got a little . . . frisky with the girl. Tried to have his way with her. He always liked the young ones. She started screaming, and I ran to her. Tried shushing her up, but she just kept screaming. I put my hand over her mouth, and she bit me. Bad."

"And that's when Frank broke her neck?" Ira asked.

Beth nodded and looked away. "Afterward we made it to town and ditched the buggy. Paid that old rummy to buy us a couple stage tickets for the gold fields."

"And Frank killed Hap?" Ira asked.

Beth nodded again. "We couldn't take the chance that he'd give our description to anyone."

She moved closer to Ira. "And if we'd made it to Deadwood, we would have just blended in, with no one the wiser." She brushed Ira's face, but he slapped her hand away. "But we can still make it to those same gold fields together, you and me."

Ira felt his legs tremble. All this time, Cassie's murderer was right inside the coach. "How the hell could you—"

Beth threw up her hands. "What choice did I have but to cover for my brother? Besides, the law would figure I was as guilty as Frank."

Logan stepped closer, but Ira cocked his gun.

"I need to see justice for my Cassie. I think you owe me that for hauling her killer this far on your stage."

"I owe you, all right—for getting my driver and the passengers killed when you should have gone to the territorial marshal. You got innocent men killed these past few days." Ira shoved Beth aside as he faced Logan. Ira holstered carefully and stood with his feet apart five yards from Logan. "The only reason I'm even going to give you a chance is because that daughter of yours didn't deserve what Beth and her brother did to her."

Logan smiled. "And, in a moment, you'll be dead. And so will the woman."

"If I thought you had a chance of beating me, I would have just gunned you down already."

"Bull—"

"That's just what Dutch thought. And he was a lot faster than you."

Logan's smile faded, his hand hovering just above his gun butt. He seemed to be weighing his chances when he brought his hands away. "You might be right."

"Of course I'm right. Now, ever so slowly, toss your gun over here."

"Ha!" Beth said, picking up Logan's gun.

"Hand it to me," Ira said, and Beth handed him the gun.

"See," Beth said, "I knew we'd make it to Deadwood, you and me. Once you kill Logan, we'll—"

Ira shoved Beth aside and stepped back. He tucked Logan's Remington into his waistband and walked to the horses. "I'm not going to kill Logan."

"But you have to kill him," Beth said. "He won't stop now."

"Yeah, just what *are* you going to do?" Logan asked.

"Three miles along this route is where I'll leave your horse and gun," he told Logan. "You make it there, and you'll be able to catch up with Beth in Custer City."

"What are you talking about, Custer City?" Beth asked.

"That little gun of yours," Ira said. "Hand it over. No offense, but I don't trust you riding with me when you've got a gun handy."

Beth handed Ira her garter gun, and he tucked it into his britches. "Custer City's as far as I'll take you. I'll drop you there, and what you do from thereon is your business."

"But he'll find me," Beth pleaded. "Logan will kill me."

"Not if you turn yourself over to the law first."

Logan smiled. "I don't cotton to walking those miles, but the woman's right—I *will* find her, and I *will* kill her for helping her brother murder my Cassie. 'Cause her kind won't never turn herself in."

"I figured as much," Ira said.

"Then why not just let her go with me right now," Logan said. "Save her and me both the trouble of some cat-and-mouse game?"

"I would," Ira said, "but a few moments ago she saved my life when she shot an Indian."

"That's right," Beth said, latching onto Ira's arm as he untied the horses. "I did. You owe me."

"What I owe you is my promise to get you to Custer City." He chin-pointed to Logan. "Now if you don't want a better chance than you gave Logan's little girl—"

"No!" Beth said and took Ira's hand to hoist her up. "It's not much of a chance, but it is *a* chance."

EPILOGUE

Deadwood, Dakota Territory
August 2, 1876, 4:10 in the afternoon

Ira dropped the reins to Dutch's beat and exhausted dapple gray, not even bothering to tie the horse to a hitching rail. Horse stealing was rampant here in Deadwood, but that didn't matter to Ira. They could have the gray, as tuckered out as he was. In a moment, his business with Hickok would be finished, and he'd relax for a day. Two at the most, before looking to stake out a claim along Deadwood Gulch. He didn't need a horse for that.

The mud clung to Ira's boots, and he had to stop every now and again, walking from plank to floating plank, to make it to the long row of saloons lining the street. Two horses rode by, splashing mud and horse crap onto his cheek. He wiped it away. Another time, he might be angry. But right now, nothing clouded his thoughts.

A team of oxen passed, the bullwhacker tossing out a stream of cuss words sharper than the whip Sally had used to coax the horses along the stage route. Ira shook the thought of the Brit from his mind. As crude and talkative as the man had been, Ira had grown to like the stage driver. But right now—with Hickok so close—he needed a clear head.

A drunk staggered out of a saloon and ran into Ira. He grabbed the man—a boy to judge by the peach fuzz lining his upper lip—by the lapels.

"Don't hit me, mister."

"I won't, if you tell me where Bill Hickok is."

"Hell," the boy stuttered. "Everyone knows where Wild Bill is this time of day—in the Number 10." He chin-pointed to the north. "Up thataway a hundred yards or so."

Ira let the kid go, as a miner in a floppy wool hat brushed past him with a soiled dove hanging on his arm, her other one somewhere deep in his trouser pocket.

Ira turned toward a mercantile and double checked his Colt. He took off the glove on his shooting hand and made his way past drunks staggering, some falling into the mud, while soiled ladies tugged on Ira's arm as he passed their cribs.

He jumped when he heard a shot from the direction of the Number 10, but he paid it no mind. Nothing could distract him from finding Hickok and killing him.

Ira saw the wooden sign dangling askew from the Number 10 Saloon by one chain just as a man burst from inside. He looked back, wild-eyed, at the door, a gun in his hand. He slipped and fell into the mud at Ira's feet, the gun burying itself in horse shit. He grabbed the reins of a horse tied to a post outside the saloon and shoved his foot into the stirrup. The saddle had been left loose, and it turned, sending the man to the mud street again.

Ira bent and picked him up. "You just come from the Number 10?"

"I did." The man struggled to get free, but Ira kept a tight hold on him.

"Is Bill Hickok inside?"

The man looked sideways at him. "Why you want to know?"

" 'Cause I'm going to kill him."

The man smiled. "Sure—Wild Bill's in there. He's not going anywheres."

"If he ain't there, I'm going to hunt you up and ventilate you."

"Oh, he's there all right, mister," the man said. "Or my name ain't Jack McCall."

ABOUT THE AUTHOR

C. M. Wendelboe entered the law enforcement profession when he was discharged from the Marines as the Vietnam War was winding down.

In the 1970s, his career included assisting federal and tribal law enforcement agencies embroiled in conflicts with American Indian movement activists in South Dakota.

He moved to Gillette, Wyoming, and found his niche, where he remained a sheriff's deputy for more than twenty-five years. In addition, he was a longtime firearms instructor at the local college and within the community.

During his thirty-eight-year career in law enforcement, he served successful stints as police chief, policy adviser, and other supervisory roles for several agencies. Yet he always has felt most proud of "working the street." He was a patrol supervisor when he retired to pursue his true vocation as a fiction writer.

The employees of Five Star Publishing hope you have enjoyed this book.

Our Five Star novels explore little-known chapters from America's history, stories told from unique perspectives that will entertain a broad range of readers.

Other Five Star books are available at your local library, bookstore, all major book distributors, and directly from Five Star/Gale.

Connect with Five Star Publishing

Visit us on Facebook:
   https://www.facebook.com/FiveStarCengage

Email:
   FiveStar@cengage.com

For information about titles and placing orders:
   (800) 223-1244
   gale.orders@cengage.com

To share your comments, write to us:
   Five Star Publishing
   Attn: Publisher
   10 Water St., Suite 310
   Waterville, ME 04901